"I WOULD NOT MAKE A GOOD HUSBAND. I DO, HOWEVER, MAKE AN EXCELLENT LOVER."

Gripping Jessye's saddlehorn, Harrison leaned over, cradled the back of her head with his other hand, and captured her mouth with his own. With a soft moan, she bent toward him, threading her fingers through the hair at the nape of his neck. His tongue delved deeply, mating with hers, conjuring up images that made sitting in the saddle increasingly uncomfortable. He wanted desperately to lay her on a blanket beneath the stars.

Drawing back, he cupped her chin and stroked a thumb across her swollen lips.

"Too bad I'm not interested in taking on a lover," she whispered hoarsely.

"Too bad indeed . . ."

Never Love a
Cowboy

Lorraine Heath

AVON
An Imprint of HarperCollinsPublishers

This is a work of fiction. Names, characters, places, and incidents are products of the author's imagination or are used fictitiously and are not to be construed as real. Any resemblance to actual events, locales, organizations, or persons, living or dead, is entirely coincidental.

AVON BOOKS
An Imprint of HarperCollins*Publishers*
195 Broadway
New York, New York 10007

Copyright © 2000 by Jan Nowasky
ISBN 978-0-380-80330-9
www.avonromance.com

First Avon Books mass market printing: April 2000

Avon Trademark Reg. U.S. Pat. Off. and in Other Countries, Marca Registrada, Hecho en U.S.A.
HarperCollins® is a registered trademark of HarperCollins Publishers.

Printed in the U.S.A.

10 9 8 7 6

For Carmel
In loving memory

I still miss you so much.

❧ Prologue ❧

August 1866

It was, beyond a doubt, the most beautiful prison that he'd ever had the misfortune to occupy.

Harrison Bainbridge, second son to the Earl of Lambourne, allowed the pillow's softness to envelop his head as he stared at the lilac canopy draped above him. During the day, a crystal chandelier captured tiny granules of sunlight, waltzing them across the walls. With the arrival of night, as now, the lit candles cast a pale glow that shimmered at the edge of the shadows.

A tiny figurine—a mother holding a child—graced the bedside table. He had never suspected that this particular woman possessed a fondness for lace and elegant adornments.

Not until he'd become a prisoner within her bed.

The wooden floor, polished to a sheen, reflected the furnishings throughout the room: a settee before the hearth, where once she may have kissed the man who betrayed her, a wardrobe that housed a green gown that he knew from experience was as silky as her skin.

1

With the whisper of the warm night wind, the white embroidered curtains billowed away from the window. Harrison tossed aside the sheet and allowed the breeze to caress his sweltering flesh as no woman had in months—as no woman ever would again.

Her faint fragrance—the tantalizing scent of lilies—wafted around him, offering comfort he did not know how to accept while bringing forth the demons that haunted him.

He had been a prisoner within her room for six weeks now, six interminable weeks filled with agony, regret, and time. Time to reflect upon what *had* been, upon what *might* have been. Six weeks to battle against accepting what *was*.

On the wall above her bureau she had hung a mirror, flowers intricately carved along its gilded edges. He caught a glimpse of his reflection—the horrifying sight of a crippled body that imprisoned him as much as this room.

Reaching out, he grabbed the figurine and hurled it with all his strength. It cracked the mirror, multiplying his reflection into a grotesque kaleidoscope of jagged shards of glass.

He heard the hurried footsteps echo along the hallway. She would be here soon, and though he prayed otherwise, he feared that as always with her arrival, his true misery would begin.

He closed his eyes, pretending for the barest of moments that he was as he had once been.

Remembering . . . remembering the fires of passion she had ignited within him. When he had been whole, strong, and healthy. When he had worn confidence like a well-tailored cloak, and life had held the promise of dreams yet untouched.

When his obsessive ambitions had blinded him to the fact that he already possessed everything of importance. . . .

PART ONE

Journeys into Hell

≈ Chapter 1 ≈

Having been raised within the bowels of hell, Harrison Bainbridge should have been inured to life's disappointments.

It irritated the devil out of him that he was not.

With a jaundiced eye, he gazed around the interior of the dreary saloon. It in no way resembled the gentleman's clubs he had frequented in London. But then nothing in this godforsaken town reminded him of England, and he readily welcomed the opportunity to leave.

Whether she realized it or not, the woman sitting across from him held the key to his salvation. Out of the corner of her mouth, Jessye Kane blew a quick burst of air, which sent into motion the radiant red curls that had escaped from her braid.

"Now don't take this personal," she said in a voice that reminded Harrison of wispy smoke curling over a log before the fire finally caught and consumed it.

7

"But I don't trust you any farther than I can throw you."

Her words flayed his heart, but Harrison knew his face didn't reflect the unexpected pain. As a lad, he'd drowned his emotions in a bottomless well, a maneuver that now gave him an edge when playing games of chance because no one—not even his trusted friends Christian Montgomery and Grayson Rhodes—could ever determine his exact thoughts.

"On the contrary," he quipped, lifting his glass of whiskey in a silent salute. "I am indeed honored. You always struck me as a woman who was adept at throwing men great distances."

He took no pleasure in the blush that flamed her cheeks, obliterating the smattering of freckles. But self-preservation was a vicious tutor, and he had learned the lessons well.

She darted a glance at Christian Montgomery, who sat beside him, before she settled her unwavering gaze on Harrison. Her eyes were the green of spring, when the first buds began to emerge. Her chin came up a notch. He knew her well enough to recognize that slight gesture as an ominous warning.

She unfolded a sheet of paper. "I'm interested in taking part in this cattle venture you two are making noise about. I'm willing to fund the whole thing just like we discussed, but the partnership will be between me and Kit. We'll split the profits fifty-fifty. I've written up an agreement that I'll need signed before I hand over any money."

Her unwillingness to accept him as a partner was yet another stroke of the lash, but his admiration for her shrewd business sense increased. It seemed *she* had also learned well the lessons of survival.

"Now, hold on a minute," Kit began.

Harrison held up a hand to silence his friend. He steepled his fingers and pressed them against his bearded chin. "Is there a particular reason you feel this action is warranted?"

"Yep. From what I can tell, Kit has done all the planning and made all the arrangements. The hardest work I've *ever* seen you do is to take a long squint at the sun and a short squat in the shade."

The lash cut more deeply.

"This is ludicrous," Kit said. "Harry carries his share—"

"And the paper?" Harrison interrupted.

"Spells out everything so we've got no misunderstandings at the end of the drive as to who gets what."

In the three months since Harrison had first met Jessye, they had developed a tentative friendship. She served drinks in her father's saloon, on occasion played poker with Harrison, and always made it well known that she had no interest whatsoever in accompanying him to a bedroom at the top of the stairs.

Not that he blamed her. Until recently, he had worked in a field like a common laborer. As he had picked the cotton, the sun had beaten him unmercifully, his hands had bled, and his back had ached in agony. Perhaps she would have admired his efforts to a greater degree if he had complained.

He and Kit had agreed that a simpler way to make their fortunes was at hand. Cattle. The northern states were desperate for the beef denied them during the war. Unfortunately, taking the cattle to market required time and money. Time was not the problem. Harrison possessed it in abundance.

The obstacle was money—or more accurately, its absence. For reasons Kit would not divulge, very little of his remained available. Harrison had gambled away the money he'd earned working the cotton fields. Yet despite his folly, he was now determined to succeed where his father deemed he would fail.

But to succeed, he needed capital, and Jessye had it. Not a great deal, but enough. Dreamin' money, she called it.

He'd played poker with her often enough to know she wasn't bluffing. She was their last hope for an investor, and well she knew it. He gave a curt nod. "Kit, sign the paper."

"But it says that you'll get nothing—"

"He'll get a hundred dollars at the end of the drive just like the other men we hire," Jessye said.

"Unacceptable," Kit said. "He is a full partner—"

"The conditions are acceptable to me," Harrison stated quietly. "Sign the paper."

"I bloody well will not."

"Sign the damn paper," Harrison ground out.

His gaze riveted on Jessye, Harrison heard Kit scratch the pen across the parchment. She squirmed slightly in her chair. Good. A bit of unease would serve her well and lessen the sting to his pride.

Kit shoved the paper toward her. "There, although I will split *my* earnings evenly with Harry."

"You can do whatever you want with your share," she told him.

"Thank God. I feared you intended to issue another mandate."

"Nothing else, other than to remind you that I'm going with you."

"I would think that contract would cancel your need to shadow our moves," Kit said tersely.

"My money's not going where I can't see it."

Harrison gave a sharp tug on the red brocade vest beneath his black jacket. "I give you my word that your money will be safe—"

"Harry, you scoundrel, I wouldn't trust your word if the good Lord carved it in stone Himself."

He didn't care whether she trusted his word, but for reasons he could not comprehend he desperately wanted her to trust *him*. From the first moment he had seen her in a faded dress serving drinks in this saloon, she had intrigued him. If she possessed any innocence at all, it was but a solitary thread woven through a tapestry that he longed to unravel. If he could personally place the money in her hands, he would definitely gain an advantage . . . and possibly a walk together up those stairs.

"Jessye love, we're not completely ignorant," he said. "We've talked with men who herded cattle before the war. I'm not certain it's wise for you to go on this journey."

Crossing her arms on the table and leaning forward, she steadily held his gaze. "Who taught you and Kit how to shoot a gun and a rifle?"

Sighing, he cursed every valid point he knew she was going to throw in his face. "You."

"What did I teach you about a remuda?"

"That it's a group of horses, and we'll have more horses than men," he recited as though reading from a boring book.

She smiled smugly. "What's an Armitas?"

"That silly leather apron that is split down the middle and ties at our waist and knees. It looks ridiculous, and I'm not wearing it."

"You will, and you'll be grateful you've got it. I doubt either of you knows which end of a cow quits the ground first. Whether you two greenhorns want to admit it or not, you need more than my money. You need what I *know*." She scraped back her chair. "I've got to help Pa—"

"Before you leave, I need your approval regarding an important matter," Kit said as he reached beneath the table and withdrew an iron rod. One end had a flattened triangle through which a man could slip a gloved hand. The other supported an L that rested on top of a T.

"Our brand was designed to represent our venture: Texas Lady. The name was Harry's idea, chosen to honor our investor. Of course, the decision was made before we realized he would not have an equal say—"

"Kit," Harrison warned, despising righteous indignation.

Kit cast him a scathing look before continuing. "If you don't like the name or the design, we can change it, but I'd like to know tonight, as I want a few more made before we leave tomorrow."

Harrison watched her tentatively touch the letters as though they were fine gems instead of iron to be heated and laid against some beast's backside. He'd forbidden Kit to mention the brand because he'd wanted to surprise her Judging by the awe on her face, he'd succeeded.

She lifted her gaze to his. "Texas Lady?"

Harrison shrugged as though the name were of little consequence. "It seemed appropriate. We'd considered the Triple E for the three Englishmen, but since Gray made the unfortunate decision to get married and has turned his endeavors toward farming, the Double E just didn't have the same ring to it."

"I'm not much of a lady." She jerked her fingers back as though the iron had scalded her. "It'll do just fine. I gotta close up."

Harrison watched her walk away without so much as a thank you. Refreshingly honest and disturbingly forthright with her opinions, she was without a doubt the most aggravating woman he'd ever known.

And his gift had touched her . . . deeply, if the tears that had surfaced within her eyes before she'd leapt to her feet were any indication.

"Correct me if I am wrong—"

"Is that not my usual habit?" Harrison cut in, turning his attention away from Jessye.

Kit narrowed his pale blue eyes. Damn, but Harrison hated his friend's scrutiny.

"I was under the impression that you and she were friends, perhaps lovers—"

"Not in this lifetime."

"Then why in God's name did you suggest we come to her?"

"Because she has money."

"We could have found it elsewhere."

"Where? The war left most of the people in this state pitifully poor. As for the conquerors streaming in, I don't trust them. Must be my Saxon heritage."

Kit scowled. "We could have sought out a banker."

"Where, pray tell, would we get a letter of reference? Our reputations are hardly pristine. We should count ourselves fortunate that Jessye trusts us as much as she does."

"She doesn't trust us at all."

"We don't need her trust. We only need her money, which we now have, and her knowledge regarding this state and cattle, which she is willing to share."

Kit shook his head. "I don't like this, Harry. I don't like it one bit."

"Why the worry? You have everything planned out."

"On paper. Putting it into practice is something else entirely." Kit rubbed his thumb along the scar beneath his chin.

Harrison had always thought it a shame that the Earl of Ravenleigh had applied a flaming hot poker to his second son so no one would mistake him for his twin brother—the heir apparent.

"I wish you could convince her not to go. I have a bad feeling about this journey," Kit said.

"Tell me where we can acquire the funds for supplies, and I'll happily cancel our arrangement with her."

"David Robertson might finance our venture."

"That Texan that visited Ravenleigh a few years back?" Harry asked.

"Yes. He was quite well-off."

"Before the war. He could be a beggar now for all you know."

"I could make discreet inquiries, determine his interest—"

"It's a moot issue. You signed a contract with Jessye." Besides, Harrison wanted more from Jessye than her money or her knowledge of cattle. He wanted her climbing those bloody damned stairs with him.

"But you just said if I were able to find another source for the funds—"

"Because I didn't think you would! Look around at these drab surroundings. An opportunity like this happens but once in a lifetime. I'd rather share the chance for prosperity with a woman who has never known wealth than a man who takes it for granted."

"It's a gamble, Harry. We could return with nothing."

"She knows that. She's risking her dreaming money, Kit. How do I tell her now that we've decided another investor would better suit us?"

"You care for her," Kit said somberly. "You might not have bedded her, but you do have some feelings for her."

"I understand her plight. Make no more of it than that."

"I'll make as much of it as I bloody well want to and pray that I don't live to regret it." Sighing deeply, Kit stood, grabbed the branding iron, and sliced it through the air as though it were a rapier. "I shall finish the preparations."

"Good. And cheer up, for God's sake. How much work can be involved in prodding a few cattle north?"

"It's not the work that concerns me, but the unknown. I don't know how to plan for it."

"You strive too hard to account for everything. An element of risk makes life worthwhile."

"I should imagine it depends upon the nature of the risk."

As Kit headed toward the stairs, Harrison heard

Jessye's throaty laughter echo over the saloon as she herded the remaining customers through the swinging doors into the night. He wondered what they had said to make her laugh so freely. The laughter she released in his presence usually carried an undercurrent of distrust.

He watched as she shared a moment with her father, smiling at him as they spoke. He couldn't recall ever smiling at his father—or his father smiling at him.

She affectionately patted her father's slightly stooped shoulder before striding through a door that led to what he knew was a back room. She'd return with a bucket of water to clean the place until it shone. His favorite moments of the night came when she got on her knees to scrub some mess. Her hips followed the circular motion of her hand, and all he could think about was how much he'd like to be beneath her.

Countless times she'd rejected *that* proposition. She'd told him that she wasn't one of *those* women, but he doubted her claims, for he had yet to meet a serving wench who wasn't.

Her father's movements caught his attention as the wiry fellow trudged across the saloon. Tufts of hair, a lighter shade of red than his daughter's, stood at various angles of attention over his head. His green eyes carried a hardened glint. "I need a word with you."

Harrison waved a hand toward the chair Kit had vacated. "By all means, then, please sit."

Jonah Kane dropped his small body into the chair. "I gotta be honest here. I ain't in favor of Jessye goin' on this venture with you fellas."

"Neither am I, but she seems to have a stubborn streak in her."

Jonah chuckled and scratched his bristly chin. "She calls it independence. Tells me that since she's twenty-one, she's all growed up. She don't realize that a father's daughter never grows up."

Harrison felt as though he'd been slapped. "She's only twenty-one?"

Jonah narrowed his rheumy eyes. "How old did you think she was?"

"A bit older." He'd never questioned her age, had always considered her closer to his own age of twenty-eight. He'd figured her to be a woman of experience, working in a saloon, surrounded by men all night, but if she were only twenty-one . . . good God, could her claims be true? Might she still be innocent? Perhaps her refusals had nothing to do with him, and everything to do with her purity.

"She's young, but she don't like to admit it," Jonah said.

Harrison was surprised to see tears shimmer in the old man's eyes before he leaned forward with a steely glare. "She's been hurt. Had her heart sliced up and tossed out as buzzard bait. I don't want to see her hurt again."

"We have no intention of harming her. She is our investor in this undertaking and will have our utmost respect and consideration."

Jonah narrowed his eyes. "There's a lot of long nights on a cattle drive. If she comes back with the smallest of bruises on her heart, I'll cut off your *cojones* and feed 'em to you."

Harrison cleared his throat. These Texans so often

threw in Spanish words that he sometimes found it difficult to follow their conversations, but he had a gist of the meaning. "Will this action render me incapable of siring an heir?"

"You'd better damn well know it."

"Then I'll keep your threat foremost in my mind as we journey."

"I don't care what you do with it, just don't forget it." Jonah stood and began stacking chairs onto tables.

Harrison rubbed his fingers over his thick beard, wondering why, of all the things Jonah had just revealed, hearing that someone had broken Jessye's heart bothered him more than the thought of being turned into a eunuch.

He'd never suspected that her tough attitude was an act designed to shield herself. A pity. He had no interest in mending hearts that had once been broken. A shattered heart would forever be a mosaic of cracked pieces, more delicate and prone to break again with less force applied to it.

Experience had taught him that lamentable truth.

Jessye Kane stood outside her father's saloon and inhaled deeply, allowing the coolness of the autumn breeze to blow the stench of spilled liquor and lingering tobacco smoke away from her. She gazed at the twinkling stars that lay upon the midnight sky like diamonds on black velvet. For the next few months, she would sleep beneath them and use them to guide her journey.

At the end of that time, if all went as anticipated, she would turn her modest savings into a considerable sum of money. Unlike Harry, who was motivated by ambition, she was inspired by fear, fear that no matter how strong she was, she would never be strong enough to protect her heart.

And her heart was definitely at risk. The image of the brand was seared in her mind. *Texas Lady*. Named for her. She'd never in her life felt like a lady, not a true lady. She'd been forced to give herself a mental shake in order to remember with whom she was dealing: a man who knew well how to cheat, a man who let it be known he wanted to bed her.

While working Abbie Westland's cotton fields during summer harvest, Jessye had learned that Harry had a tendency to sit in the shade, eat watermelon, and entertain the children with card tricks. He only went into the fields when Grayson Rhodes brought him an empty sack. And when next she looked, there he was again, sitting in the shade.

He was in for a rude awakening. He wouldn't find much time to squander on a cattle drive.

Turning slightly, she lifted her gaze to the windows on the second floor that looked into the rooms reserved for paying guests. Harry and Kit rented rooms that faced each other across the long, narrow hallway.

She saw the pale lamplight spill out of a window—Harry's window. She didn't want to think about what Harry might be doing, but she seemed unable to stop herself.

He'd take off those fancy clothes he wore, clothes that would make any other man look like a dandy. It aggravated her that whenever she joined him at a table, she felt like the east end of a westbound mule, while he possessed an abundance of charm and sophistication.

Sauntering through the cotton fields had bronzed his skin. When he shuffled the deck, his deft fingers mesmerized her. He had such a light touch that the cards barely whispered when he sorted them, and she had to fight against imagining those hands skimming over her body with as much expertise as they handled the deck.

She enjoyed their verbal sparring, was challenged by his ability to always win with the hand he dealt. Out of deference to her suspicions, he played with his sleeves rolled up so she knew he didn't sport any extra pockets or devices that would give him the cards he needed. But she also knew his forearms weren't puny and white like those of a man who'd spent his life pampered. The veins bulged beneath his skin, and his muscles appeared hardened even when his arms were at rest. Made no sense, but little about him did.

Damn, but she wished she could figure out how he cheated. Maybe then she'd stop watching him with an intensity that bordered on obsession. Lord help her, she had almost every inch of him memorized, trying to catch him in the act of swindling her.

He swore he never cheated when he played her, but she knew that was an outright lie—otherwise, she'd occasionally win a hand. She wasn't that poor of a poker player.

Now he needed her—or more accurately, he needed her money. She might have given it to him with no strings attached if he didn't always call her "Jessye love." She trusted the endearment as much as she trusted the man. She knew he didn't love her, and using the word made a mockery of an emotion that had the power to wound unmercifully and heal unconditionally.

The light from his window faded into darkness, and she realized he'd gone to bed. She dared not contemplate what he might *not* wear while he slept. Every time she changed the sheets on his bed, she wondered if they'd known the touch of his bare back . . . stomach . . . buttocks . . .

Or did he sleep with nothing but the night air to caress his flesh?

Squeezing her eyes shut, she spun around. She'd sworn never again to become involved with a man until she was a woman of independence, although Harry had a disconcerting way of making her regret that vow.

She'd lost count of the number of times he'd invited her to join him beneath the blankets. His voice carried a teasing lilt, but his eyes, Lord, his emerald eyes held a vulnerability that intrigued and frightened her. He wasn't nearly as simplistic as he appeared.

A high-risk gambler, he manipulated cards, enjoyed strong words, and indulged in strong liquor. Yet there was another facet to him, like turning a diamond and seeing it sparkle from a different angle. A haughtiness in the way he said his name. He was the second son of an earl, sent here to make his way in the world.

With cattle, she thought he had a good chance of succeeding. She knew a lot about cattle. Before the war, she'd known a man who herded longhorns to California. Gerald Milton. He had loved to talk, and she had loved to listen.

He hadn't looked at her the way most men did—like whiskey that was to be enjoyed during the evening and forgotten come the light of day.

She had learned too late that his innocent eyes shielded an abundance of faults.

"Jessye?"

Glancing over her shoulder, she smiled warmly. "Hey, Pa."

Her father strolled through the door that led to the rooms they lived in at the rear of the saloon.

"Don't guess I can talk you out of goin'," he said.

Turning her gaze back to the stars, she wrapped her arms around her waist. "Nope."

"Gonna be a lot of men—"

"I can handle myself around men. Besides, I'll be dressed like them. After a few days, they'll forget I'm a woman."

"Long stretch of miles between towns. Men ain't likely to forget anything."

"I'll be fine, Pa."

She heard his sigh travel on the wind. "You're like your ma, you know. Strong-willed, determined. I can't help but believe things woulda worked out different if she hadn't died on us when you was seven."

She pivoted slightly so she could face him. "Things didn't turn out so bad."

He shook his head. "Shouldn't have had you working in a saloon."

"I like working in a saloon. I'm thinking if I make enough money on this cattle drive, we can add that stage you've always talked about—with the red velvet curtains that open and close. We could get some shows in here. A singer or two. That would draw a crowd and increase profits."

In the moonlight, she saw her father's wrinkles shift

until he looked much older, so much older. "Is that why you're doing this crazy thing . . . on account of my dreams?"

"No, Pa, I'm doing it for me."

She heard him sniff. "You just take care then, girl, 'cuz if somethin' was to happen to you . . . wouldn't be no reason for me to live."

She slung her arms around him, hugging him tightly. "Nothing's gonna happen to me."

His thin arms circled her. Once upon a time, she'd thought all men loved as unconditionally, as fiercely as he did.

He patted her back and stepped out of her embrace. "Just so you'll know, I told Bainbridge I'd castrate him if he hurt you."

She laughed lightly. "He won't hurt me, Pa."

No man ever would because she wouldn't let any man get close enough to do so.

He sniffed again and rubbed his eyes. "I'm gonna go talk to your ma for a spell. She might have some words of wisdom for me to share with you before you go."

She watched him walk into the night shadows, toward the church at the far end of town and the small cemetery behind it. She wondered if her mother had truly known how much her father had loved her.

Jessye had once dreamed of giving and receiving that kind of powerful love. But not any longer.

At seventeen, she'd had her heart ripped from her chest. She'd vowed then that she'd never again be dependent on either a man or money. This arrangement with Harry and Kit would ensure that she kept that promise.

"He's right, you know," a deep voice rumbled into the night. "You should stay here."

Jessye spun around, her heart thundering. Harry stood at the edge of the shadows, a silhouette guarded by darkness. His jacket and vest were gone. Several buttons on his white shirt were loosened as though he'd been undressing and changed his mind. His black hair and beard framed his face, accentuating his emerald eyes, holding her captive. She swallowed hard. "Figured you'd gone to bed."

"I thought as much, since I saw you watching my window."

"I wasn't watching your window. I was just looking around, and your window happens to be there. Besides, it's going to be a long while before you sleep in a bed again. You ought to be up there enjoying the comforts of a mattress."

A lazy grin spread across his face. "I *never* enjoy being in a bed when I'm in it alone."

She chuckled low. "And the next words you speak are going to be an invite to join you. I've served drinks long enough that I've heard it all, and I know that the sweet talkin' stops as soon as the whiskey wears off."

"Mine wouldn't."

She laughed. "You're smoother than most, Harry. I have to give you credit for that, and if I had a dollar for every time you invited me to climb those stairs with you, I wouldn't have to go on this cattle drive."

He took a step toward her, effectively closing the distance between them until she felt the warmth of his body battling the cool night air. "Why are you going,

Jessye? You must realize that traveling alone with men is bound to ruin your reputation."

"I've worked in a saloon all my life. I've got no reputation to ruin."

"From what I hear, the nights on a cattle drive are not only long, but lonely."

"Nights in a saloon are just as lonely."

He slowly trailed his finger along the column of her throat. The intense heat surged through her like flames igniting with the promise to consume.

"Then come upstairs with me," he murmured in a low, seductive voice. "Physical pleasure can ease the loneliness without involving the heart."

She felt her body and resolve melting, but bittersweet memories kept her from reaching for him and allowed her to speak in a calm voice that hid the turbulence swirling within her. "Not for me, Harry. I've told you before that I'm not one of *those* women. I can't be persuaded by a silver-tongued scoundrel. Besides, I've already marked you as a man who can't afford me."

"Name your price."

"Love."

A heavy silence permeated the air, and she knew she'd named the one thing he'd never give her. His touch retreated, and the coldness swept in like a blue north wind.

He bowed slightly. "I bid you goodnight."

She wrapped her arms around her middle and watched him walk up the stairs, knowing both he and her father were right. She should stay behind.

Because if she were truly honest with herself, Harrison Bainbridge had the power to destroy the fragmented remains of her broken heart.

❧ Chapter 2 ❧

*W*ith *Kit and Grayson Rhodes flanking*
him, Harrison strolled through the fields where cottons bolls had once quivered in the wind. He thought
Grayson had done rather well for himself when he'd
taken Abigail Westland as his wife. In addition to the
land, he'd gained three children from her first marriage and her fierce, undying love.

"Abbie says it's bad luck to have a woman on a
cattle drive," Gray murmured speculatively.

Harrison stopped walking and faced his friend
squarely. "Without Jessye's money, we would have
no hope of pursuing a cattle drive."

"I cannot fathom why she would risk ruining her
reputation by going with you."

"Did Abbie not risk her reputation when she allowed you to live here without the benefit of marriage?" Harrison asked, finding it odd to defend a
stance he did not support.

"I slept in the barn."

"Jessye will sleep on her own pallet," Harrison assured him.

Gray narrowed his blue eyes. "For two or three nights perhaps—"

"For the entire duration of this venture." Harrison glanced toward the front porch, where Jessye was talking with Gray's wife. Jessye wore clothes similar to his: plain flannel shirt, simple vest, boots, red bandanna, woolen trousers. Dear Lord, but he already missed his finer garments. Once this drive ended, he would never go another day dressed as a commoner. "She has no interest in men."

"But they will no doubt have an interest in her," Gray assured him.

Harrison feared that would be the case. Since she'd stepped out of the saloon and he'd seen the perfect outline of her hips and legs previously kept hidden by a skirt, he'd been unable to take his eyes off her. "She thinks dressed as she is that the men won't notice she's a woman."

"That's not bloody likely," Kit said. "I'm thinking all women should wear trousers. I like the way the garment shows off their rounded bottoms."

Harrison had an irrational desire to gouge his friend's eyes. "She's your partner," he snapped.

Kit jerked his head around. "Yes, and she should be yours as well."

"What's this?" Gray asked.

"It's unimportant. Will you let it go?" Harrison demanded, glaring at Kit.

"It makes no sense not to accept you as a partner, and your willingness to blithely accept the terms of that agreement aggravates the devil out of me. It's not like you to surrender without a fight—"

"I have not surrendered."

Interest gleamed within Kit's pale blue eyes. "I should have known. By God, why didn't you argue your case last night?"

"Because when we play poker, I absolutely adore the expression of disbelief that crosses her face when she calls my bluff . . . only to discover I wasn't bluffing. She has deemed me a laggardly jackanapes. But I have no doubt, a moment will come when she realizes that I hold a true winning hand. And then, watching the truth dawn in her eyes will be a balm to the"—he searched for a word that would not reveal the true extent of what he'd felt: humiliation, anger, resentment—"*sting* to my pride and will make the gamble worthwhile."

"I hope it doesn't take long," Kit said. "Even with your acceptance of the deal, I'm not happy with it."

"But you will strive to protect her," Harrison insisted.

"I should think with that gun strapped to her thigh she can protect herself."

"Since she taught me how to handle a gun, I can assure you she knows well how to use it," Gray said.

Harrison touched the butt of the gun housed against his own hip. "She taught us as well." It had unnerved him to see the ease with which she managed the weapon.

"Why aren't you wearing a gun, Kit?" Gray asked.

"I prefer the Henry rifle. It's more accurate and holds fifteen shells for repeated firing. Besides, I don't like the weight of the pistol on my person. Makes me feel lopsided."

"You could wear one on either side," Harrison suggested, grinning.

"Other than hunting for game, I can't imagine we're going to use the blasted things anyway. So uncivilized."

"I agree," Gray said quietly. "The day when I faced Abbie's husband, I realized no honor is found in using the damn things. I swore then to never wear one again."

"You should come with us," Harrison said, wanting to steer the subject away from the past.

Gray shook his head. "I was forced to leave Abbie before. Only death will take me from her now."

"How maudlin," Harrison muttered.

"It's the truth," Gray assured him.

Harrison didn't doubt the words, but he found he envied his friend's vehement defense. He nudged a blackened cotton stalk with the rounded toe of his boot. "You're not going to plant cotton, are you?"

Gray shrugged. "I'm not sure what we're going to do." He glanced at his hands. "I hate harvesting the crop."

"What would you say to using the land for grazing the cattle?" Kit asked.

Gray removed his straw hat and combed his fingers through his blond hair. "You want to go into a bit more detail?"

"According to Jessye, we can't move the cattle north until spring. She says only a fool would herd cattle in winter."

"Then why leave now? Why not wait until spring?" Gray asked.

"The cattle are spread over the state, particularly to

the west and south. We need to round them up and move them to one place where we could keep them until we're ready to herd them north."

"I suppose you'll tell me all I need to know to take care of these cattle."

Kit grinned. "Basically you'll keep them from wandering off."

"I'll need a fence."

"Jessye says a wooden fence isn't practical," Harrison told him, "although I can't see where it would hurt to have some sort of barrier."

"I can't imagine that Abbie will want to give up cotton completely, but holding the cattle here might work well," Gray said. "We could use their manure for fertilizer."

"Then it's settled. Once we begin encountering cattle, we shall probably hire men. I'll send them along with a letter of introduction."

"What am I to do with the men?" Gray asked.

"Feed them. Give them a night's lodging in the barn. Then they'll head back to round up more cattle."

"A moment ago I was only required to watch cattle. Now I must feed and lodge your men? I want the details, Kit, every one of them."

Harrison stepped away from his friends and the murmur of their voices. Details held no interest for him. Jessye, however, was another matter. His last night in a bed had been an uncomfortable affair. He'd been unable to sleep with thoughts of her constantly tumbling through his mind.

He'd tried to concentrate on other women he'd known, graceful, beautiful, genteel. Women who smiled sweetly, laughed softly, and judged his wisdom to be far greater than theirs.

Dull. Every image had bored him. Those women were completely opposite of the woman who would travel with them. He could not imagine her dressed in finery and attending a ball. He was certain she would curtsy to no one, and her forthright language would have the matriarchs swooning, although her smoky voice with its slow drawl would no doubt attract the ear of every gentleman in attendance. He didn't much care for *that* image.

He watched Jessye plop to the ground and talk to Abbie's youngest son, obviously not caring that she would begin their journey covered in dirt. She grabbed Micah. He yelled, and then his deep laugher mingled with Jessye's throaty chuckles as they tickled each other, stirring up a cloud of dust.

A dull ache spread through Harrison's chest. Never in his life had anyone tickled him. Never in his childhood had he laughed.

The pain intensified to an unbearable tightness.

Last night, Jessye had revealed her price with one shattering word that he knew he could never pay.

Love.

He knew nothing of it except to scorn its deceptions and mock its false virtues.

But as the dawn captured her within a halo of muted sunlight, he could not deny that something drew him to her.

Not making her one of his conquests would challenge his moral fiber.

Unfortunately for them both, he feared the fabric was frayed and worn thin.

* 　 * 　 *

Capturing Micah's eager hands, Jessye held him against her. "I give up!" she cried, laughing. "You win."

He scrambled from her lap and pointed to the spectacles that enlarged his violet eyes. "And see, they didn't come off." He tugged on a tiny braided strip of leather attached to the wire that circled his ears and tied together at the back of his head. "Pa made this to hold 'em on so when I'm bein' a knight, they don't go flyin' off."

"Your pa's a smart man."

He nodded, his dark hair flapping against his brow. "We just gotta learn him how to talk right." He jumped to his feet and loped toward his older brother and sister, who were watching the horses.

Jessye rose to her feet, brushing the dirt off her backside and smiling at Abbie. "I can't imagine with your husband's education that your children don't think he talks right," she said.

"It's not the words so much as the way he pronounces them. They find his accent peculiar," Abbie admitted. She was the only woman in Fortune who'd ever made Jessye feel welcome. It was the reason she'd helped pick her cotton during the late summer.

"Do you find it peculiar?"

"No," Abbie said wistfully. "I love his accent, but then I love everything about him."

"It's good that they think of him as their pa."

"It's not hard, when he gives them so much attention. Watching him with the children is like watching you with Micah just now. You would make a wonderful mother, Jessye."

The anguish of inescapable regrets threatened to pummel her. She held it at bay with thoughts of Harry's offer, an offer other men had made as well: the joining of bodies without hearts. "That's not likely to happen, Abbie. A woman needs a husband to have children, and I'm the kind of woman men proposition for the night, not for life."

"Don't sell yourself short, Jessye. You have a lot to offer."

A lot of baggage that she didn't think any man in his right mind would willingly help her carry.

"You just haven't met the right man," Abbie added. "You should meet a lot of men on this cattle drive."

Jessye felt Harry's disconcerting gaze settle on her. She ignored the desire to stare him down, turned slightly, and pressed her shoulder against the post. "I'm not searching for a husband. I'm looking for independence."

"I can't believe you're actually going on this adventure," Abbie said, her voice laced with excitement.

"I was afraid Harry might get his hands on the money and gamble it away before they got the cattle to market," she admitted.

"You don't trust him, then?" Abbie asked, surprised.

Jessye glanced down at her boots. "I don't trust him with money. Don't think he'd hurt me, though. If he tried, I'd shoot him." She lifted her gaze. "How well do you know him?"

"Not well at all. He and Grayson are friends, but Harry hated picking the cotton, and he seldom came to visit."

Jessye snorted. "I remember him sitting in the shade more often than not."

Abbie smiled warmly. "Grayson used to get so angry when he did that."

"Can't say as I blame him."

"Grayson said Harry was a master at cards, so his deft fingers could pluck the cotton more quickly. It was amazing to watch."

Jessye felt as though someone had just spun her until she was dizzy. Were they discussing the same man, the same thing? "I'm talking about Harrison Bainbridge, here."

"I know. He and Grayson had a pact. Harry didn't want to pick the cotton, but he agreed he would fill as many bags as Grayson did. So when Harry's bag was full, he'd sit in the shade until Grayson caught up."

Jessye turned and stared at the fields, thinking back to the long, hot, arduous days of summer. "I never saw him with any full bags," she said quietly.

"Grayson used to tell him that if he'd just continue picking, we'd all be finished that much sooner. Harry didn't think he should have to do more than his share. I couldn't really complain, when he matched Grayson's efforts, which was more than I did."

Jessye felt the prick of guilt as she remembered Kit's defense of his friend last night. He was still angry. His greeting this morning had been clipped and extremely British. Harry, on the other hand, seemed to hold no ill will toward her. Was that because he recognized that she was correct in her assessment of him, or did he have plans to manipulate her as easily as he did cards?

"He'll have to do more than his share on the cattle drive," she said absently. "Can't have any slackers."

"I told Grayson he should go with them, but he won't leave . . . because of the baby."

Jessye darted a glance at Abbie's stomach and was hit with a sharp stab of envy. "I think you're both likely to be the reason he's staying."

"Whatever the reason, I'm glad he's not going. I just don't want him to look back in later years and regret that he missed this great cattle drive."

"Your marriage sure took me by surprise. I thought these Englishmen were just passing through."

"That's what I thought, too, but Grayson found a reason to stay."

The tender expression of love that glowed in Abbie's eyes as she gazed across the land to where her husband stood caused an unaccountable ache deep within Jessye's chest. For what she thought she'd once possessed, for what she now knew she'd never held.

"We'd best get going. We're burning daylight," Jessye announced.

Abbie wrapped her arms around Jessye and hugged her tightly. "Be careful. There's more to these Englishmen than meets the eye."

Jessye nodded, suddenly aware that was her greatest fear.

Sitting on a log, Harrison watched the sparks shoot up from the campfire while the stars looked down. He'd never known such peace.

"I swear, Harry, I'm beginning to think you're on

a first-name basis with the bottom of that deck of cards."

Harrison gazed into Jessye's lovely green eyes. Although he'd never seen her bright red hair unbound, he had a feeling it was as untamed as she was, because curling strands constantly sought their freedom, circling her face, offering the hint of a glorious crown.

She was currently skewing her luscious mouth in such a way that she could blow a constant breeze over those loose strands—an indication that she was holding three of a kind or better.

He loved poker. After his arrival in Texas, he had quickly mastered the game. It contained so many possibilities, and the challenge was to make certain that he barely beat his opponent. He had learned the hard way that a royal flush was never drawn three times in one evening.

He was fortunate the gambling gentlemen of Galveston had only broken his hand and not drowned him in the Gulf waters. He wasn't certain his father would have seen the irony in his demise. His father had feared his gaming debts would land him in the River Thames and had sent him to Texas as an alternative.

He flexed his fingers, trying to work out the stiffness that occasionally crept in to serve as a reminder of his foolishness.

"Is your hand hurting?" she asked.

"It gets a bit stiff if I don't move it often. Did you want to kiss it and make it well?"

Her response was a look of disgust designed to send him scurrying to a corner in shame. It never worked.

"I can't believe you cheated some fellas—and got caught."

"They did not catch me cheating. They assumed I was dishonest because I was blessed with three royal flushes that evening. I could not convince them it was only luck."

"You couldn't convince them because no one is that lucky. You had to be cheating, no two ways about it. Makes me doubt my wisdom in financing this cattle venture."

"I'd never cheat you, Jessye love."

"Prove it." She slapped her cards on the ground. Three queens.

Unfortunately, he could not now reach for the deck and swap his cards without her noticing. "Lady Luck is smiling on me tonight," he said as he laid down a full house.

She snorted in a very unladylike manner. "I don't know how you do it, but I know that you cheat every time."

"Jessye love, I would never cheat you."

She scoffed. "You'd cheat the devil if you could."

He gave her a disarming smile. "Now that I would do, but I'd never cheat an angel."

"I'm no angel."

He pressed his aching palm over his heart. "I beg to disagree."

He scraped his meager winnings across the ground. She wouldn't wager more than two bits per hand, which made accumulating wealth a slow process. "Another hand, Jessye, and I shall attempt to prove I don't cheat."

"Nope. You've won enough from me tonight."

He watched as she crouched before the fire and poured coffee into her tin cup. He tried to imagine the women he'd known in England riding from dawn until well past dusk without complaining once—and the image simply would not take shape in his mind.

He couldn't see them setting up camp or building a fire by which to cook the hare they had shot and skinned only moments before. But Jessye did it, seeming to relish the independence that her iron stomach gave her.

"If you two could keep your voices low tonight, I'd appreciate it," Kit said as he spread his blankets over the ground near the supply wagon. "I'd enjoy a good night's sleep."

Jessye glanced over at Harry, and he saw the faintest blush creep up her cheeks. He liked the camaraderie that settled between them as the night deepened.

"I'll take the first watch," she said as she planted her bottom on the ground and worked her back against the log.

He cursed himself for envying the dirt and rotting wood, but Kit had been right. The clothes she wore did nothing to help a man forget she was female. The absence of petticoats and corsets only made her that much more alluring because so little separated her skin from the open air. With but the flick of a button or two, his palm could meet her flesh. With great effort, he shoved his errant thoughts aside. She did not want his body without his heart, and he had no heart to give.

"I know we've done this two nights before, but I haven't quite figured out exactly what we're watching for," he said.

She lifted a narrow shoulder. "Critters. Desperadoes. Stampeding cattle." She cut her gaze over to him. "Once we round up some cows, you'll need to sing to them to calm them through the night."

"Sing to them? Surely you jest."

"Nope. That's the way it's done."

"Kit's singing is likely to make the animals run off."

"I heard that," Kit grumbled, continuing to arrange his blankets. "I'll have you know that I was a choirboy."

"That doesn't mean you can sing," Harrison pointed out. "It only indicates your mother didn't want to have to bother with you during the church service."

"My mother adored me. She would have kept me at her side until I was eighty. More than likely it was Father who didn't want to be bothered with me."

He heard the touch of wistfulness in Kit's voice, so slight as to be as elusive as a shadow. How hard it must have been for him growing up to see someone who looked exactly as he did receive all the Earl of Ravenleigh's love and attention while he received none. Still, he had known his mother's adoration.

Harrison had only known his mother's hate.

"If we're successful in gathering those cattle we saw late this afternoon, I'll put you both to the test tomorrow night," Jessye said sternly, as though sensing the tension in the air.

Harrison had noticed that she spoke harshest when most women would have coddled. From the window of his room at the saloon, he'd watched her hug her father the night before they were to depart—but the next morning when the leaving actually took place, she'd issued orders to him as though she were a general. She hadn't hugged him then, even though the old man's chin had trembled. Harrison had a feeling it was her own chin she had hoped to prevent from quivering.

"So we'll have cattle here tomorrow night," Kit said.

"Yep. I don't want either one of you forgetting my instructions."

"Instructions?" Harrison snorted. "They sounded like mandates to me."

"Call them what you want. Just be sure you follow them."

"I don't understand why we can't take a cow that has a brand on it. Surely if the owner were about, it wouldn't be roaming the wilds," Kit said.

"I told you before that it's not practical to build a fence. Ranchers just let their cattle graze on the open range. When it's time to take them to market, they gather them up and divvy them accordingly."

"What if the rancher was killed during the war?" Harrison asked before taking a sip of coffee.

"We'll keep a tally of the brands we see. If we discover that a rancher was killed, we'll drive the cattle to market for his widow."

"*What?*"

"We take her cattle to market and bring back her money."

"What percentage does she get?" Kit asked.

"The whole kit and caboodle."

"But why?" Kit fairly yelled, clearly incensed at the idea. "She did nothing—"

"Her husband did it all by sacrificing his life for

Texas," Jessye insisted, a stubborn set to her chin.

Harrison enjoyed watching the passion with which she defended her beliefs. If he could but harness it and unleash it at his will, with his touch . . . and without involving their hearts.

"It was my understanding that the cattle were free for the taking—" Kit began.

"Not if they're branded."

"Yes, even if they are branded, because it's assumed after this length of time if no one has gathered them, there is no one *to* gather them so we can have them," Kit ended on a note of finality that would have ended any discussion among gentlemen. Unfortunately, his adversary was an obstinate female.

Jessye shook her head so hard that Harrison was surprised it didn't fly off. "That's not the way we're doing it."

Kit waved a dismissive hand in the air. "Harry, talk to her."

"Only a moment ago, you forbid me to talk to her."

"I asked that you not talk to her until the wee hours of the morning. Right now, I need you to convince her that this isn't going to be a charitable endeavor. We are not going to adopt the cattle of every widow we run across."

Harrison shifted his backside on the log and met Jessye's challenging gaze. "I know you want to save our blackened souls—"

"You're past saving, Harry."

"And that, Jessye love, is our point."

"I am not stealing a dead man's cattle!"

"But if the man is dead, you can't steal from him." She jumped to her feet. "I can steal from his widow, steal from his children. I am *not* stealing from his children."

Harrison slowly rose. "And if he has no widow or children?"

She pressed her mouth into a hard, straight line until her lips disappeared. "Then they might be free for the taking—"

Harrison breathed a sigh of relief.

"—unless he has grandchildren."

"Good God, woman!" Kit yelled.

Harrison took a step toward her. He knew by the slight jerk of her body that she wanted to move away, but she stood her ground. "Jessye, in order to make the fortune we've envisioned, we *must* get the cattle to market before anyone else. That won't happen if we spend our time hunting down a man's ancestors."

"If we take branded cattle, there's a good chance that they'll string us up."

He shot his gaze over to Kit before returning it to Jessye. "String us up?"

"Hang us—as cattle thieves."

Amused, Harrison shook his head. "Once we explained our mistake to the magistrate—"

"You'll get no chance to explain anything. This isn't civilized England. If we are caught with a cow bearing a brand, we'll be judged as thieves and hanged. Half the time we're our own law here. I'm not saying I approve of it—but that's the way it is."

"Then we shall only take cattle that have no brands—and we'll let the merry widows take their own herd to market."

"It just seems to me that if we're going that way anyway—"

"We have to be the first."

She tucked her arms beneath her breasts and tapped her booted foot on the ground. "All right. We won't help any widows, but it seems selfish to me." She crossed the short expanse, dropped to the ground, and leaned against the log.

Grateful Kit had the good sense not to gloat over their small victory, Harrison sat beside her. He watched Kit settle into his makeshift bed before turning his attention to Jessye. He lowered his voice. "Sometimes, you have to put yourself first."

"Doing that doesn't come easy for me."

"I know."

She slanted her gaze his way. "Seems to come easy enough for you."

He gave her a devilish smile. "Only after years of constant practice."

She released a burst of laughter before covering her mouth and looking toward Kit's supine figure. "He's right, you know. You shouldn't talk to me during my watch. You should sleep."

"I enjoy talking with you. You're not like any woman I've ever known."

"That sure says it all, doesn't it?"

"No, actually, it doesn't say anything."

She gave him a warning glare. "Don't start flirting with me, Harry."

With a sigh, he settled against the hard log and rubbed his beard. He'd considered shaving it. Now he was glad he hadn't. Few amenities existed in the wilderness they traversed. "How is it that you know so much about cattle?"

She looked at the stars, and he wondered if she was

searching for memories or something to replace them.

"Before the war, I knew a fella who herded cattle. He talked about the things he did. I listened. I used to be good at listening."

"You still are."

She sliced her gaze to him, her lips curling into a mockery of a smile that had his chest aching. "Harry—"

"Why do you think every compliment I give you is an attempt to seduce you?"

"Because I'm the only woman out here, and you admitted you're not a man who likes sleeping alone."

"Do you enjoy sleeping alone?"

"Yep. I plan to sleep alone until the day I die."

"What of children?"

She jerked her gaze back to the stars, but not before he saw the pain in her eyes.

"You gotta get married before you can have children. No man in his right mind is gonna tie the knot with me."

"Why? You're bright, spunky—"

"Hardheaded, bossy—"

"Curvaceous—"

"Good with a gun—"

"Soft—"

"Better with a knife."

Harrison chuckled. "Your father has already threatened me with that."

"He'll do it, too. So stop your flirting, because it won't get you anywhere but frustrated."

"This fellow you knew before the war . . . what was he like?"

"He was a long drink of water."

Harrison didn't like the way she'd said that, as though she were parched and this fellow could quench her thirst when no one else could. Jealousy was not an emotion he'd ever encountered before, but if he were to make a wager with himself, he might speculate that he was experiencing it now. He didn't much care for the sensation or the thought.

"Were you . . . involved with him?"

"I'm not one to kiss and tell."

By not telling him, she'd told him exactly what he'd already surmised. But how involved? Had a kiss evolved into an intimate embrace? Had she gifted this fellow with her innocence?

"Did he break your heart?"

She chuckled. "You English are such a romantic bunch. No, he didn't break my heart."

"But you *have* had your heart broken."

An infinite sadness touched her eyes. "Yeah, Harry, I had my heart broken."

⚘ Chapter 3 ⚘

Someone had broken Jessye's heart. Recognizing the depth of pain reflected in her eyes, Harrison had wanted to draw her into his embrace and comfort her, but he had no skill at offering solace.

Sometime later during the night, no doubt seeking comfort—or perhaps more—she had come to him. He felt her weight resting on his chest. He hadn't realized how dainty she was—so much so that he couldn't feel her along the length of his body. That would change the moment he rolled over and tucked her securely beneath him.

With his eyes closed, he slowly lifted his arm so he could cradle her—

"Harry, don't move!" Jessye whispered harshly.

"Jess—"

"Don't move. Don't talk," she ordered. "Don't breathe."

Strange how her voice seemed to come from some distance away when he knew she lay curled upon him. He opened his eyes and stared into black orbs immersed in death—instead of the green of spring he'd expected. A forked tongue slithered out of a mouth that had no lips.

"Don't panic. Kit's aiming his rifle—"

He heard a rattle that sounded like a thousand wooden chess pieces toppling to the ground. The serpent lifted its head—an explosion ripped through the air.

The head disappeared.

Scrambling to his feet, Harrison shoved off what remained of the vile creature. Breathing heavily, his eyes locked onto the scaly beast that jerked and writhed over the ground before settling into death's stillness, Harrison backed up until he slammed against a tree.

Jessye grabbed his arm. "You all right?"

He wrenched free of her hold. "Bloody damned hell, no I'm not all right. What in God's name was that, and what was it doing on me?"

She took his arm again. "A rattlesnake. It's not unusual for one to crawl on a person while he's sleeping. I've heard tales of men waking up to find the critter coiled on their chests—"

He snapped his gaze to Kit, who still held his rifle. "What if you'd missed?"

"Then I would have shot again. It's like the Texans say. I can load this rifle on Sunday and shoot all week."

Harrison pointed his finger at Kit. "You were supposed to be on watch. Why didn't you shoot it before it crawled on me?"

"Because I don't keep my gaze fastened on your

sleeping form like you watch Jessye while she sleeps!" Kit shot back.

Jessye's hold on him slipped away. "You watch me while I sleep?" she asked.

"I keep a close guard on everyone and everything," Harrison lied. In his mind, as long as Jessye was safe, the camp was safe.

"So do I," Kit said. "I was walking the perimeter—"

"A lot of good that did." Harrison took a deep breath, trying to stop his heart from pounding with such ferocity. Rattlesnakes. He'd heard of the poisonous creatures. No one had mentioned they were huge or that they enjoyed using a man's chest as a bed.

Thank God, his wits were returning along with his better judgment. He reluctantly admitted that he unfairly blamed Kit. Truthfully, he never cast a glance Kit's way during his own watch. "I didn't realize you were *that* skilled with a rifle."

"I saw little point in carrying a weapon I couldn't use effectively," Kit said. "Jessye taught me the basics, and the rest came with constant practice."

Harrison rubbed his sweating palms along his trousers. "I suppose I should thank you."

"Yes, you should."

He groaned. "I suppose you intend to hold this little episode over my head—"

"Indeed I do," Kit assured him with a mischievous smile.

"At least we don't have to hunt for breakfast," Jessye said.

Harrison watched as she retrieved her knife and

knelt. "Surely you're not implying that we're going to eat it."

She glanced over her shoulder at him. "It's not half bad. Tastes like chicken."

"I don't care what it tastes like. I do not eat serpents."

"You do if you're hungry. There's a lot of things you'll eat if you're hungry."

She began skinning the snake. He shot his gaze toward Kit, grateful to see that his friend looked a bit queasy.

Kit glanced his way. "Would you like to share a can of beans?"

Harrison nodded, disconcerted to discover that he suddenly wished he were in a field picking cotton. None of the cattlemen with whom he'd spoken had ever mentioned the snakes. He wondered what else they'd failed to mention.

Stubborn, obstinate, pigheaded. A litany of other unflattering words ran through Harrison's head as he shoved his shoulder against the beast's backside. He stood knee-deep in the mud of a small pond while it sat thigh high in the muck and refused to budge.

He had damn near been gored when the animal had unexpectedly jerked his head in Harrison's direction. It could easily thrust those long horns straight through a man, and it looked mean enough to try. He didn't know if he was dealing with a bull or a steer, but he refused to accept that a neutered animal could get the better of him, so as far as he was concerned, the animal was a bull. That status would end shortly after he got it out of the mud.

"He's not worth the trouble. I say we leave him."

He glared at Jessye, who dismounted from her horse and stood at the edge of the pond. While Kit was driving the supply wagon to a predetermined destination, Harrison and Jessye were searching for cattle. Thus far, they had only rounded up six. "I am not leaving forty dollars wallowing in the mud."

The bull released a low bawl.

"He doesn't want to move," Jessye said.

"Then we cheat." Harrison trudged through the sludge, the dank odor rising to suffocate him. It reminded him of the stench of the dungeon, with its mold, dead rotting rats, sweating stone walls, constant dripping, cold—he fought back the images. He refused to succumb to their nightmarish power, and he wasn't going to let a wayward bull have his way.

His feet bare, he stepped back onto firm ground, stalked to his horse, and loosened the rope from its mooring on the saddle.

"What have you got in mind?" Jessye asked.

On one end of the rope, he created a noose as he walked to her. "I've got to figure out a way to get this end around his horns"—he held up the noose—"and you'll tie the other end to your saddle horn. You'll climb onto your horse and pull while I push."

"How are you gonna get that rope around his horns without getting yourself gored?"

"With great care."

"I wouldn't do that iffen I was you fellas."

Harrison jerked around at the unfamiliar voice. A young man sat astride a gray pony. He spit out a stream of tobacco before lifting his hat off his brow with his thumb. "You're gonna pull them horns right offa his head. Makes a bloody mess."

"How would you know?" Harrison asked.

"I was a bogger afore the war—"

"A bogger?"

"Yep. I was the one sent to get the cattle out of the muddy bogs and thickets." The man slung his leg over the saddle and slid to the ground. His long, slender legs curved out, so he walked as though he still had a horse beneath him. "It was a damn lonely job—"

Staggering to a stop, he jerked his hat off so quickly that Harrison felt the air riffle. He also noticed that the man's gaze had fallen to the gentle swells of Jessye's flannel shirt.

"My apologies, ma'am. I thought you was a fella."

Jessye smiled warmly. "No apologies necessary. I'm Jessye, and this is Harry."

"Folks call me Magpie. Don't know why. Reckon it's on account of my legs bein' as skinny as a bird's." He dropped his hat on his head. "I'll learn you how to get this here beast outta the mud."

"Do you know if he belongs to anyone?" Jessye asked.

Deep within his soul, Harrison groaned. He was not exerting all this effort for someone else's bull.

"I don't imagine he belongs to anyone. Ain't a damn, pardon me, ma'am, soul within fifty miles of here."

Thank God for that.

The young man approached him and held out his hand. "Iffen I could have your rope."

"Certainly," Harrison muttered, handing it over.

The man smiled. "You ain't from around here, are you?"

"He's from England," Jessye offered, and Harrison gritted his teeth. He wanted the man to finish his business and be off.

"Now ain't that somethin'," he said before jerking off his boots and trudging into the mud.

Magpie chattered to the bull as he tied the rope beneath and behind the animal's shoulders. Harrison decided the man's mouth, not his legs, had earned him his nickname.

Holding the other end of the rope, Magpie walked to Jessye's horse with a loose-jointed movement of his hips that made it seem as if hurry was a stranger to the man. He secured the rope around the saddle horn. Bending over, he cupped his hands near the stirrup and motioned toward Jessye. "Ma'am, iffen you'll just mount up here and guide the horse back, me and your husband there—"

"He's not my husband," Jessye told him.

A welcoming grin crept onto the man's face. "That so?"

Incensed at the camaraderie developing between Jessye and this stranger, Harrison stepped forward. "She is, however, the investor and, therefore, I would take great offense if she was not treated with the utmost respect."

"Investor? In what?" he asked, his gaze never leaving Jessye.

"Cattle, Mr. Magpie—"

"No mister to it. Just a front name. Ain't got no back name."

Jessye smiled warmly. "We're gathering cattle to take them north."

"Now if that don't beat all. I know cows like I know the back of my hand. Here I was wondering what I was gonna do with the rest of my life—"

"Do you think we might attempt to get this beast out before the sun sets?" Harrison asked.

"Yes, sir," Magpie said.

Jessye slipped her booted foot into Magpie's cupped palms, and Harrison had to restrain himself from snatching it back. Magpie hoisted her into the saddle, a feat Jessye performed on her own every morning.

The man tipped his hat at Jessye. "You do the pullin', and we'll do the pushin'."

Magpie trudged into the mud as though it weren't the most disgusting substance in the area. "You comin'?" Magpie asked.

Harrison glanced at Jessye, the challenging glint in her eyes irritating him more than the damned beast's stubbornness. The slimy mud eased between his toes as he made his way to the back end of the creature.

"Give him a tug!" Magpie ordered just before he leaned his shoulder against the animal's rump. Harrison did the same. The animal released a bawl, followed by a snort.

The bull lurched forward. Harrison lost his leverage and landed facedown in the muddy bog.

"We got him!" Jessye cried.

"We sure did," Magpie yelled.

Harrison twisted his head to see Magpie standing beside him, grinning like the village idiot.

"Reckon I forgot to mention that when they get

good and ready to move, they move fast."

Harrison gave the man a forced grin. "*Reckon* you did, at that."

While he watched Magpie slinging mud as he made his way toward solid ground, Harrison contemplated various methods of torture that his ancestors had developed, trying to determine which one would offer the best revenge.

Jessye quietly wended her way through the trees and shrubbery to the edge of the river and crouched at its bank. Within the moonlight, she saw Harry scrubbing his body with that fancy-smelling soap of his. Sandalwood, he called it. She couldn't understand why that scent mingled with the sweat of his labors always made her want to stand closer to him. Maybe because it was so different from the stench of drunks.

His clothes, now free of mud, were draped nearby over some low-hanging branches. The man sure put a lot of stock in the way his clothes looked. Most cowboys put on their clothing at the start of a roundup and took them off when the trail drive ended and they had money with which to purchase a new outfit. But not Harry. His clothes would be worn thin from washing, not wearing.

The water lapped at his hips as he rubbed briskly with the soap, his back to her. She enjoyed watching the light from the moon and stars chase the shadows over his broad shoulders. She hadn't wanted to touch a man in a long time. Curling her fingers until they bit into her palms, she cursed them for wanting to play the shadow dance over Harry's back. She imagined her lips joining the game. Did Englishmen taste like Texans?

Her tongue circled her lips. She didn't think kissing Harry would be a hardship, and she contemplated that thought more often than she should. Would his beard tickle or caress? Would his mouth distract her so she wouldn't notice?

Therein lay one of her fears. If she gave in to a kiss, she might give in to everything—and she was unwilling to pay the price that came with giving everything, especially to a man who thought a woman could separate her heart from her body.

Still, if she was honest with herself, she liked a lot about Harry. Except the beard. He'd been clean-shaven the first time she'd set eyes on him, with his gleaming black hair falling past his collar and those long, thick lashes framing his emerald eyes. His features were strong, as though chiseled by a hand intent on perfection. She remembered everything about him from that first encounter—even the little indentation in his chin that was no longer visible.

Yep, she liked that intriguing dent. She thought it was a shame he'd grown a beard that hid half his face. She needed to find a subtle way to get him to shave it off just so she could take a little additional pleasure in gazing at him. A pity that the few pleasures on a cattle drive made her resort to contemplating the merits of a man's whiskers.

He'd surprised her today. She hadn't expected him to work so diligently to get a bull out of the mud when he earned the same money with no effort. Her mind longed to understand him; her heart dreaded the knowledge.

"You still angry?" she called out.

She saw him stiffen, and thought that if she were closer, she might have seen his muscles tighten.

"I am not angry." He raised an arm and scrubbed viciously at his skin.

"You've hardly spoken a word since we got that bull out of the mud."

He glanced over his shoulder and nearly cut her with his glare. "It's a bit difficult to speak when someone else is constantly chattering. I'm surprised the man's jaws stay hinged."

"You're upset 'cuz I invited him to join us."

"I thought we had agreed to keep our cadre small until we'd gathered more cattle."

Sighing deeply, she wrapped her arms around her knees. "I know, but he seemed lonely."

Harry spun around, the water swirling out. "Lonely? Are we now to become a haven for lonesome souls as well as lost cattle?"

"No, but he knows a lot about cattle—"

"Which would be fine if he told us exactly what he knew *when* we needed to know it!"

Jessye bit back her laughter, knowing she'd only rile him further if she released it. But Lord, he had looked funny covered in mud—especially since he took pride in looking like he could sit in a widow's drawing room with only a moment's warning. "I know he was sorta unkind not to warn you about slipping in the mud, but some men enjoy pulling harmless pranks. He wants me to send you snipe hunting."

"What in God's name is a snipe?"

"That's the point. There's no such thing, but you send a greenhorn out into the night with a flour sack and tell him he's gotta find one . . . and well, it's funny 'cuz you know he never will—"

"You believe this activity to be humorous?"

"Some folks do."

"Do you?"

Avoiding the question, she cracked her knuckles, wondering if she'd have knotty fingers when she was old like her father constantly warned her.

"Do you?" he prodded. "Do you think it's funny to embarrass someone?"

"No. I just understand that some men never grow up, and I try not to hold it against them."

He waved his hand in the air. "Be off with you. I need to get out of the river."

"Afraid I'll see your shortcomin's?"

With a distinct purpose to his stride and an unmistakable challenge in his eyes, he waded through the water toward her. She jumped to her feet and headed into the bushes. She ought not to tease him. Men were sensitive about certain aspects of their bodies . . . but she couldn't help but wonder exactly what Harry looked like in the altogether. She had a feeling he'd make accepting the challenge worth it.

Harrison walked into the camp, his mood unimproved and threatening to worsen. Magpie was still talking, and Kit, by God, was taking notes. Everyone, it seemed, was intent on betraying him.

Kit looked up. "Fifteen cattle today. Not a bad beginning."

"Not a good one either if you want two thousand head come spring."

Kit glanced at Jessye and rolled his eyes.

"What was that?" Harrison demanded.

Kit looked back at him, his gaze a reflection of innocence. "What?"

"That signal between you two." Harrison pointed his finger first at Jessye, then at Kit.

"Miss Jessye was just sayin' that you was actin' like you was raised on sour milk. Reckon Kit here was agreein'," Magpie offered.

"Sour milk?" Harrison inquired, taking a step toward Magpie.

Jessye lunged between them, smiling guiltily before spinning around and placing her hands on Magpie's shoulders. "I reckon you can tell these Englishmen are a little green when it comes to herding cattle."

"Yes, ma'am, I surely knew that for a fact this afternoon, what with him thinkin' to wrap that rope 'round them horns—"

"I know," Jessye agreed quickly, cutting him off. "Which is the reason I was wondering if you'd be able to keep watch over the herd the entire night."

Magpie's eyes blinked rapidly, and Harrison thought with any luck a fly might pop into the man's open mouth. Jessye had apparently found a way to silence him.

"Usually a watch is only four hours—"

"Yes, I know, but I thought you could stay with the herd all night, and we'd make a place in the wagon for you to sleep during the day."

Magpie shook his head. "You're thinkin' these fellas ain't gonna know how to stop the cattle from wanderin' off or keep 'em from stampeding."

"Exactly."

"Yep, I'll do it."

"Wonderful. I'll bring some coffee out to you later."

Magpie gave her that idiotic grin. "I'll be lookin' forward to it."

He sauntered into the darkness. Jessye spun around, her triumphant smile withering as she met Harrison's hardened glare.

"Were you implying that I have a sour disposition?"

She cleared her throat. "Yes, that's what the phrasing means."

"You sent him to watch the cattle all night so we wouldn't have to endure his constant jabbering."

She nodded. "Just for tonight. Until you learn to appreciate him."

Harrison scoffed. "Appreciate him—"

"He's a fountain of information, Harry," Kit interrupted quietly. "This herding cattle is much more involved than I was led to believe. Besides, he swears he can guide thirty cows single-handedly, which means while we continue to gather more, he can take them to Gray's land."

"You don't think he'll take the cattle for himself?" Harrison asked.

Kit shook his head thoughtfully. "No."

"I despise your blasted instincts."

"They have nothing to do with my faith in the man."

"Upon what, then, do you base your confidence in his trustworthiness?"

"I listened while he told me about a battle he fought in 1863 at a place called Gettysburg."

Harrison shrugged. "Most of the Texans we've met

fought battles during the war. What makes this one so special?"

"It was a bloodbath. Three days ago that lad who irritates you with his constant talking just turned twenty. Think about what we were doing when we were seventeen."

"Harry?" Grabbing her pallet, Jessye eased a little closer to the man lying on his side, his back to her. "Harry, I know you're not asleep. You're not snoring."

"I do not snore."

"Yes, you do. Just a slight purring—"

"Jessye, I am not in the mood for conversation," he tossed over his shoulder.

She disliked the wall he was building between them since Magpie's appearance. It was one thing for her to keep a wall between them. Hers wasn't as thick or as strong. She had a feeling Harry could build a fortress that she'd never be able to breach. "Harry, what *were* you doin' when you were seventeen?"

He rolled over and met her gaze. "What difference does it make?"

She raised up on an elbow. "I can't figure you out. From the minute I met you, I knew you despised being here—but here you are, being someplace you don't want to be, doing something you don't want to do. Why don't you just go back home?"

He set a deck of cards between them. "Cut the deck. If you cut to a higher card than I do, I'll tell you."

"You'll cheat."

He waved his hand over the cards. "How can I

cheat if I'm not holding them in my hand? I can't see through the stack."

She narrowed her eyes in suspicion, reached out, and grabbed half the cards. She turned them to reveal the eight of spades. Harry simply turned over the top card. A nine of hearts.

"Sorry, Jessye. Guess I'll hold onto my reasons a while longer," he murmured as he took the cards from her, put his deck together, slipped it into his pocket, and shifted into position, presenting her with his back.

Damn, obstinate, stubborn man. Leaning toward him, she whispered harshly, "I hate your beard."

He jerked around so fast, came so close, that his hot breath fanned her cheek. She saw the rage burning within the depths of his eyes as he dug his fingers into her upper arm. His breathing grew ragged, uneven.

"Hate!" he spat through clenched teeth. "I should teach you a lesson in hate."

Dear God. She realized clear down to the depth of her soul that he could indeed teach her more about hate than she'd ever known existed. Cold fear rippled along her spine. What had she been thinking to travel with men she barely knew? She'd never seen anger this raw, this intense. She wanted to lash out at him, but some inner instinct warned her that she was safe as long as she held her tongue.

"Harry, you're hurting her," Kit said quietly, laying his hand over Harry's. "She meant no harm."

Harry shifted his gaze from her face to her arm. Slowly, mercifully, he unfurled his fingers. She saw the taut lines of his jaw, watched his throat muscles work, and was both surprised and relieved when he ground out, "There's no reason that lad should have to stay awake all night. I'll take a turn watching the herd."

He shot to his feet and stalked from the camp. She'd never been more grateful to see someone disappear into the darkness. She rubbed her arm, wincing as her palm passed over the tender flesh.

"Are you hurt?" Kit asked.

"No," she lied, the ache surrounding her heart far outweighing the pain in her arm. In the few months she'd known Harry, she'd never seen his temper flare. She had no desire to ever witness that sight again. "Didn't realize he was so fond of the beard."

"It'll be gone when next you see him." Kit stood, walked to the fire, crouched before the low embers, and stirred them to life.

Jessye eased from her pallet, pulled her blanket around her, and huddled closer to the fire. The chill of the night had little to do with the cold swirling through her. "I never knew Harry had such a temper."

Kit stared into the low flames, his pale blue eyes giving away none of his thoughts.

"His anger had nothing to do with the beard, did it?" she asked hesitantly.

"A man's soul is his alone to bare to others." Kit turned his head slightly and met her gaze. "Harry and I are friends because he holds my secrets well . . . and I hold his."

"And I'm just your business partner."

"You're only my business partner."

"And Harry is just one of the hired hands," she said more sharply than she'd intended.

"That was your decision, not mine. If you had any wisdom, you would keep your distance. But I fear the heart has a way of sending wisdom to hell."

She glared at the flames as Kit unfolded his body and walked away. She heard him settle onto his pallet.

"You should at least pretend to be asleep before Magpie returns," he said with a touch of teasing laced in his voice.

She nodded but remained hunched in front of the fire, fearing that if she moved away from the flames, she wouldn't return to her pallet. Instead, she'd search for the man whom she now feared had the potential to hurt her far worse than Gerald Milton had.

She was drawn to Harry for reasons she couldn't comprehend, reasons that were beginning to go beyond the handsome face and the beautiful physique. She wanted to know what had shaped him into a kaleidoscope of inconsistencies. She wanted to be his friend. But she wanted a friendship deeper than the one he shared with Kit. He and Kit were friends because they had shared secrets.

But to reveal her secrets might very well shatter her heart all over again.

❧ Chapter 4 ❧

As *dawn eased over the horizon, Jessye* stared at her reflection in the water, which lay still against the bank of the river. She looked like a hoyden. If she had any sense, she'd chop off her unruly hair. It wasn't as if she'd ever use it to entice a man into her arms. She didn't understand men, didn't want to—

"How badly did I bruise you?" a quiet voice asked behind her, startling her, nearly sending her leaping into the water.

She took a shaky breath. "Didn't notice."

She sensed more than saw Harry kneel beside her. Lord, she didn't want to look at him.

"Let me see," he ordered.

She jerked her head around. "Look, Harry—" His beard was gone, just as Kit had predicted. She dug her fingers into her palm to stop herself from touching the strong line of his jaw. She shrugged. "Bruises heal."

"Only those you can see. I bruised more than your arm—"

"You're making too much of this."

64

"Your eyes are unable to shield your lies. I regret that I harmed you."

"No need for regrets. Last night you said you didn't want to talk. I should have left you alone. Next time I will. After all, we're just business associates, not friends. We don't have to bare our souls to each other."

He gave her a long, thoughtful nod. She turned her attention back to her task, dipping her canteen into the water. "You'd best get ready to ride."

"You asked what I was doing when I was seventeen. I was gambling, drinking to excess, and I took my first mistress."

She tried to concentrate on the gurgling water making its way into her canteen, anything but the words he'd just spoken. She didn't want to know anything about the women who had shared his bed.

"She was a beauty . . ."

Jessye snatched her canteen from the water and stood. "Harry, I don't care."

She took a step away before he curled his hand over her shoulder with a tenderness that stilled her motions, her breathing.

"She was as cold as ice. She wanted nothing more of me than what she could see. She set the standard by which I selected future mistresses."

Jessye glanced over her shoulder at him. "You loved none of them?"

"I know nothing of love, but I know all there is to know of hate."

She faced him squarely. "When I said I hated your beard—"

He touched his finger to her lips. "You meant no

harm. I know that." He cradled her chin within his palm and trailed his thumb along her mouth. "I have never wanted to have a woman beneath me as much as I want you, and therein lies the source of my anger, for I can never give to you the one thing you require. Magpie, on the other hand, could probably give you love in abundance."

She watched him disappear into the thick brush that ran along the stream. Her chest tightened, and tears stung her eyes. Yes, Magpie could probably give her love. Too bad Harry was the one her obstinate heart cared about.

"It's colder than a witch's caress," Magpie pointed out, quite unnecessarily, in Harrison's opinion. But he kept his thoughts to himself as they huddled around the campfire. He was growing accustomed to the lad's constant chattering . . . and missing like the devil the easy conversations he'd once shared with Jessye.

Occasionally, he caught her watching him. While most women would blush and look away, she challenged him with a tantalizing gaze that hinted she sought the secrets to a puzzle. A puzzle he could help her solve. He found it increasingly difficult not to offer her the solution.

"The cold weather shouldn't last but a few days," Jessye said. "This far south, it comes and goes."

"Unfortunately, our supplies aren't lasting either," Kit said. "I propose we head back to Fortune with the cattle we have on hand, spend the holiday with friends, and finish rounding up our herd in the new year."

"You're talking about spending over a month sitting on our asses when we could gather more cattle," Harrison said.

"We're nearly halfway to our goal—"

"Nearly is not close enough as far as I'm concerned."

"We won't start herding the cattle north until March. That'll give us two more months—"

"I'm not sitting in Fortune while someone else is out here gathering the strays I might have found. Leave me enough supplies to get by. I'll bring what I find to Fortune before Christmas."

"You can't herd the cattle alone—"

"He won't be alone," Jessye said quietly. "I'll stay with him."

Harrison jerked his head around. "You are not staying. I am fully capable of herding a few cattle—"

"I know that, but it's my money that's invested in this venture. Every cow we find adds to my profit. I've got no desire to spend a month serving whiskey in Pa's saloon when I could gather cattle."

With the darkness of midnight surrounding him, Harrison drew up the collar on his duster and huddled within his clothing as the rain pounded his back. He should have insisted that Jessye return to Fortune with Kit and Magpie. The warmer weather had yet to make its return. Instead, colder winds had been joined by torrential rains.

Riding beside him, Jessye sat hunched in her saddle. They needed a warm fire, but he'd had no luck finding a dry spot. If she complained, he couldn't hear her over the howl of the wind.

But he seriously doubted that she was complaining.

They had traveled to the west and south for ten days and had yet to find a single cow. It seemed the beasts were more intelligent than either he or Jessye. Setting up camp was pointless when their saddles were warmer than the ground.

She had told him that towns were few and far between, but he had expected to find some sort of shelter. Even after spending several months in Texas, the absolute lack of civilization in this state astounded him. Perhaps they should look into building proper roads and decent taverns where a man could get a stiff drink and a soft, feminine body to warm him through the night.

Guilt pricked his conscience with that thought, and he cast a sideways glance at Jessye. Did she ever long for a hard, masculine body to warm her through the night?

She had asked no more personal questions of him since his fit of rage. They were business associates in the truest sense. If they talked at all, they discussed the cattle and the journey they would make come spring. In truth, he found the conversations utterly boring. The only consolation they afforded him was the opportunity to hear her raspy voice. He imagined that smoky inflection moaning with pleasure, urging him on with whispered words of passion. If only her price was one he could afford to pay.

She sat a little straighter and leaned forward slightly. She pointed her gloved hand. Her mouth moved, but the wind captured her words.

He sidled his horse closer to hers. "What?"

"A house!"

He squinted through the rain. In the distance, a faint

light beckoned. He nodded, not certain if she saw his actions. Not that it mattered. She was already guiding her horse toward the light. He hoped it was an inn, or at the very least a farm with a dry barn in which they could spend the night.

The rain and darkness distorted the light. A few times he lost sight of it, then it reappeared as though by magic. The trees had lost their leaves to winter, and the bare branches snagged his clothing as he followed Jessye. When they passed into the clearing that surrounded a house, he took the lead. He drew his horse to a halt, dismounted, and tethered the reins to the porch railing. Beside him, Jessye followed suit.

He slipped his hand beneath his duster and wrapped his frozen fingers around the cold handle of the revolver. He'd never used it other than to shoot cans. He prayed he wouldn't be forced to use it tonight. Jessye stepped onto the porch. With a frustrated sigh, Harrison leapt over the steps and grabbed her shoulder. He felt her glare even though her hat brim shadowed her face.

"We don't know what we'll find. Let me stand in front," he insisted.

He expected an argument, but she merely nodded, probably as anxious to escape from the cold as he was. He slipped in front of her and knocked. Lightning flashed in the distance, thunder rumbled, and a woman's scream echoed on the other side of the door.

Shoving him aside, Jessye pounded on the wood. Harrison jerked her back. "What do you think you're doing?"

"Someone needs help."

"You haven't a clue—"

The door flung open, and a man who looked as white as freshly fallen snow filled the doorway. Another scream ripped through the house, and the man blanched. "You know anything about birthin'?"

"Not a thing—" Harrison began.

"I do," Jessye said as she sidled past the man and trudged inside.

The man followed her, leaving Harrison with no choice but to do the same. He closed the door behind him, welcoming the warmth of the fire burning within the hearth.

"You got some water heated?" Jessye asked as she removed her hat, gloves, and duster. She rolled up her sleeves.

"Yes, ma'am." The man fetched it for her, and she washed her hands.

"How long has she been in labor?" Jessye asked.

"Goin' on two days." The man turned his attention to Harrison as though seeking understanding. "I thought it'd be like a mare givin' birth to a foal. Ain't nothing like it at all."

"A woman isn't a horse," Jessye said, disgust woven through her voice. "Where is your wife?"

"Back here in the bedroom," the man said, leading the way.

Jessye glanced over her shoulder at Harrison. "Wash your hands."

His stomach tightened at the command, and dread ripped through him. "Why?"

" 'Cuz I'm gonna need your help."

Harrison had grown up listening to his mother's constant badgering. She'd never missed an opportunity to point out that her second son was useless. Until this moment, however, Harrison had not understood the full measure of the word.

Nor resented the fact that he was exactly that—useless.

He hadn't a clue how to bring a child into the world.

But Jessye knew. The knowledge was evident in the defiant set of her chin and the calmness that settled within the green depths of her eyes. When she wiped the sweat from her cheek with a bloodied hand, a darkened brown smear remained. His gut clenched, and his only thought was, *Thank God, it isn't her blood.*

"Help her sit up, Harry," Jessye ordered.

He stared helplessly at the woman gripping the iron railings of the headboard. "I would think that is the last thing—"

"She's gonna need to bear down, and it'll be easier if she's sitting up some. Just put your arms behind her shoulders and help her up."

The determination in Jessye's eyes had him wedging his arms between the woman's back and the sweat-soaked mattress. He didn't know how the woman's trembling body could bear what was to come.

"Oh, Lordy," the woman moaned. "I can't do this."

"Yes, you can," Jessye assured her. "Just push down, push down as hard as you can."

He felt the woman straining, heard her grunts. It was all he could do not to bellow along with her. The sweat streaming down his face stung his eyes as though he was the one caught within the throes of labor.

"It's almost here," Jessye said softly. Her gaze snapped to the woman's, and he was surprised to see tears shimmering within her eyes. "It's got black hair."

"Like her pa," the woman said, panting.

"Give it another push," Jessye urged.

He didn't know where the woman found the strength, or how everything that had been happening so slowly occurred with such speed—but suddenly, a beautiful smile graced Jessye's face as she held a bawling babe in her arms.

"It's a girl," Jessye announced as she placed the child within her mother's arms.

"Ain't she purty," the woman whispered reverently, as though she'd forgotten the pain and trouble the child had just caused and would probably cause for the remainder of her life.

Harrison stepped back, not liking at all the way his gaze seemed to caress the child, as though he might forgive her as well. He swept his attention to Jessye, and the longing he saw reflected in her eyes caught him like a punch to the jaw. In the short time he'd known her, he'd never seen her yearn for anything, but he knew beyond a doubt that right now she wanted to take that child back into her arms.

She turned toward him, and the longing retreated like a shadow touched by the sun. "Why don't you see about warming up some more water? I'll finish in here, and then we'll wash the baby."

He gave a brusque nod and strode from the bedroom. He had no desire to learn exactly what "finishing" entailed.

Before, he'd had little time to notice the plain main room or the furniture held together by rope and wood wedging one piece into another.

The front door opened, and the man stepped inside, his eyes reflecting worry. "I tended to your horses. Put 'em in the barn." His gaze went to the bedroom door.

"You have a daughter," Harrison said quietly.

"A daughter," the man repeated. "And Jo Beth?"

"She seems fine."

The man stuck out his hand. "I'm obliged to you."

Harrison slid his hand into the man's strong grasp. "The ladies did all the work."

"I'm obliged just the same. I'm Peter Haskell. Don't recall that we was properly introduced. Don't recall much but worryin'." His gaze slid back to the bedroom door. "You reckon I could go see my wife and daughter now?"

"I don't know why not." The moment Peter Haskell disappeared into the bedroom, Harrison dropped into a chair. He no longer heard the baby wailing or the woman moaning, but he still envisioned the longing in Jessye's eyes.

He heard the bedroom door open and the soft footfalls. He glanced over his shoulder. Contentment etched within the lines of her face, Jessye held the child curled against her breast.

"I've neglected my duties," Harrison said as he stood. "I haven't warmed the water—"

"That's all right. We're in no hurry."

As he set a pot of water on the stove, from the

corner of his eye he watched Jessye sit in a rocker. She hummed as she rocked the child, holding her close to her bosom. He thought he would carry that image of peace with him until his dying day. Had his mother ever held him with such reverence? Such love?

He crossed the room and crouched before Jessye. A smile eased across her face. "Isn't she perfect?"

"It's a good thing the woman didn't have to depend on me to help her. I hadn't a clue as to what I should do. I suppose birthing comes naturally to women."

Jessye shook her head slightly as she gazed at the child. "Gave birth to one of my own once, so I knew what to do."

Harrison felt as though someone had just punched him in the midsection. "I never realized you'd been married—"

"I wasn't." Her voice carried no shame, no quest for pity. "The fella ran off. The war had just started. Reckon he figured he'd rather face a Yankee bullet than marriage to me."

"The man was a fool."

"I was the fool, Harry. I lapped up his smooth talking the way a cat laps up cream."

"What of the child?"

Closing her eyes, she shook her head. Harrison placed his hand over hers. "Jessye, what happened to the child?"

Tears shimmered in her eyes when she opened them. "I gave her up."

"Gave her up? You hated her that much?"

Reaching out, she dug her fingers into his forearm,

her eyes pleading for understanding. "No, I loved her that much."

He jerked free of her touch. "Love does not abandon."

He stalked to the stove and watched the water, drowning in memories he seemed unable to hold at bay. The softening he'd begun to feel toward Jessye had vanished. He had experienced moments when he'd actually believed her to be warm and loving, moments when he'd thought perhaps she could show him the way to love.

But she had abandoned her child. She was no different from his mother or his mistresses. She was a woman without a heart.

Jessye lay on her side before the hearth, staring at the dancing flames, her back to Harry. She didn't know why she bothered to care about the man. He had a habit of wounding her with words . . . and tonight those words had sliced open a wound that she thought had long ago healed.

Jo Beth and Peter Haskell had offered them the floor in their front room because the barn was wet and cold. She heard Harry's breathing, felt his presence, and was contemplating moving to the barn. She didn't think she could feel any colder there than she did lying here next to him.

She listened to him shifting his body over the puncheon floor. Would he never settle in to sleep?

She heard the tiny wail of hunger in the next room—the sweet echo of innocence—followed by silence as a mother took her child to her breast. Jessye had only held her daughter and nourished her for three days . . . touched her soft hair . . . breathed in the pure scent of her small baby's body. A hot tear rolled toward her temple. How could memories that brought such joy hurt so painfully?

The rustle of Harry's movements intruded on her thoughts. "Will you be still?" she demanded, jerking her head around to glare at him. He sat on his knees, staring at the bedroom door, his hands balled into tight fists on his thighs.

"The baby was crying," he murmured. "Then she stopped. What do you think they're doing to her?"

Jessye eased into a sitting position, folding her legs beneath her. "She was hungry. They're no doubt feeding her."

"They didn't come out here to get any food."

"Her mother . . ." She felt the heat suffuse her face. "Her mother is probably nursing her."

Harry's glance darted to Jessye's breasts before he shifted his gaze upward to her eyes. He gave a short nod. "Oh, yes. I . . . I hadn't thought of that. Did you . . ." He waved his hand in front of his chest. "Did you feed your baby like that?"

"While I had her. Before I *abandoned* her." She couldn't prevent the bitterness from tainting her voice.

He flinched, but his action failed to ease her hurt. "Go to sleep, Harry, and for God's sake stop twisting and turning." She started to lie down.

"I was afraid that they might be hurting the baby."

She stilled, studying his profile as he kept his gaze focused on the door. Little wonder the colonies rebelled. The English were a stupid bunch. "You don't give birth to a baby and then hurt it."

"My mother did."

Her stomach knotted at the surety in his voice. "Not intentionally—"

"When I was four, she led me to the cellar. She demanded that I tell her that I loved her. When I did, she said she hated me, shoved me into the dank storage room, closed and locked the door. In the darkness, I heard the rats squealing, the patter of their paws clicking over the cold stone—"

Jessye's stomach roiled as the bile burned its way up her throat. Touching his arm, she felt the tenseness in his muscles. "Did she do the same to your brother?"

He released a mirthless laugh. "To the heir apparent? To the boy who would become the man who decided where she lived and what her allowance would be once Father died? Of course not. I, on the other hand, was of no value except for the pleasures she found in torturing me."

"Did you tell your father?"

"I tried, but I'd made the mistake of crying while I listened to the rats and waited for them to feast upon me. A serving girl discovered me when she went to the cellar to fetch some of his favorite brandy. He overlooked my mother's transgressions and focused instead upon my red, swollen eyes. After that, he fancied me a popinjay and would have nothing to do with me."

"But you were only a child—"

"A male—even one as young as I was—does not cry. Ever. An earl's son is never a child. He is born a man."

Shuddering, Jessye longed to wrap her arms around him, but she feared his reaction. His voice carried no emotion. His body was coiled tighter than a snake's. Little wonder he knew nothing of love.

"Did she ever take you to the cellar again?"

"Ah, yes," he replied as though no other answer could exist. "Our journey became a weekly ritual. Even when I stopped telling her that I loved her."

"How could she do that to you?"

He slid his gaze to her. "Haven't a clue. I rather suspect she might have been insane."

Taking a deep, steadying breath, she touched her fingers to his cheek, holding his gaze. "She was insane. No mother would have done such a horrid thing to her own child—to any child. A mother's love—"

He shifted his body so quickly that she nearly fell backward. Facing her directly, his emerald eyes were hard as stone, his face set in rigid lines. "Yes, Jessye, tell me all about a mother's love. Explain to me how a mother could abandon her child."

❧ Chapter 5 ❧

"*Looks like you had a rough night,*" Jo Beth said. "I know sleepin' on the floor can be hard on a person. We should have offered you our bed—"

"Don't be silly," Jessye said as she held the bundle of joy within her arms. She hadn't slept after Harry had asked his accusatory question. A bed wouldn't have made any difference. She'd asked herself the same question a thousand times in the passing years, but the words coming from him had hurt her more than she would have thought possible. "A new mother needs all the comforts she can find."

"Well, I sure don't know what I woulda done if you hadn't happened along," Jo Beth said as she eased out of bed.

Jessye stroked the child's soft hair. "You would have managed."

"Not likely. My Pete's a good man, but he worries something fierce."

Jessye smiled at the woman. "Appreciate that he does. Most men don't." She handed the child to her mother.

"You oughta think about staying until the weather warms," Jo Beth said.

Jessye settled her hat into place. "It'll warm up in a day or so, and we'll be that much closer to finding the cattle."

"You watch that fella you're traveling with. I think he has an eye set on you."

"He has his eyes set on my money." With that honest truth nipping at her heels, Jessye strode from the house.

She saw Harry talking with Pete near the saddled horses. Although Jessye had protested, Jo Beth had insisted they take some of the canned goods from her pantry. Jessye slung the saddlebags over the horse's rump before mounting. "Come on, English, we're burning daylight."

Grinning broadly, Pete took a step toward Jessye. "Did Jo Beth tell you we was naming the baby after the two of you? Jessica Harriet."

Jessye felt the tears sting her eyes. "I'm honored. It's a right fine name. I hope the world always treats her kindly."

Harry slanted his gaze toward her. They held no warmth for her. They were as cold as those of the rattler that had curled on his chest. "Pete said he saw unmarked cattle to the south."

"How many?"

"A dozen or so."

Jessye nodded. "Fine."

Harry shook Pete's hand. "Thanks for the tip." He pulled himself onto the saddle and urged his horse south.

With disappointment swirling through her, Jessye kicked her horse's sides and followed Harry's lead.

With a blanket wrapped around her, Jessye stared at the fire blazing within the hearth of the small vacant shack they'd discovered earlier in the evening. They'd traveled three days without rain, three days without sighting cattle.

Three days without speaking to each other.

Strange how they could work side by side, do what needed doing, and never utter a word. She'd always imagined love worked that way—allowed people to communicate in ways that went beyond speech.

But no love existed between her and Harry. She could see in his eyes exactly what she'd seen in her own for over a year after she'd given up her daughter: disgust, revulsion, disrespect.

When she'd returned to Fortune, she'd removed every mirror from her room. She'd been unable to tolerate the sight of herself.

That Christmas, her father had given her a beautiful mirror, edged in gold. "I don't know why you left," he'd said, "but I do know until you face yourself in that mirror, you'll never really be home."

The first time had been the hardest. Each time, it grew a little easier . . . and each time she looked in the mirror, she forgave herself a little more.

But with Harry, she'd find no forgiveness. He was indeed teaching her a lesson in hate, one she would have preferred not to learn.

She heard the thunder rumble. The storm had hit just before they'd spotted the rustic cabin. But even with the fire and the dry clothing she'd changed into, she still trembled from the winter festering within her heart.

Tomorrow, whether or not the frigid winds stayed, the cold within her would leave. She'd wait until Harry started forward, then she'd turn and go in the opposite direction.

She neither wanted nor needed Harry's company. She'd find her own cattle and to hell with him and his judgments.

She heard him roving around the shack, scavenging for odds and ends. Their supplies were sorely depleted, but as long as she had bullets for her gun, she'd have food for her belly.

"You should get some sleep," he said quietly as he dropped beside her.

"You should mind your own business."

"I've been trying to understand how the Haskells determined that they'd named their daughter in my honor when my name isn't Harriet."

"Reckon that's why you've been so quiet these past few days—you can't think and talk at the same time."

"And what's your excuse?" he asked.

"I haven't been in the company of anyone I thought was worth talking to."

He cleared his throat. "Is Jessye short for Jessica?"

"Nope."

"Is it short for anything?"

"Nope."

He sighed deeply. "Jessye, I am striving to mend this rift between us—"

"Some things can't be mended."

"We cannot continue going on as we have been—"

She spun around and faced him. "You got that right. Tomorrow, I'm looking at the back end of your horse and heading in the other direction."

"You bloody well will not. I'm not going to allow you to travel alone—"

"I traveled alone when I was seventeen. Went from Fortune to a mission east of San Antone. That's a long stretch of miles. I gave birth to my baby alone, with no one to hear my screams, hold my hand, or wipe my brow, and I alone decided what was best for her. So don't go telling me that I can't do things alone!"

She grabbed his saddlebag and began rummaging through it.

"What are you looking for?" he asked.

"That dang mirror you use when you shave." She pulled it out and looked at her reflection.

"Why in God's name do you want that?"

"Because I need to see someone look at me without hate in their eyes."

"I don't hate you."

She shoved the mirror in front of his face. "Look inside those eyes, Harry, and tell me that's not hatred lookin' back."

He grabbed the mirror from her hand and threw it into the fire. "I asked you to explain how you could abandon a child you claimed to love, and you answered with silence. I learned the hard way that silence mirrors hatred."

"Go to hell!" She surged to her feet, rushed across the room, flung open the front door, and escaped into the night. The cold winds buffeted her, the harsh rain pelted her unmercifully, tears blinded her as she ran, ran with only one thought: to escape the guilt that gnawed at her constantly, the doubts that plagued her.

She screamed as strong arms snaked around her. She twisted and pounded her fists against Harry's shoulders. "Let me go!"

"You foolish woman! You'll die out here!" he yelled over the howling winds.

"Do you think I give a damn! Don't you understand? I had nothing of value to give her. Nothing! And, God, it hurt, it hurt so bad . . . and it still does. Do you know the agony of waking up every morning wondering if she's happy? Can you imagine the grief of knowing you'll never tuck her into bed and kiss her goodnight?" She bucked. "Now let me go!" She wrenched free of his hold. She managed to take three steps before he grabbed her and pulled her against his body. His arms closed around her, pinning her against him, chest to chest. She tilted her head back. Through her tears, the rain, and the darkness, he was only a blur. "Let me go and leave me alone."

"I can't," he rasped.

Dipping down, he slipped an arm beneath her knees and lifted her. She cursed her arms that betrayed her and slid around his neck, cursed her shivering body that pressed against his, seeking warmth. She doubted she could have run much farther. And what was the point in escape? Sooner or later, she would have to face him. He held the key to her future security; she held the key to his present needs. Money. Money when she would sell her soul for love.

He kicked open the door, carried her into the shack, and set her in front of the fire. She eased forward, extending her hands toward the heat, waiting for it to work its way through her body. She heard him slam the front door. From the corner of her eye, she watched him kneel and riffle through her belongings. "What are you doing?"

"Trying to find you some dry clothing."

"This is all I've got."

He glared at her over his shoulder. "Wonderful." He reached for the clothing she'd worn when they'd first arrived at the shack, clothing she'd hung near the fire so it could dry. "It's still damp," he murmured before reaching for his own bag. "You can wear some of my clothing." He snatched out a shirt and a pair of britches.

"How many outfits . . . did you bring?" she asked, her teeth clattering.

"This is it," he said, turning to face her. He reached for the button on her shirt, and she slapped his hand away.

He sighed deeply. "You have got to get out of those wet clothes before you catch your death."

She hated the wisdom of his words. "Get outta here, and I'll change."

"I am not leaving the warmth of the fire," he explained as he set his clothes beside her. He lifted his blanket, forming a woolen wall between them.

With shaking fingers, she unfastened the buttons on her shirt. "What are you going to wear?"

"It's acceptable for a man to be without a shirt— not a lady. Although I've never understood the reasoning. A woman's chest is so much lovelier to gaze upon."

Jessye fought back her smile as she slipped into his shirt. His words were as deft as his fingers when it came to dealing a winning hand. He'd melt her anger like butter on a biscuit if she allowed it. His shirt swallowed her, but it was dry, warm, and welcoming. She ran her fingers over his trousers. "Your britches are way too big. You wear them, and I'll wrap myself in a blanket."

He lowered the blanket. "I want you out of everything that is wet."

"You are not my boss."

"Jessye, for God's sake, there are moments when stubbornness is not an asset."

She thrust his britches toward him. "Change outside."

He rolled his eyes. "Only if you promise to pray that nothing of importance freezes off."

"I'll pray just the opposite."

He gave her a smile that set her heart to fluttering.

"No you won't. Your words are always tough, but your eyes usually betray your softness."

She waited until he'd walked out of the shack before she shucked her drenched britches, wrapped the blanket around her waist, and tucked it around her legs. The door swung open, and Harry, barefoot and bare-chested, rushed inside.

"It's freezing out there," he snapped as he draped his clothes over the rickety chairs near a rotting table. "I do wish the warmer weather you promised would return."

He moved her damp clothes to the chairs before snatching up her wet clothes and placing them near the fire. Her clothes would be dry by morning, but he'd no doubt be traveling in damp attire.

Damn the scoundrel for being nice when she wanted to remain angry with him. He crouched before her saddlebag. Hampered by the blanket, she couldn't peer far enough around him to see what he was about. "What are you doing now?"

"Looking for your brush. Your hair looks like a rat's nest."

"It always looks like that. It's the way nature made it."

In triumph, he held up her brush and scooted toward her.

"What do you think you're going to do?" she asked.

"Remove the tangles from your hair. I'll be very gentle."

He reached for her braid, and she grabbed his wrist. "Why are you doing this, Harry? Why are you being so nice?"

He dropped his gaze to the brush, running his thumb up and down the bristles. "Because I've hurt you, and apologies are not in my vocabulary."

"All you gotta say is 'I'm sorry.' "

He lifted his gaze to hers. "I'd rather brush your hair."

She lifted a shoulder. "Fine, but I won't forgive you until you say you're sorry."

"You've already forgiven me," he said as he unraveled her braid.

"Have not."

"Have so."

She snorted. "We sound like a couple of children."

"I fear we acted like children as well. What were you thinking to run out into the storm like that?"

She felt his gentle touch as he draped her hair over her shoulder and worked the brush through the snarled ends. Her heart tightened with the knowledge that he'd done this before, no doubt for countless other women, because only a man of experience would know the best way to work the tangles free. "Obviously, I wasn't thinking. I just wanted to get away from the memories."

"Because of the guilt?"

She gritted her teeth. "Harry, I don't want to talk about this."

He stilled the brush and ran his thumb along her chin until she turned her head to meet his gaze. "Jessye, I've pondered your words for three days, and I can't understand them. You said you abandoned her out of love—"

"I did not abandon her. I gave her up. There's a difference."

"Explain it to me."

"Why do you care? It was almost four years ago. What difference could it possibly make to you?"

He cradled her cheek with infinite tenderness. "The pain reflected in your eyes when I said what I did would have brought me to my knees had I not already been sitting. Kit confided to me once of the love he held for another. As his friend, I accepted his words, but I could not fathom his actions or his feelings. What I know of a mother's love is tainted because my mother was an expert in revealing the ways of hate. As for my mistresses . . . they were no better." He slowly trailed his gaze over her face as though searching for something he'd never known. "I have a feeling you're an expert in the ways of love."

"I'm not an expert, Harry. If I was, I wouldn't have

found my belly swelling with the child of a man who wouldn't stand beside me."

"Outside, you said you had nothing of value to offer her. You had yourself, *your* love."

She gave him a sad smile. "I had no husband, no father for her. Back then I had no money. I work in a saloon. I didn't want my baby raised around drunks and gamblers. I didn't want children to taunt her because her ma got caught in a sin."

"I'd say the fellow who left you was the one who sinned."

She shook her head. "He didn't force me. He sweet-talked me. I would have followed him into hell. Guess in a way, I did. When I discovered he'd hightailed it out of Fortune, I was ashamed—not of the baby, never of the baby. But of myself. I didn't want any witnesses to my stupidity, so I ran off. Got to a mission just east of San Antone. The baby was born there. She had the reddest hair, the bluest eyes. That's all I remember about her."

"You left her at the mission?"

"I was gonna take her with me. The priest took care of me until I was strong enough to travel. I was packing to leave when he came to see me. He simply said, 'The Lord works in mysterious ways' and told me to look out the window. A man and woman had stopped by the mission to bury their baby, who had just died. I saw them standing in the cemetery. It was raining. I didn't get a good look at them, but I could tell they wore fancy clothes. Then the man put his arms around the woman and drew her close . . . and I knew they'd take good care of my baby."

"So you gave her to them," Harry said.

"I gave her to the priest and watched as he gave her to them. You asked me once if I'd had my heart broken. Giving her up shattered it into a thousand pieces."

❧ Chapter 6 ❧

Resting up on an elbow, Harrison listened to the logs crackle within the hearth, a sweet harmony enhanced by Jessye's even breathing as she slept curled on her side, a hand tucked beneath her cheek.

In silence, he'd finished brushing her hair. The rat's nest she detested was beautiful in the amber glow from the fire.

Careful, so as not to wake her, he rubbed several strands between his fingers. From a distance, her hair looked like tangled wire, but in truth, it was as soft as gossamer, much like its owner. Jessye was undeniably strong and incredibly vulnerable. A woman with a shattered heart. And he had unmercifully gouged those shards into her time and again.

It had hurt to love his mother and to know only her hate. He had shackled the emotion in the darkest pit of his soul where none could touch it, where it could not threaten to taunt him with what he could never possess.

Just as he had learned to cheat at cards, he had mastered cheating at love. Love could be imitated with baubles, flowers, and hollow words. A touch here, a kiss there, a whispered endearment. Until Jessye, he had always taken great care in choosing his gaming partners. He always selected those who understood the rules and cheated as well.

Jessye had played the game of love with a cheater once before—and she had paid dearly for her innocence. She was not likely to play the game with him.

For the first time in his life, he wished he understood love, so he could play fairly without manipulating her heart . . . in order to gain her body.

"I'm thinking we should head west," Jessye said. The rain had stopped, and she felt the new direction of the wind, bringing the warmth.

"South." Harry extended his deck of cards toward her. "Cut the deck. If you get the high card, we go west. Low card, we go south."

"Cutting a deck is not the way to make a business decision."

"But you won't compromise."

She slammed her eyes closed. Why was she even considering cutting the deck? She could just head west and he'd follow. She knew from last night's conversation that he was too much of a gentleman to let her ride alone. Releasing a frustrated sigh, she opened her eyes and cut the deck a quarter of the way down. Nine of hearts.

Harry cut to a card in the middle. Jack of clubs.

One of these days, she was going to figure out how he cheated.

Sitting astride her horse atop the rise, Jessye stared at the cattle roaming the land. "How did you know they'd be here?"

"I didn't."

She narrowed her eyes. There were too many long-horns to count. Their coats differed in shading, but they were all lean, bony creatures. "They have to belong to someone."

"I don't see any brands."

"How many do you reckon there are?" she said, her voice low, disbelieving.

"A hundred at least. Probably more. It'll take more than the two of us to drive them back to Fortune."

She cast a sideways glance at Harry. He was unfolding a map. After a week of traveling, he was unshaven, covered in dust and grime. But he looked over the herd as a conqueror might have, with the slightest smile of triumph. "Why were you so sure the cattle were here?"

He studied his map. "I wasn't."

"We just got lucky?"

He sighed heavily. "If you must know, I tried to think like a bull."

She stared at him. "What?"

He cast his arm out in a circle. "Look about you. The weather is warmer. There is plenty of water, and the grass is plentiful even though winter is upon us. If I were a bull, this is the haven I would seek."

"Harry—"

He held up a hand. "To ease your doubting mind, we shall take a slow, cautious ride around the perimeter of the herd. You may keep a sharp lookout for brands. If you spot none, and if we find no one living about who can lay claim to these cattle, then we shall head to the nearest town"—he looked at his map—"which I judge to be a day's ride away if we ride in haste. There we will hire a few men to help us herd the cattle back to Fortune."

"If men are that close, why haven't they already rounded these cattle up and claimed them?"

"Because, Jessye love, not every man is willing to risk everything when there is a chance he will gain nothing. Look at the men of Fortune. We offered them this opportunity, and they turned it down, preferring to pick cotton." He urged his horse forward. "Come along. Let's ease your mind."

Nudging her horse to follow, she wondered why she felt that Harry was somehow cheating.

For the first time, Jessye wished that she'd brought a dress. A foolish thought, when the town was mostly populated with men. She and Harry sat at a corner table in a log cabin saloon that made her father's place look grand.

They had taken advantage of the bathhouse next door. Her clothes were clean and pressed, but they were the clothes of a man, and she knew deep in her heart that it was for the best. Still, she wished she had something pretty to wear, even if it was nothing more than a colored ribbon.

Harry, on the other hand, was dressed in a black waistcoat, a red brocade vest, a black cravat, and black britches that hugged his thighs. He had shaved and looked deliciously wicked. When he'd stepped out of the bathhouse, he'd literally stolen her breath, and she had yet to recover it.

Damn the scoundrel for distracting her when all her attention needed to remain focused on the men they were interviewing. A man approached the chair across

from them, turned it, straddled it, and braced his forearms along its back. He was ruggedly handsome, with
broad shoulders and the roughened hands of a man
who worked outdoors. He slid his hat from his head
and gave a slight nod. "Ma'am."

She smiled softly. "I'm Jessye Kane. This is Harrison Bainbridge."

His grin revealed a dimple in his left cheek. "Dan
Lincoln, but I'm hoping you won't hold the name
against me."

"We won't, Mr. Lincoln," Harry said before Jessye
could respond. "Have you herded cattle before?"

Dan Lincoln shifted his gaze away from Jessye to
Harry. "Yes, sir. Before the war, I herded cattle to
San Francisco. During the war, herded 'em east."

Harry raised a brow. "So you were too cowardly to
enlist?"

Jessye gasped. "Harry—"

"Confederate soldiers needed to eat," Dan Lincoln
cut in, his voice taut. "I saw to it that they did until
July of '63 when Grant took Vicksburg. He sliced the
Confederacy in half. That's when I enlisted."

"You took cattle across the Mississippi?" Jessye
asked.

Lincoln hesitated before gazing back at her. "Yes,
ma'am."

"That took a great deal of courage, Mr. Lincoln."

"Yes, ma'am. Reckon it did. Many a man drowned
in the Mississippi trying to get meat to the Confederacy. I dadgum guarantee you that I'm a strong
swimmer."

"That's all well and good, Mr. Lincoln," Harry said
curtly, "but we don't need swimmers. Thank you for

your time, but we can't use your services."

Lincoln narrowed his eyes and started to rise. Jessye laid her hand over his forearm. The strength she felt there astounded her. "Please wait." She turned her attention to Harry. "May I speak to you outside for a moment?"

Harry tugged on his brocade vest. "Certainly, Jessye love."

Clenching her teeth to keep from mouthing her thoughts, she stood and strode from the saloon. She heard Harry's footsteps following as she rounded the corner into the alley between the saloon and the bathhouse. She swung around and faced him. "What are you doing?"

"I am attempting to hire some men to help us herd the cattle to Fortune."

"Why didn't you hire Dan Lincoln?"

"I didn't like the man."

"Why? Because he smiled at me? Harry, the men who herded cattle to the army during the war were some of the bravest this state produced. He's exactly the kind we need on this trek. You've talked to over a dozen men and you've hired two. One is old enough to be my grandpa—"

"He has experience."

"And the other is as homely as a sack of potatoes."

"I don't think we should judge a man's abilities based on his looks."

"You're right. You can't turn a man away because he's handsome, has a nice smile, or his gaze drops to my bosom!"

"His gaze did more than drop. It lingered!"

Jessye laughed. "You're jealous."

"I am not jealous."

"Would you hire Dan Lincoln if I wasn't here?"

He pressed his lips into an invisible line, his jaw tightly clenched.

"Would you hire him?"

"Yes, damn it, but you are here. I am simply trying to protect you from scoundrels. I know one when I see him."

"So do I. You know I'm not innocent, Harry."

"You've had experience with one man. That does not make you a woman of the world."

"But it makes me a woman who knows the cost of lifting her skirts for a man. It's a price I'm not willing to pay ever again—no matter how attractive the smile, no matter how long a man stares at my bosom." She wrapped her hand around his arm. "Don't you understand that I invested my money in this venture because it will guarantee me the independence I've never truly had? A woman of poverty has to say no a thousand times. A woman of wealth has to say no only once to be heard. We have to hire the best if we want to meet with success. I've known failure. I don't care to repeat the experience."

He cradled her cheek, his gaze sweeping over her face. "There are moments when I wish to God that I wasn't a scoundrel. We shall hire whomever you want, and I shall kill anyone who harms you."

She watched him stride back to the saloon. And damn the man. He carried a portion of her heart with him.

➥ Chapter 7 ➥

A soft glow spilled into the night from the windows that circled the house. Harrison gave a hard knock on the door. It swung open, and he grinned at Grayson Rhodes. "Merry Christmas."

Grayson took his hand and pulled him inside, into a large front room that smelled of cinnamon and apples. "You scoundrel, why didn't you let us know you were coming?" He looked past Harrison, and his smile widened. "Jessye, come in."

Harrison stepped aside so Jessye could enter.

Abbie rushed across the room and took Jessye within her arms. "You survived."

Jessye laughed. "Barely."

"Was it worth it?" Kit asked as he approached and handed them each a cup of warm apple cider.

Harrison dipped his head toward Jessye. "Tell him."

She grinned like a child who had just discovered her Christmas stocking didn't contain a lump of coal. "We just added a hundred and fifty head to the herd."

"Do tell?"

She nodded. "And six men."

"To the herd? How much do we get for them?"

Her face was aglow, her cheeks bright red. Harrison didn't know if it was from the cold winds that had started to blow again or the excitement regarding their accomplishment. He only knew he wished he had the power to sustain the lust for life emanating through her at this moment. It was almost contagious, even for a soul as jaded as his.

"No, we hired six men. They're outside—"

"Get them in here," Grayson ordered. "It's chilly out there."

"We're all a bit rank," Harrison explained.

"What does that matter? It's Christmas. Get them inside," Grayson insisted.

"I'll help 'em with their horses," Magpie said as he peered around Kit.

"Magpie!" Jessye cried. "I didn't see you standing there."

"Didn't want to impose on the homecomin'."

"Enjoy your holiday, lad?" Harrison asked.

"If only he'd taken a holiday," Kit said. "Every day, he searches for stragglers and strays from dawn until dusk. He seems to have a nose for finding them."

"I just try to think like 'em is all."

"That's what Harry does," Jessye said, grinning. "That's how we found so many."

Harrison stifled a groan. He'd preferred for his method to remain a secret. "Why don't you get warm while I get the men?"

He ordered the men to take the horses to the barn and tend to their needs before they came into the house. Introductions were made. Grayson and Abbie's home was not large, but the main room was comfort-

ing. The candles flickering on the cedar tree in front
of the window were responsible for the welcoming
light he'd seen as they neared.

With the exception of Magpie, the men preferred
quiet to gab. Jessye sat on the floor before the hearth,
Abbie's three children gathered around her as they
proudly displayed the gifts they'd received for Christmas. Johnny was eight. He demonstrated a fishing
pole that had a wooden contraption on it that allowed
him to wind the string that held a hook at the end.
Lydia, six, was placing a fabric doll in a wooden cradle. Micah, the youngest at five, was holding a
wooden shield and blunt-tipped wooden sword.

"Care for something a bit stronger than apple cider?" Kit asked, extending a glass toward Harrison.

"Appreciate it." He relished the sip of burning
whiskey and tilted his head toward the children. "I
didn't think to bring gifts."

"Not to worry. Your presence is gift enough."

Harrison chuckled. "For you and Gray, perhaps, but
not for the children. It suddenly dawned on me that
this is our first Christmas away from England. I hadn't
expected to miss it."

"Ah, yes. The grand halls, magnificent feasts, ser-
vants scurrying to answer our every beck and call, the
pageantry. The hypocrisy of having so much and not
appreciating any of it."

"Is that why our fathers sent us here?"

"Perhaps. Do you know I think Gray made those
toys?"

"You're joking."

"No, he has become quite the father. He adores

those children. You would think they were his," Kit said.

Harrison glanced across the room to the far corner, where Grayson talked with his wife. Her hand moved to her slightly rounded stomach as she smiled. His hand covered hers, and he brushed a kiss across her lips.

Harrison returned his attention to the people before the hearth. Jessye watched the exchange with longing in her eyes, similar to what he'd seen the night she'd delivered the baby. Micah, the youngest boy, shoved his shield in front of her face. She laughed and hugged him.

He wondered if she thought of her own child every time she hugged one who belonged to someone else.

"So how did things go between you and Jessye this past month?" Kit asked.

"Things went . . . not well enough."

"Has she decided you deserve to be a full partner?"

Harrison sliced his gaze to Kit. "That arrangement does not bother me. Why in the bloody hell must it drive you to distraction?"

"Because you deserve better."

"So does she. She's a remarkable woman, Kit."

"Have you fallen in love with her?"

"Don't be an ass."

Kit nodded with an irritating smirk and crossed his arms over his chest. "Are these all the men you hired?"

"Yes. That Dan Lincoln is a good man, a natural leader. I think he would make an excellent choice for trail boss."

"I'll trust your judgment on that. We have over

nineteen hundred cattle. If we hire more men and continue to scour the countryside for the next two months, we should have an impressive herd to take north."

"Impressive, yes." Harrison studied the amber liquid in his glass. "Actually something did happen while we were away. Jessye delivered a baby."

"Good God! She was with child? She didn't look it."

Harrison rolled his eyes. "No, you dolt. We came to a farm where a woman was in labor. Jessye helped deliver the baby."

"Ah, well, that's a different matter entirely, isn't it?"

"Of course, it is. The dilemma, however, is that a bond developed between us that night that I can't explain, a bond so strong that we've shared a bit of our pasts."

"Danger lurks in secrets revealed."

"Must you always be so damned philosophical? I'm trying to understand. All I know of love, I learned from you."

"A shame, since my experience resulted in tragedy."

"Still, I thought perhaps you could explain to me what I am unable to comprehend."

"Love cannot be explained. It cannot be taught. It cannot even be understood, but when it touches you, when it takes hold of your heart and your soul . . . you are the better for it." Kit's gaze circled the room. "Perhaps you should try again to convince Jessye not to travel with us."

"I could just as easily turn back the wind."

Kit released a melancholy sigh. "You know, my trusted friend, it is not Jessye's heart that concerns me, but yours. You have known the pain of hatred, but not the pain of love. It is far, far worse."

"That's just what I want to hear."

" 'Tis better to be forewarned than to be caught unawares."

∽ Chapter 8 ∽

Spring, 1866

*A*s dawn hovered beyond the horizon, Jessye stood and looked with pride at the herd she'd helped round up. With diligence and the additional men they'd hired after they'd returned to Fortune, they'd managed to increase the size of the herd considerably in the two months since Christmas.

She'd noticed, however, the way a few of the men studied her, and her confidence in her ability to handle them had faltered. She'd stuffed her hair beneath a beat-up broad-brimmed hat and wound strips of cloth around her chest until she was almost as flat as a flapjack.

The cattle would stretch out for miles, the men along with them. She closed her hand around the gun she wore strapped to her hip, although she knew in her heart that it was unlikely she'd find the courage to use it against a man—regardless of the circumstances.

She heard a horse whinny and spun around. She forced bravado into her smile as she faced Harry. "I can't believe we're finally ready to take them north."

His gaze slowly traveled from the brim of her hat to the toes of her boots. "Have you lost weight?"

The heat of embarrassment scalded her face. "No, I...I bound my..." She cleared her throat as his gaze captured hers. "I thought it best to remove temptation with so many men about."

He gave a long, thoughtful nod. "Don't suppose you'd reconsider the wisdom of staying."

She shook her head briskly, her smile broadening. "Nope. I wanna be there when they tally the cattle and hand over the money."

"We'd bring back your share of the money, Jessye."

"I just want to be there to see it, Harry."

He released a deep sigh. "Then mount up, Jessye love."

She pulled herself into the saddle. "Who's going to lead the herd?"

"Kit is the man with the details. He wants to have a few words with the men gathered at the supply wagon before we head out."

Her heart swelled with self-satisfaction as she followed him. Half the cattle belonged to her. Half the profits would go into her pockets...along with an independence that no man could ever take from her.

The cool March air surrounded them, and she saw wisps of smoke curl in front of Harry's face as he breathed. She knew in her heart that he was probably right. She should stay behind. What sort of investor was she not to trust her comrades?

One who had paid a dear price for betrayal.

As they neared the wagon, she saw the men mingling around, talking, waiting. None were mounted. It seemed odd to see the trail hands without horses beneath them. She noticed Kit standing near his bay gelding. Harry gave his friend a brisk nod as he drew his horse to a halt and dismounted. Jessye slipped her foot out of the stirrup.

Harry wrapped his hand around her ankle. "Stay where you are. Kit will join you."

She watched him walk toward the other men, leading his horse behind him. The lonesome image he created surprised her.

Kit mounted his horse and guided it around to Jessye's side. She'd never realized how small she was in comparison to him as he sat tall in the saddle. Even though Kit was beside her, Harry's presence dominated the camp. He spoke not a word, but the men who had been mumbling fell into silence. Other men stopped fidgeting. Into the autocratic stillness, Kit finally spoke.

"We have close to three thousand head of cattle and a short span of time in which to move them to Sedalia, Missouri. The days will be long, the nights longer. My father taught me that a man was better able to meet his expectations when he knew what they were so here is what I expect: hard work, no grumbling, no cursing, no drinking. You men spent three months burning our brand into the hides of those cattle. A T that rests on top of an L. The Texas Lady. She's traveling with us because she's financing this venture. She's your boss as much as I am. Her voice carries as much authority as mine. Display any disrespect toward her, and you'll find yourself on a long walk back home with no coins jingling in your pockets. If you have any problems with my expectations, don't bother to mount up."

Silence grew thick until Harry swung up onto his saddle. Magpie quickly followed his example, then Dan Lincoln. One by one, the men mounted their horses.

Kit gave a brusque nod. "Gentlemen, let's take these cattle to market."

He started to guide his horse away. Reaching out, Jessye grabbed his arm. He glanced back at her.

She swallowed, her mouth dry, her heart pounding. "Thank you for that."

"Don't thank me. They were Harry's words."

Jessye walked through the camp, her muscles protesting. The first day of their journey had begun before dawn, and they'd continued moving until dusk. The cattle were settling down for the night, several riders circling the herd to calm them.

She smelled the aroma of baked beans and fresh coffee. Her stomach rumbled, but she wanted to remove some of the dust before she ate. Kit was talking with the young wrangler he'd put in charge of the remuda. She had to give Kit credit. He left no details to chance.

Slim walked away as Jessye approached. Kit smiled. "Rough day?"

"You'd think after all these months I'd be used to it."

"We pushed a bit harder today, plus there's the excitement of actually being on our way."

She jabbed the toe of her boot into the dirt before

peering up at him. "You're still upset with me over that contract I wrote up."

"I think you've misjudged Harry."

"He doesn't seem to have a problem with it."

Kit scratched his chin. "He wouldn't let you know if he did. British pride and all that rubbish."

"Maybe you've been his friend for so long that you no longer see his faults."

"Or maybe I've simply learned to see beyond them."

"Then you have an advantage over me, but I'm not going to change the terms of the contract." She angled her chin defiantly. "But I *am* going to mosey down to the creek and clean up a bit."

"I think most of the men are either with the herd or at the wagon eating."

"If you hear gunfire, come running."

"Did you want me to accompany you?"

"I'll be fine. I'm just gonna wash up, not take a real bath. Have you seen Harry?"

"Not since we stopped for the night."

Nodding, she glanced around the campsite. The men they'd hired were all respectful toward her, but deciding where to bed down wasn't going to be easy. "I'll be back in a bit for supper."

"If you see Harry, tell him he has first watch."

She smiled broadly. "He'll love that."

"No, I imagine he'll find some unsuspecting man and gamble his way into a full night of sleep."

Laughing, she strode into the copse of trees near the camp. Kit was no doubt right. Until the men learned that they couldn't trust Harry with a deck of cards, he would probably never have a watch.

She heard the gurgling of the nearby brook, smaller, more secluded than the river beside which they'd left the cattle. She should have some privacy here. She was on the verge of stepping into the opening when she spotted Magpie sitting on a log near the edge of the water, poking a stick into the mud. She'd never seen such a dejected soul. She took a step forward.

"Magpie," Harry called out, striding along the bank, "I've been looking all over for you."

Jessye stepped back, hiding in the brush, watching as Harry crouched beside the young man.

"What's troubling you, lad?" Harry asked.

"Nuthin'." Magpie tossed the stick into the creek.

"You've been awfully quiet."

"Got nuthin' to say."

"Kit's going to be disappointed to hear that."

"I doubt it. I ate dust most of the day." Magpie jerked his hat off his head and scrunched it. "I ain't complaining."

"Of course, you're not."

"I just . . . I just thought since you hired me first that I'd get to be trail boss. Instead you give the job to Dan Lincoln."

"Kit and I discussed it late into the night. It wasn't an easy decision to make, but Lincoln has a lot of experience herding cattle in very unfavorable conditions."

Magpie nodded solemnly. "And I'm just a bogger."

"On the contrary, you're our chief advisor."

Magpie snapped his head around. "What?"

"Kit's concern was that if he gave the responsibility of trail boss to you, you wouldn't have time to advise him, and he wouldn't know for certain if he was making the right decisions. Why, this very moment he is waiting on a report regarding your thoughts on the progress we made today."

"You're joshin' me, right?"

"Certainly not. Kit values your opinion and writes down every word you say."

"There was a few things I noticed today that I think we oughta do different."

"Then you'd best let him know."

"On account of me being the chief advisor?"

Harry placed his hand on the young man's shoulder. "Let's keep the title of your position between us, shall we? We don't want to cause discontentment or rebellion among the men."

"Yes, sir. You're right about that. You reckon I oughta tell Kit everythin' I'm thinkin'?"

"Every thought."

Jessye waited until Magpie had disappeared through the brush before stepping from her hiding place. "Chief advisor?"

Groaning, Harry glared at her over his shoulder. "How long were you there?"

"Long enough." She sat on the log Magpie had vacated. "Didn't think you liked Magpie."

"I don't, but it's bad enough riding at the back of the herd without having a morose rider beside you. Besides, I needed to punish Kit. He botched his speech this morning."

"You mean he botched *your* speech."

He narrowed his gaze. "That's exactly how he ruined it—by telling you they were my words. I wanted to throttle him when he told me this evening. Instead

Magpie will do it with constant chatter."

"Don't you worry about losing Kit's friendship?"

"Our friendship was forged within the fires of hell. It can withstand the heat of anger."

"You're incredibly lucky," she said quietly.

His eyes widened. "*I* thought *you* thought I cheated."

She scowled at him. "I do think, no, I *know* you cheat at cards, but I meant you were lucky to have the friendship with Kit that you do. The closest thing I've ever had to a friend is Abbie, but I've never bared my soul to her."

"I would think that you would have an abundance of friends."

She frowned. "Working in a saloon? Men were only willing to be friends if I was willing to give them more than friendship, and women always worried that I was flirting with their men. Abbie had no worries because her first husband never came to the saloon."

"And neither does her second."

"Not now that he's married to her."

"Must have been lonely," Harry said with a hint of speculation in his voice.

She shrugged. "I had my pa. Reckon he was always my friend, but there are some things you can't tell your pa."

"Like finding yourself in a troubling situation?"

She stared at the small creek. "Yep. I never told him about all that. I was afraid he might go after Gerald—"

"Gerald?"

Grimacing, she felt the heat burn into her cheeks.

"The man I loved." She jerked her head around and held his gaze. "I *did* love him."

"Of course you did. You wouldn't have lain with him otherwise."

She pressed her hands between her knees. "You believe that?"

"Why shouldn't I? Good God, Jessye, you've got two dozen men out there, and you're doing your damnedest to make certain none of them think of you as a woman. Your morals are commendable. Your judgment . . . questionable."

"You never knew Gerald. He was such a dreamer, and he had me dreaming right along with him. But then the dream turned into a nightmare. I never told Pa anything. I was afraid it would hurt him too much. He never asked me why I left or why I came back."

"I suspect he knew. He was aware your heart had been broken."

"But I don't think he knows the specifics." She held his gaze. "I suppose you mentioned my shameful past to Kit. He told me once that you bare your souls to each other."

"I would bare *my* soul to him, but never yours. As for your *shameful* past, I've told you before that the shame rests with the man who abandoned you."

"I can't figure you out, Harry. You only let me see tiny parts—"

"Believe me, you would completely dislike the whole portrait."

"I'm not so sure. Kit wants me to make you a partner."

"There are many things that Kit wants. Ignore him."

She averted her gaze, trying to find the words.

"Jessye, you worry about things that are of no consequence."

She twisted around and faced him. "I trust you more than I once did."

He grinned wickedly. "As well you should."

"But you gotta understand that this cattle drive is everything to me, and I can't afford to make errors in judgment."

"I do understand. More than you realize."

She nodded. "I'm a little curious. What were your father's expectations?"

Harry looked toward the water. "That I would fail, and I was quite successful at meeting those expectations."

"I wish I could make you a partner, Harry, but I just can't. Not on this cattle drive." She rose to her feet and walked away, wondering why the guilt continued to fester.

The camp grew quieter as the darkness deepened. Jessye sat on the fringes of the camp, close enough to hear, far enough away so she wouldn't be noticed. She enjoyed watching the camaraderie between the men, wanted to be part of it, but knew she was safest if she kept herself apart from them.

Some of the men slept, preparing for their watch. Most were studying the cards Harry had just dealt them. She'd considered banning gambling—after all, Harry had banned cursing and drinking—but what else was there for a man to do but stir up trouble?

And trouble they didn't need.

Kit sat beside her, his ever-present pad of paper and

pencil in hand. The man did more writing than a school marm.

Jessye pointed her spoon toward the circle of men. "So how come you never join them?"

"Because I value the worth of my dollar more than they do."

She cast him a sideways glance. "Because you know Harry cheats." She moved the beans around on her plate. "I don't like to see him taking their money."

"He doesn't win every hand."

"He wins enough. He doesn't realize that the money these men make at the end of the trail has got to last them all year."

"I would say that was their problem, not his. He offers the game. He doesn't force them to play."

"But gambling is like whiskey. Some men just can't say no to it."

"So perhaps your father should close down his saloon."

Jerking her head around, she narrowed her eyes. "Your point being?"

"You can't condemn one vice without condemning them all. Life is a series of choices, and as my father taught me, you live the remainder of your life with each choice made."

"You always think with your head?"

"No. Unfortunately, when the situation warrants it, I tend to think with my heart. It is not so wise, and the regrets are—"

"Hot damn!" Magpie cried.

Jessye returned her attention to the men. Magpie wore a grin that spread from one ear to the other.

"Two aces. Who would a thought I'd beat you with

two aces? How much do I owe you now?"

She watched Harry glance at his tally sheet. Playing on credit was another idea she didn't approve of, but she wasn't about to start doling out anyone's pay until they reached Sedalia.

"Let's see, lad," Harry said, making notations. "You owe me eighty-three dollars."

Magpie's smile eased. "Well, at least I can still get me a new pair of boots. Reckon I ought to call it a night."

"You ain't gettin' them boots if you play him tomorrow," one of the men sneered.

"Don't know why you're so uppity," Magpie retorted. "You owe him ninety-six."

"Yeah, but I feel Lady Luck is about to kiss my cheek," Red said.

"That's the only lady what'll kiss you," Magpie said with a guffaw.

"That's one more than will kiss you," Red told him.

"Now, gentlemen," Harry said, raising a hand. "Enough with the insults. Who wants to play another round?"

Jessye watched the men toss in their rocks. Rocks instead of coins. She should have known Harry would work out a way to gamble with men who had yet to earn any dollars. She sighed. "Three weeks on the trail, and he's already got most of their money in his pocket. No wonder it didn't bother him when I wouldn't sign him on as a partner. He's gonna end up with a bundle of money anyway."

"They only owe him on paper. If a good wind snatches it from his hand, they'll have to start over."

"You think he'd do that?"

"I know he would. He cares nothing for the money, Jessye. He cares only about winning."

Jessye watched one of the hands amble into camp, a worried expression on his face. "Cows are restless tonight, Dan. I think we need a few more riders circling the herd to lessen the chance of a stampede."

Dan looked toward Kit. "It'll make the men tired tomorrow, but a stampede could leave a few of them dead tonight."

Kit nodded. "Take as many as you need."

Without hesitation or complaint, the men tossed their cards into the circle and scrambled to their feet. The one thing they all knew and feared was a stampede. Jessye was surprised to see Harry gather up his cards before standing and heading for his horse. She didn't want any of the men in harm's way, but at least the Texans knew how to handle a stampede. The Englishmen . . . she didn't want to think about what might happen to them if the cattle took off at a haphazard run. "We don't need all of them out there," she said.

"Harry?" Kit called. "I want to talk with you."

She felt her stomach loosen. Why she worried about the scoundrel she'd never know, but she was grateful he wouldn't be circling the skittish cows.

Harry strutted over like the lord of the manor. Only a contract kept him from officially being recognized as one of the partners. No man in the outfit questioned orders he gave, and he gave them as though he had the right. She'd considered putting him in his place a time or two, and she would if he ever gave an order with which she didn't agree. Unfortunately, he had yet to make that mistake.

He hunkered down in front of them. She wondered

if he realized how much like a cowboy he actually looked posed as he was, his trousers tight across his thighs. Certainly not the way a man would sit in a lady's parlor.

"What did you need?" Harry asked.

Kit reached into his pocket, withdrew his map, unfolded it, and spread it over the ground. "Do you remember my mentioning David Robertson?"

Harry narrowed his eyes. "Yes, but I thought we'd agreed—"

Kit smiled. "Hear me out before jumping to conclusions. They live near Dallas. By the end of the week, we'll be close enough that I'd like to pay them a visit if you have no objections."

"Why would I object to having an opportunity to engage in a meaningful conversation with people who appreciate the finer aspects of life?"

Jessye felt the sting of his words as though he'd delivered each one with a bullet into her heart. She knew nothing of the finer aspects of life, and she wondered if he found conversations with her meaningless. But if he did, then why did he talk to her at all?

The answer hit her with an unerring truth: she was the only woman around.

"I have no idea how the war might have changed their financial situation. I did write him about our cattle venture. He views it as a great folly. Still, I would like to see for myself that they are well," Kit said.

"Then we shall do so with my blessing."

"Good. I thought we'd also let the men draw lots and give a few of them the night off. I have no idea what Dallas offers in the way of entertainment, but it must offer more than the open prairie."

Harry glanced at Jessye. "Do you know anything about Dallas?"

She shrugged. "I only know the Shawnee Trail takes us by it."

"Then it'll be an adventure for us all," Harry said as he unfolded his body.

"Where are you going?" Jessye asked, her gut tightening.

"To watch over the herd."

"We've got enough men out there."

"One more can't hurt. Besides, I saw that young lad Slim head out with the others. If stampedes are truly as horrifying as these men indicate, he should be here at the camp."

Jessye leapt to her feet. "But you won't know what to do. You've never seen stampeding cattle."

"Dan has recited the procedures so often I could handle the situation in my sleep."

He walked off, and Jessye dropped to the ground. She knew he was right. Their wrangler, Slim, shouldn't be out there, but durn it, she didn't want Harry out there either.

"Put the stampede out of your mind, Jessye," Kit said quietly. "It's unlikely to happen with all the precautions we're taking. Think of Dallas instead and the fine time we'll have in the city."

❧ Chapter 9 ❧

Jessye gazed out the window of her hostelry room and watched the people walk the dusty streets of Dallas. The town consisted of little more than crude buildings, but a promise of greatness permeated the air.

She yearned for a hot bath and a soft bed. She'd enjoy both later tonight.

But this afternoon, she wanted to walk through the town, and she thought she'd be safe as long as she looked like a dirty, trail-weary cowboy—which she certainly was.

She longed to stroll into a saloon and take a look around, gather mental notes regarding the walls and the arrangement of the room so she'd have ideas on ways to improve her pa's saloon once she returned to Fortune. She'd make good money on this trail drive, but it wouldn't last a lifetime—she wanted to invest it in something that would.

She left the room quietly. The hostelry wasn't fancy. Little in this town was. The hostelry had no back steps that she could use to slip out unnoticed. She descended the stairs into the main foyer. The clerk behind the desk gave her a tight smile. She gave him a brusque nod. She cursed her hands for growing damp. What did it matter that he thought she was beneath him?

When this cattle drive was over and she held an abundance of money, she'd be the one looking down her nose. With a purpose to her stride, she started toward the double front doors.

"Jessye!"

She staggered to a halt at the echo of Harry's voice. She turned to see him marching toward her. He *had* cleaned up, and her heart almost stopped beating as she took in his appearance. Cleanly shaven and dressed in his gambler's clothes, he made her feel like a rag doll that should be tossed out. "Why are you all gussied up?" she asked as he stopped in front of her.

"Because there is some evidence of civilization in the area." He cupped her elbow and leaned low so only she could hear. "I need an advance on my earnings."

She narrowed her eyes. "Why?"

She watched as his jaw clenched, and she knew he didn't like that she controlled the purse strings, but damn if she'd hand her money over to him without good reason.

"Kit fears we might not have enough money to purchase all the supplies we need to reach Sedalia. A man has invited me to participate in a private poker game later tonight, and I intend to ensure that we do have enough—"

"By risking what little we've got left on the turn of a card?"

"By risking my allotment," he said in a taut voice.

"The rules are that every man gets paid when we reach Sedalia and not before. If I pay you, I'll have to pay some amount to the others, and then I guarantee we won't have enough for supplies."

"Then give me a loan. I promise I'll pay it back tenfold."

"Harry, I know all about promises."

"You know nothing about my promises—"

"Jessye?"

Her breath hitched at the familiar voice from her youth. She twisted her head slightly. Gerald Milton stood beside her, a hesitant smile on a face that was more rugged than she'd remembered, but still as handsome. Where was quicksand when she needed it to swallow her whole? She cleared her throat as quietly as she could. "Gerald?"

His smile grew. "What in God's name are you doin' here dressed like that?"

She cast a quick glance at Harry and saw suspicion slowly dawn within the emerald depths of his eyes. She forced herself to speak past the knot tightening her throat. "Herding cattle."

He laughed. "Jessye, everyone knows that a woman does not herd cattle—"

"I'd be mindful of what you say regarding my fiancée," Harry commanded in a tightly controlled voice.

Gerald snapped his gaze to Harry. "Your fiancée? Why I had no idea when I invited you to join us in a little poker game that you knew Jessye . . . so well."

His voice hinted at an intimacy shared between a man and woman. He reached out to touch her cheek, and Jessye jerked back. She saw the flash of anger in the blue eyes she'd once drowned in.

"Me and Jessye go way back, don't we, darlin'? Maybe Bainbridge here would like to know exactly how well we know each other."

"Jessye and I share our secrets," Harry said as he slipped his arm around her and pulled her snugly against his side. She'd never been more grateful for the support in her life. If he felt her trembling, he gave no indication. "I know you chose the South over her."

"So you're willing to take tarnished goods and a bastard—"

"The baby died," Jessye lied.

For the barest of moments, Jessye thought she detected regret in his eyes before his smile returned. "I imagine that was for the best." He looked to Harry. "You still gonna join us tonight?"

"No, I've decided you've taken enough."

"It was good to see you, Jessye." He winked. "You keep tellin' people you're just herdin' cattle. Hell, lookin' like that, maybe you are."

He started walking away. She took a step toward him, and Harry jerked her back against his side. "Let him go. What in God's name possessed you to fall in love with that?"

She shook her head. "He wasn't like that before the war. He was sweet—" Blinking back the tears burning her eyes, she bit her knuckle to keep herself from saying more. She swung around. "What possessed you to say I was your fiancée?"

"Haven't a clue, but it seemed the thing to say at the time. Besides, I thought it might offer you a little protection from the lust emanating from him."

She snorted. "Lust? The way I'm lookin'? He was right. No man would want me."

"It's your spirit that attracts men. You could be covered from head to toe in mud, and men would find you attractive."

"Desperate men, maybe. And that's the last thing I want. That and you gambling away my money."

"When he invited me to play, I didn't realize who he was. You never told me his last name . . ." Harrison shrugged. "It's just as well. We have a party to attend this evening."

Her breath hitched and her eyes widened. "What?"

Harry looked at her casually. "You were there when Kit mentioned that he wanted to visit with the Robertsons. As it turns out, they're hosting a small party this evening, and we've been invited."

With her heart pounding, Jessye took a step back. "I don't have a dress to wear."

"I realize that. I assumed you were on your way to find a seamstress. You knew Kit planned for us to visit—"

"I knew you and Kit planned to visit them. I didn't know you meant for me to go." She released a nervous burst of laughter. "Besides, a seamstress can't make a dress in a day."

"For someone as small as you, she could no doubt make it in an afternoon, which she will need to do, since we have to be there at seven."

"I'm sure the invitation didn't include me."

"I'm certain that it did."

She shook her head vigorously. "I've got nothing to wear, and I'm not spending our supply money on a dress just to impress some rich folks." She shoved her way past him, heading back to her room. Suddenly, she was grateful that they were only spending one night in Dallas. So far, she thought the town should be more aptly named Hell.

As though he handled a newborn babe, Harry pulled the wooden box out of his bag. He ran his fingers over the carving that reflected his family's coat of arms. He lifted the lid and smiled at the pair of dueling pistols housed inside. The box and pistols had been a gift from his grandfather.

With his palm, he cupped one of the pistols. He'd like to use it to send Gerald Milton to hell. But these Texans knew little of the proper way of dueling.

Besides, the pistols were of more value if left inside the box. Gently, he closed the lid, relishing the distinct, audible click.

A man could be hurt in many ways. His mother had taught him that physical pain resulted in the least anguish, the memories of the agony diminishing over time—but emotional pain could last forever, the torment increasing as moments passed into years.

He'd seen the pain reflected in Jessye's eyes when she'd first caught sight of Gerald Milton. He would find a way to ease her suffering even if it cost him his life.

Jessye lay on her side, her knees almost touching her chest, curled as she imagined her child had been as she grew inside her. She didn't know what had possessed her to tell Gerald that the baby had died. Maybe she'd feared that he wouldn't care that their daughter had lived and that Jessye had been forced to give her up. Or perhaps she hadn't wanted her short-comings to be viewed through his eyes.

Had she been stronger, more independent, maybe now she would enjoy her child's smiles and wipe away her tears. She could only pray that she'd been right to give her to the couple at the mission, could only hope that her child was well and truly loved.

A hard tap on her door brought her out of her reverie and self-pity. She despised these weakened moments when she doubted the actions she'd taken four years before. She'd done what she thought was best at the time. She gained little in looking back.

She swung her legs off the bed, crossed the room, and flung open the door. A woman stood before her, her silvering hair pulled back so tightly that it caused the skin across her face to tauten, giving her face a skeletal appearance. The woman hugged a brown package against her chest.

"Are you Jessye Kane?" she asked.

Jessye furrowed her brow and hesitated before responding. "Yes."

"Good," the woman snapped and walked briskly into the room. "I'm Gwen Harper. We haven't much time." She dropped the package on the bed and untied the string.

"Much time to do what?"

Gwen Harper folded back the brown paper and spread the most beautiful green material Jessye had ever seen across the bed. "Sew your gown."

Jessye stepped back. "My gown?"

Gwen looked over her shoulder. "The gown you're going to wear to the Robertsons' party tonight."

Jessye shook her head. "I'm not going to the Robertsons' party."

The woman knitted her brows together. "Mr. Bainbridge said you were. He told me to make you a proper gown to wear for this evening. He suggested the emerald silk, and I can certainly understand why. With your green eyes and red hair—"

"I am not spending my money on an outfit I'm only gonna wear one night—"

"Mr. Bainbridge has already purchased it."

Instinctively, Jessye pressed her hand to the hidden pouch that circled her waist beneath her clothes. Thank God, she still felt the pouch bulging. Harry hadn't found a way to pilfer her money. "What did he use to buy it?"

"Lincoln skins."

Jessye stared at the woman, wondering where Harry had managed to latch on to Yankee money. She scolded herself. There was no longer a division between the states or the currency. Confederate money was useless. All they had was Yankee money, simply money, but accepting that reality was hard for some folks.

"Now, come on, we ain't got much time before my daughter gets here to fix your hair—"

"Mrs. Harper, I am not going to the Robertsons'—"

"But you've been invited. They're nice people and generous to the town, but not everyone gets an invite." She took a step and leaned over slightly as though imparting a secret. "They're richer than Midas, and their brick house is the most beautiful in the area, surrounded by so many oak trees you can barely see it. Some folks say they got an oak lawn."

"I can't—"

"You can," a deep voice boomed behind her. She spun around and glared at Harry. "And you will," he finished.

"Where did you get money?" she whispered harshly, fearing he'd stolen it. Hadn't she heard somewhere that the English picked money out of people's pockets? With Harry's deft fingers—

"Mrs. Harper, could you give us a moment alone?" Harry asked.

The woman glanced at the watch pinned just above her heart. "My girls will be here soon to help me sew, but we're barely gonna have time to get this gown made as it is. If I don't get it cut out—"

"One moment. That's all I need."

Mrs. Harper hurried past him, and Harry clicked the door shut. Jessye took a step back. She didn't fear him, but the impropriety of being in a hostelry room alone with a man, a bed only a few feet away . . . "What have you done? Where did you get the money?"

"I bartered away my grandfather's dueling pistols."

Her heart battered against her chest. She'd seen the pistols when he'd offered to let Grayson Rhodes use them in a duel against Abbie Westland's husband. She'd never seen a finer pair of guns. She shook her head, trying to clear the confusion. "But why purchase me a gown? Why not use the money for that poker game—"

"Because life is a game of chance. Every decision involves some risk. The magnitude of the return should always either equal or exceed the magnitude of the risk." He crossed the room, and she watched as he fingered the satiny material. "My grandfather's words. He would not have approved of me trading his pistols for a game of poker where I could stack the odds in my favor." A smile touched his lips. "But he would have approved of this venture, which has so damned little chance of success."

He spun around. "I told you that Kit has concerns regarding our financial situation. We are driving more cattle than he anticipated; we've had to hire more men than he originally planned, which means the purchase of more supplies. You know what our money situation is like. It may become necessary to add an investor in order to gain what we need. Robertson thinks our cattle venture is doomed to failure. We must convince him otherwise. You are Kit's partner. It's imperative that Robertson meet you."

"I hate parties."

"We won't stay long. Once you've taken a measure of each other, you and I will be free to leave."

"And if this David Robertson finds me lacking?"

His gaze slowly traveled from the top of her head to the tips of her soiled boots. She hated his scrutiny but refused to cower before it. Finally, after what seemed an eternity, his emerald gaze met hers. "If I thought for one second that his finding you lacking was a possibility, I would have never traded the one thing in my life that I ever treasured."

He stalked across the room and jerked open the door. "I shall knock at precisely seven o'clock. Be ready."

Her breath whooshed out as though he'd punched her in the gut. He was *still* gambling, betting on her to make a good enough impression that David Robertson would invest in their business if need be. The risk was higher than drawing to an inside straight. How dare the man put the burden on her. . . . The irritation swelled, bringing her obstinacy to the surface. She'd show him that the risk wasn't nearly as much as he thought.

Gwen swooped into the room. "Ready to begin?"

Jessye gave her an uncertain smile. "You know you're working with a sow's ear here."

Gwen laughed. "I have a reputation for creatin' silk purses the likes of which you won't find anywhere else."

Harrison paced within his room, the ticking of the clock keeping perfect rhythm with his steps and his doubts. What had he been thinking to suggest that Jessye attend this little party tonight?

That she intrigued him, he could not deny. That he wanted to bed her, he *would* not deny.

But to risk causing her embarrassment . . . dear God, what had he done? The women she would meet tonight did not drink, swear, or watch men bathe. He released a mirthless laugh. With Jessye's stubborn streak—which he adored—she'd no doubt wear her trousers regardless of how hard the seamstress worked to finish the gown in time.

The tick of the clock finally struck seven, and he smiled. It was a good thing that he enjoyed creating scandal—because he had little doubt that tonight he and Jessye would create one that this town would never forget.

Straightening his black jacket, he opened the door

to his room and crossed the hall to hers. He knocked lightly.

The door flung open, and his lungs forgot how to draw in air. Jessye stood in the emerald gown, her cheeks a bright red, her hair piled on top of her head with curling strands framing her oval face, her breathing heavy.

"You didn't purchase enough material!" She stalked to the mirror and tugged on the bodice of the gown. She'd been wearing her breasts bound for so long that he'd nearly forgotten she had them. This gown was a remarkable reminder as the gentle swells rose and fell with each breath she took.

And dear God, her waist. He could have spanned it with his hands. The male clothing she wore, which he thought revealed everything, in truth revealed nothing. It hid the delicateness of her features, the alabaster softness of her bare shoulders.

She spun around. "Harry, I can't wear this."

"Jessye, it would be a sin for you not to. I had forgotten exactly how lovely you are," he said quietly.

"Lovely?" she snapped. She stared in the mirror and tugged once again on the bodice. "This gown doesn't cover enough of me to be lovely. It's downright indecent."

Swallowing hard, he walked slowly across the room, enjoying every angle, every nuance of femininity revealed to him. The temptation to stay within this room and remove the gown was almost more than he could bear.

He came to stand behind her and caught the wisp of her fragrance: wild lilies flourishing in a field.

"You've been wearing a man's shirt for too long. The gown reveals hardly anything."

She took a deep, shaky breath. "But you can see my . . . my . . ."

"Soft feminine curves." He trailed his fingers along the column of her throat and felt the quickening of her pulse as she met and held his gaze in the mirror. His mouth grew dry and her eyes darkened as he slowly, seductively lowered his hand and outlined the swells where cloth met alluring flesh. Not a freckle in sight. Dear God, but he longed to kiss her where the sun had never seen the hint of her glory. He hadn't purchased too little material—he'd purchased too damned much.

He slid his gaze past her to the bed reflected in the mirror. Desire such as he'd never known clawed through him.

"Did I mention earlier that I hate parties as well?" he rasped. "We could stay—"

She slid away from him. "So I can lift this pretty skirt for you?"

"Why do you equate desire with insult?"

"Because there's no love attached to it. You could have what you want, and we could still get to the party on time."

"To have what I want, Jessye, we would not leave this room until dawn."

Jessye backed into the dresser. She'd seen lust in the eyes of a thousand men—but desire? For the first time in her life, she thought she was actually looking at desire, and the sight terrified her. "Thought we had a reason to go to this party."

He bowed slightly. "We do. For a moment your charms made me forget."

"I bet you say that to all the ladies."

He smiled wickedly. "I never expected to hear you refer to yourself as a lady."

"I didn't mean *I* was a lady."

"But you are. Look in the mirror."

"I've looked."

"Look again."

Defiantly, she did as he bid. He stood slightly behind her in his strikingly white shirt, cravat, red vest, and black jacket. And durn his hide, within his eyes, she saw understanding—his understanding of her fears and insecurities.

"Tonight, Jessye love, no one will mistake you for a saloon owner's daughter." He withdrew something from his pocket. With one fluid motion, his sleight of hand laid a necklace against her flesh, a small teardrop emerald resting just below the hollow at the base of her throat.

She met his gaze in the mirror. "What are you doing?"

"Cheating."

She narrowed her eyes. "Want to explain that?"

"My grandfather taught me that when life deals the cards unfairly, you cheat. A man is more likely to invest in our enterprise if he does not think we are desperate for his money."

"I thought this man was Kit's friend."

His eyes hardened as they captured hers. "Jessye love, you're the one who drew up the contract on our enterprise. I would think you of all people would understand that within the boundaries of business, friendships do not exist."

☙ Chapter 10 ☙

Harrison took great delight in watching
Jessye's eyes widen as he drew the carriage to a halt
in front of the large brick house. He had rented the
vehicle for the evening because he didn't want Jessye
to have to walk the mile or so to the Robertsons'.
Their home lay beyond the outer edges of Dallas
proper, but he thought someday the town would
stretch its boundaries and its influence.

For a fleeting instant, he wished she could visit his
father's estates. Although it was unfair to compare a
fledgling community to a country with centuries of
history behind it, he could not help but feel a measure
of pride in his family's homes. Next to them, this
place was tiny.

He assisted Jessye out of the carriage, led her up
the steps, and knocked soundly on the door. A stern-
faced butler opened it and bid them to enter. Harrison
hadn't expected Jessye's eyes to widen further. Her
fingers tightened their hold on his arm. "I can't do
this," she whispered beneath her breath.

"You can and you will."

"I ain't never been in a place this fancy. I don't know how to act."

He leaned low until his lips were but a whisper's breath from her ear. "Just be yourself, and you'll charm them. Besides, if we get the cattle to market as planned, you'll be able to build a house grander than this one."

She snapped her gaze to his. "We won't be that rich."

"Yes, we will. The risks are high, which means the rewards shall be as well."

"Harry! I expected Kit to arrive with a beautiful woman on his arm, not you." Tall, with gleaming black hair, David Robertson strode across the foyer like a man who had no doubts that he owned his place in the world.

Harrison smiled broadly. "Kit has yet to take a fancy to these strong-minded Texas ladies. David, allow me to introduce you to Kit's business partner"— he caught a movement out of the corner of his eye. Gerald Milton was strutting across the foyer like a bloody peacock—"and my fiancée."

Jessye would have protested the introduction if she hadn't spotted Gerald. She smiled brightly, when she preferred to retreat. David Robertson was younger than she'd expected, but deep furrows creased his brow and his brown eyes told her he'd seen much of life. "It's a pleasure to meet you," Jessye murmured.

"The pleasure is all mine," David said as he took her hand and brought it to his lips. Jessye wished to God that she wasn't trembling like a leaf caught in a tornado.

"Southern gallantry," Harrison murmured. "I suppose it's a good thing you're married."

David's eyes twinkled. "No, it's a good thing I love my wife as much as I do." He turned slightly. "Gerald, I'd like you to meet—"

"We've met," Harry cut in.

Gerald smiled, but it wasn't the smile of his youth, the one that had lured her to him. This smile was cold and calculating. "You gonna join us later for that poker game?"

"No," Harry said. "I thought to retire early. I've been too long without the softness of a bed."

Jessye felt Gerald's gaze sweep over her, and it was all she could do not to shudder.

"Yep, I can see that the softness has improved."

Jessye wanted to slap the sneer off his face, but it disappeared the moment David looked at him as though trying to decipher his words.

"Let's go into the parlor. Madeline managed to locate a couple of fiddle players. Do you dance, Miss Kane?"

With Harry at her side, she followed David. "No—"

"Yes, she does," Harry broke in. "But I'm a possessive sort. All her dances are reserved for me."

"She didn't dance before the war," Gerald stated boldly.

Harry stopped abruptly, and Jessye felt the tightness in his arm, which mirrored that in her stomach. "She was a mere slip of a girl when last you knew her. Fortunately for me, since then she has acquired a taste for the finer aspects of life."

Gerald narrowed his eyes as though he was trying to determine if he'd been insulted.

"Harry!"

Harry's cold smile turned warm as he released his hold on Jessye and hugged a dark-haired woman. "Madeline." He placed his hands on her shoulders and held her at arm's length. "You seem to have survived the war looking more beautiful than ever."

"Only because David survived. You have no idea how many times I regretted that we returned when he heard that war had erupted."

Jessye watched as David brushed a light kiss near her temple. "It's over now."

"Thank God for that. Everyone is in the parlor. Please join us."

The parlor was the most beautiful room Jessye had ever seen. Standing before the hearth, Kit was dressed similarly to Harry, only his black vest and shirt gave him the appearance of being in mourning. People surrounded him, listening to his tales, but it was the young woman sitting in a chair watching him who caught Jessye's attention. She could only hope that she never looked at Harry with that much adoration reflected in her eyes, even if she felt it.

David approached the woman, and she rose elegantly. Her blond hair and pale features gave her an ethereal quality.

"I don't believe you've met my sister Ashton," David said. "She's the reason we're having this party tonight."

Ashton smiled warmly. "I'm so glad you could come."

Gerald stepped beside her. "Ashton is the reason

I'm here," he said as though he'd just won a victory over the North.

The bile rose to burn Jessye's throat. The woman appeared so innocent. She prayed Gerald would not take advantage. "So the two of you are friends?" she asked.

"Ashton wrote me during the war," Gerald replied. "That's how we met."

Ashton blushed. "During the war, I wanted to do something, so I wrote letters and simply addressed them to 'any Confederate soldier.' "

"And I was fortunate that one fell into my hands," Gerald said.

Ashton's blush deepened. "I corresponded with many men, but so few returned. Gerald came by to thank me. I thought that was very kind, and Madeline agreed to have a party. And I'm so glad. Kit has been here most of the afternoon telling us the most outlandish stories about him and Harry picking cotton."

Harry groaned. "Bless his black-hearted soul."

Jessye glanced at Gerald and wondered if Harry's statement didn't more aptly refer to the man she'd loved in her youth.

Jessye relished the booming laughter reverberating around the dining room. David Robertson obviously appreciated life. Beside him, his wife smiled and constantly touched his hand, arm, or shoulder.

Gerald sat slightly across from Jessye. A shudder ran through her every time his gaze fell upon her.

David took a deep breath to control his laughter. "So your fathers paid this Winslow to bring you to Texas?"

"Yes," Kit admitted. "It seems the exploits of Gray, Harry, and myself were becoming quite legendary— and embarrassing to our families."

"Surely, you didn't truly mean to embarrass them," Ashton said softly.

Kit shook his head. "Not intentionally, no. But we decided if the only title we were to be given was that of 'black sheep,' then we needed to develop reputations worthy of the honor. We were quite successful at our endeavors."

David chuckled. "Yes, I can imagine you were. Although I know your goals often lacked height, I've never known the three of you to fail at anything you set your minds to achieving."

Jessye couldn't have been more stunned by the man's words if he'd suddenly spoken in Latin.

David leaned forward slightly. "But the cattle will be your downfall."

Madeline clicked her tongue against her teeth. "Surely you men will wait to discuss business."

"Men and lady," Harry said. "Jessye is our cattle expert."

Jessye felt, more than saw, Gerald's gaze boring into her.

"Just a touch of business, then we'll move on," David assured his wife. "As your friend, I must speak honestly. This cattle venture is doomed to failure."

"At the risk of being rude to our host," Harry said, "I disagree with your assessment, David. Texas's future lies in cattle."

David studied him thoughtfully. "Your confidence intrigues me. The railroad stops at Sedalia, Missouri."

Kit nodded. "That's our destination."

"How are you plannin' to get through Kansas?" Gerald asked.

Jessye's heart bounced against her ribs. Why did the smoothness in his voice have to remind her of warm summer nights beneath the stars?

"We'll guide our three thousand head of cattle through Kansas in the same manner that we guided them through Texas," Harry said, his voice calm. "With success."

"Them longhorns carry tick fever. Kansas passed a law forbidding Texas cattle to go through the state. Jayhawkers are working to enforce that law."

"Jayhawkers?" Kit asked.

"Vigilantes," David answered, his voice rife with disgust. "I heard of some smaller outfits trying to cut across Kansas. The jayhawkers told them they had to pay a fine or turn the cattle back."

Jessye was familiar with that particular Kansas law. She hadn't heard that anyone was serious enough about it to stop the Texas cattle from going through Kansas. "What did the outfits do?" she asked.

"One paid a hefty fine," Gerald said even though she'd directed her question to David. "The other turned their cattle back after some of the men were beaten."

Harry met Gerald's challenging gaze. "We shall neither pay a fine nor turn back our herd."

"Then you'd better find a trail to follow besides the Shawnee."

"David, perhaps you can offer us an alternative," Kit said.

David shook his head. "My interest in your cattle venture is pure curiosity. The people in the north can starve for all I care. Starve as they starved us. There isn't a man at this table who would lift a finger to benefit the north."

"And our taking cattle north benefits them," Kit said quietly. "That's why you consider our errand foolhardy, and perhaps a bit of a betrayal to you."

"Puts food in them Yankee bellies," Gerald said vehemently.

Jesse had worked in a saloon long enough to recognize the signs of an impending brawl. Dear Lord, she wished they'd never moved on to this topic.

Harry lifted his glass and swirled his wine. "And money in *our* pockets." He shifted his gaze to David. "Surely you've heard of William the Conqueror."

"Who hasn't? He conquered England."

Harry stilled his glass. "He conquered the land, not the people. His Norman forces spoke French, and yet, here Kit and I sit before you today speaking our mother tongue—English. The Union may have defeated the Confederacy. Do not allow them to defeat *you*. The North has money. You do not. Find ways to get their money into your state and build it into the greatness that its forefathers envisioned. The depth of your defeat is determined by your willingness to accept it."

Jessye swallowed hard to stop the tears from surfacing in her eyes. There were times when she thought Harry had as many layers to him as a deck of cards.

David narrowed his eyes. "If I didn't know better, Harry, I'd think you had been to war."

"Wars are not always defined by the size of the opposing forces, nor battles by the amount of blood shed. I doubt a man or woman who sits at this table has not fought at least one battle. Victory or defeat is of little consequence when the true test is whether the encounter strengthens or weakens us."

"It seems to me," Kit said, "that if the northern states truly want Texas beef, the simplest solution would be to bring the railroads into Texas."

"Railroads would just bring the carpetbaggers into the state that much quicker," Gerald said.

Kit raised a brow. "Along with their money."

David smiled. "You're suggesting we find a way to relieve them of it."

Kit raised his wineglass in a salute. "I'm suggesting you find a way to make their greed work against them. If our drive north is successful this year, I shall pursue the advantages of railroads."

Madeline released a delicate sigh and rolled her eyes. "Now, we're moving the topic of conversation from cattle to railroads. Miss Kane, I admire your ability to endure the stifling conversations these men must put you through."

"I don't mind talking cattle or railroads," Jessye admitted. Railroads were an avenue she hadn't considered. If they invested—

"Jessye is used to men's conversations," Gerald said. "She worked in a saloon."

Jessye wanted to crawl beneath the table, thought she might have if Harry's hand hadn't at that moment come to rest on her thigh. She didn't know if he was offering comfort or signaling her to keep her mouth shut.

"You worked in a saloon?" Ashton asked with interest. "What in the world did you do exactly?"

Tilting her chin defiantly, she spoke with pride.

"My father owns a saloon in Fortune—"

"Jessye would serve up drinks, smiles, and anything else a man wanted," Gerald finished.

Within Jessye, the anger swelled to the point that she wanted to toss her wine right into Gerald's face. She knew what he was leading people to believe. She just didn't understand why he'd want to shame her.

"She didn't serve up *everything*," Harry said, the coldness in his voice causing her to look away from Gerald.

"She did to some," Gerald contradicted.

Harry's hand spasmed on her thigh. She watched as he ruthlessly brought his gaze to bear on Gerald. "Milton, Jessye led me to believe that you were a bright fellow so I'm going to share a little story with you. A few years back, a gentleman insulted my mistress. I called him out. A duel at dawn. I shot him high on the inside of his left thigh." Harry narrowed his gaze. For the first time in her life, she understood the meaning of the expression "If looks could kill."

"You can no doubt fathom where I would have shot him had he been insulting my fiancée."

She jerked her gaze to Gerald in time to see him swallow.

"I meant no insult," he said. "I was just sayin' how things were is all."

"I'd suggest you keep Jessye's past where it belongs: in the past." Astonished, she felt Harry's hand close around hers. He brought it from beneath the table and pressed her fingers to his lips, his gaze never wavering from Gerald. "Although Jessye is fully capable of taking care of herself, I protect what's mine."

His warm breath skimmed across her knuckles,

sending shivers along her spine. For an insane moment, she almost believed he meant the words, forgot that they really weren't betrothed.

Kit cleared his throat. "Madeline, you seem to have gotten your wish, and Harry with his usual aplomb has steered the conversation away from business."

Madeline chuckled. "I suppose next time I should allow Mary Ellen to stay up and join us, only I fear we'd have no conversation at all then."

Harry loosened his tight hold on Jessye's hand and gave her a small smile. She clutched her hand in her lap, trying to avoid Gerald's gaze. "Who is Mary Ellen?"

Madeline smiled warmly. "Our daughter. She'll be four next week."

Jessye's stomach tightened. Her own daughter would have been four. "I would have liked to have met her."

"She's precocious," Kit told her.

"She's an angel," David countered.

Kit grinned. "She's an expert at wrapping people around her finger."

"Speaking of children," David began, "has your brother given your father the heir to Ravenleigh he was craving when last I saw him?"

Jessye watched in somber fascination as Kit's grin abruptly faded, and he turned pale.

"No." He quietly cleared his throat. "No . . . Christopher's wife took ill and died shortly before I left England."

"I'm sorry to hear that. It's not often among the nobility that one sees a love match. They looked to be in love."

Kit nodded slightly. "Yes, Christopher and Clarisse were fortunate in that regard. They did love each other." He stiffly picked up his glass and downed the remaining crimson wine in one long swallow before holding the glass out to the butler who was keeping the glasses filled.

Madeline folded her napkin and placed it on the table. "Why don't we adjourn to the parlor so we can enjoy the music?"

"Dance with me."

The seductiveness in Harry's voice shimmered along every nerve in Jessye's body as she watched the other couples waltzing in the parlor. She crossed her arms beneath her breasts, then uncrossed them. "I meant what I said earlier. I don't know how to dance."

"A woman doesn't need to know how to waltz. She only needs to follow her partner's movements. Think of a cow following the herd—"

She narrowed her eyes. "Are you comparing me to a cow?"

"God, I find you incredibly appealing when you get angry."

"Is that why you work so hard to keep me mad?"

He smiled, and she thought the warmth in his eyes would eliminate the need for a fire on a cold winter's night.

"All the couples are dancing. People might doubt our betrothal."

She glanced quickly to the corner, where Kit was refilling his wineglass. "That would leave Kit alone."

"Believe me, he's alone anyway." He cradled his palm against her elbow. "Come along."

"Harry—"

"Trust me. It will be as simple as walking."

"Do you have any idea how many times I fell on my butt before I learned to walk?"

His smile deepened. "I'll catch you before you fall."

With reservations, she gave him a sharp nod, fearing he might be catching her heart. His hand came to rest on the curve of her waist, and he swept her onto the dance floor. Her breath caught at the smoothness of his motions, as though he carried her on air.

"Not so bad, heh?" he asked, his eyes twinkling.

"You've done this before."

"Many a time. It's required of an English gentleman to know the art of sweeping a lady off her feet."

"Gentleman." She scoffed. "More likely it's a requirement for scoundrels."

"One must be a gentleman before he can be a scoundrel. It's an unwritten law."

"Did you really shoot a man for insulting your mistress?"

"Indeed I did."

"You must have cared for her a lot."

He shook his head slightly. "She was fun. I enjoyed her company, and she understood how to play the game."

"The game?"

"Pretending affection so that for a while we could both forget that we were pretending."

"Haven't you ever really loved anyone?"

"If I did, it was so long ago that I have no memory of it."

As much as loving a man had hurt, of late she'd

longed for the moments when love seemed to make life worthwhile. She couldn't imagine never knowing the experience of love, the giving of it, the receiving of it.

"Telling Gerald that story about the duel seemed to shut him up. Why did it matter that you shot the man in the left thigh?"

She'd never expected to see a red tinge creep into Harry's cheeks. "How can I put this delicately? Most men have a tendency to . . . hang to the left."

"Hang?" she asked, furrowing her brow.

"Their . . ." His eyes brightened. "Shortcomings."

Awareness dawned, and she widened her eyes. "You mean that you shot off his . . . his . . ."

"It was my intent. Fortunately for him, he hung to the right. Now if your former lover continues to insult you, I shall shoot him dead center and relieve him of his family jewels."

"Or as my father would say, 'his cojones'?"

"Exactly."

She laughed lightly. "You know, I think you would."

His face grew incredibly serious. "Make no mistake. I did not issue an idle threat, and he well knows it. He hurt you once. I assure you that he will never harm you again."

She glanced past Harry to watch Gerald dance with Ashton. His steps were awkward, ungainly as he held Ashton at a respectable arm's length.

"Do you wish to switch partners?" Harry asked, his fluid movements mirroring poise and confidence.

She jerked her gaze to his. "No. I sorta prefer to keep my toes from getting hurt."

"I shall take that as a compliment."

She licked her lips. "That's how I meant it."

She swallowed hard as his hand tightened on her waist and drew her closer until she felt the brush of his thighs against hers. "Isn't it scandalous to dance this close?" she asked, breathlessly.

"Incredibly, but it is the way I prefer."

The warmth from his body seeped into hers. "I reckon you've danced with a lot of women."

"Too many to count, but I give you my word on this: I never waltzed with one of them because I *wanted* to. You are the first with whom I have actually relished dancing."

"You danced with them because you wanted to entice them into your bed."

She started to jerk free, but he maintained his hold, bringing her closer. "I forget how well you know men, and you forget how little you know me."

"Do you deny my words?"

"No. But since we began dancing, I have given no thought to bedding you."

She felt the sharp sting to her pride. "Maybe you ought to dance with Ashton. She seems like a fine lady."

"She holds no interest for me. You, on the other hand . . . I am aware of you in ways that I've never been aware of another. You are a seductress simply because you don't realize you are one."

"You're dealing your words from the bottom of the deck—"

"I've never given you false words, Jessye."

He swept her across the dance floor as though no one else were in attendance. No false words. No false hope. She could have his body, but not his heart.

Someday, he would find love, she was sure of it, and she could well imagine the woman who would capture his heart. She would be beautiful and refined, her words uttered poetically, her manners impeccable. She wouldn't have to keep darting her gaze around the table as Jessye had done earlier to make certain she was eating in the same manner as everyone else. She would never wear men's clothes or serve men whiskey with a saucy smile that might add an extra coin to her pocket.

But tonight it didn't matter. She wore a gown that made her feel like a lady, and Harry gazed at her as though she was the only woman in the room. He'd asked her to dance when he'd asked no one else.

"Why didn't you like the beard?" he asked quietly as the music continued to fill the room.

She studied the perfect lines of his face. "Because it hid the strong curve of your jaw and that little dent in your chin."

He brought her closer, the curves of her body molding against the hardened planes of his. Desire, deep and burning, illuminated his eyes, and his hands tightened their hold. "Tell me that you never wonder what it would be like to lie within my arms with nothing but shadows between us."

Her mouth grew dry, her throat tight. She wondered so often that she considered abandoning her vow, but she feared the disappointment that would reel through her when she had to finally acknowledge that she'd gained his body without his heart. "I've thought about it," she whispered hoarsely.

"Do you realize how long it'll be before we have

another opportunity to sleep in a bed?" he asked in a low, captivating murmur. "And you know how little I enjoy a bed when I'm in it alone."

She nodded mutely.

"We can leave this party at any time . . . discreetly . . ."

"Harry, I can't. You're offering me your body without your heart. It would be like dancing without music. I know the cost, and it's a price I'm not willing to pay—ever again."

Disappointment clouded the emerald depths of his eyes. "Attending this party was a mistake. You look ravishing, and I am a starving man. Fortunately for us, the night will soon end—"

She nodded. "And so will the pretense. We'll just go back to being who and what we are."

The music drifted into silence. Jessye stepped out of his embrace. "Thank you for the dance."

He cupped her chin. "I am halfway tempted to kill Milton for what he did to you. Tonight, you think you are pretending to be a lady, while in truth, you spend the greater portion of your life pretending that you are not." He bowed slightly. "If you'll excuse me, I want to talk with David for a moment."

She watched him walk off, his stride graceful with confidence, his words echoing through her mind. She hated to admit that Harry did a lot less bluffing than she realized. She'd judged him to be a scoundrel, but there were times when she thought he was anything but one. It was much easier to be around him when she didn't trust him, much harder to guard her heart when she did.

She spun around and came up short, jerking back
to avoid ramming into Gerald.

"Dance with me, Jessye," he said as he grabbed her
arm.

She wrenched free. "I only dance with my fiancé."

A corner of his mouth lifted into an ugly sneer.
"You don't think I honest to God believe you're betrothed to that fella, do you? Didn't you hear what
Robertson said? He's nobility. During the war, I saw
plantation houses that make this one look like an out-
house. And I hear tell that in England, the nobility
live in castles. Why would a man who grew up rich
settle for the likes of you?"

She didn't care that Harry hadn't actually settled
for her. She only wanted to convince Gerald that he'd
made a mistake in leaving her. "Maybe he likes my
spunk."

He laughed. "He doesn't want anything more from
you than what I wanted: a quick roll in the hay."

Jessye balled her hands into fists, pressing them
against her sides to keep from ramming them into his
nose. Tonight—for Harry—she would be a lady. "The
war changed you, Gerald. I don't recall you bein' so
mean spirited."

He glanced down briefly as though shamed by her
words. But when he lifted his gaze, the hardness she
saw in his eyes shook her to the core. "I'm just trying
to spare you some hurt. I recognize my own kind
when I see him. Bainbridge ain't the type to settle
down. He'll use you like I did, only this time maybe
you won't be as lucky. Maybe the baby won't die."

The crack of her palm hitting his cheek echoed
around the room, and a heavy silence descended. Jes-

sye wanted to throw out words that would wound him as much as he'd gouged her heart, but her blank mind wouldn't cooperate. His shocked expression gave way to a cocky grin.

"If you didn't want to dance with me, Jessye, all you had to do was say no."

He strolled away, leaving her to feel like a fool.

Madeline approached and gently touched her arm. "Are you all right?"

Jessye nodded mutely, her voice trapped behind a wall of shameful memories. Madeline studied her, and she knew she should apologize for disrupting the party, but she couldn't find the words. Madeline made a slight waving motion with her hand, and music once again filled the room.

"I'm sorry," Madeline said quietly. A sadness touched her eyes. "When Gerald stopped by to thank Ashton for the letters she wrote, I thought it might be nice to have a small party. But if I can be quite honest, I'm not very comfortable around him. I don't know why you slapped him, but I seriously doubt it had anything to do with his request for a dance."

"We go a long way back. He seems bound and determined to destroy whatever good memories I had of him."

"The war hurt our men in ways we can't even imagine. I know David grew stronger in some ways, weaker in others. And we women did the same. I admire the fact that you've undertaken this venture with Kit and Harry."

"It's an honest venture."

"Of course, it is. For reasons beyond my understanding, Kit took great delight in aggravating his father, but deep down he's not the rake he would have everyone believe."

"Harry's a scoundrel. He cheats at cards."

"Can you prove it?"

"No," she admitted reluctantly.

"Then perhaps he's just lucky, and he'll no doubt want another dance once he's finished his conversation with David. Perhaps you'd like a moment to freshen up," Madeline suggested kindly. "If you walk out of this room and past the stairs, you'll see a door to your left. It's a small room with a vanity. You should find everything you need there."

"Thank you."

Madeline smiled warmly, her brown eyes glowing. "You know, it's so odd, but whenever you tilt your head like that I am left with the oddest notion that we've met before."

"Don't see how that could be unless you've been in my father's saloon."

"No, no, I've never been to Fortune. Have you traveled much?"

Jessye shrugged. "Went to San Antone a few years back, but didn't stay long."

"San Antone," Madeline murmured. "I doubt that we met there. Still, something about you is incredibly familiar. I'll probably figure it out long after you're on the trail." She waved her hand. "But I'm delaying you. You wanted a few moments alone. I'll let Harry know where you've gone."

Jessye headed into the hallway. Although the conversation with Madeline had helped, she was still haunted by the ugliness of Gerald's remarks. To distract herself, she concentrated on the mundane. How many hands did it take to polish the wood trimming that lined every floor and ceiling? She could almost see her reflection in the floor as she walked out of the main parlor.

She shook her head. She'd best not think about fancy things. Even if this cattle drive paid off as well as Harry thought it would, all the fancy things in the world wouldn't give her the one thing she wanted most.

As she neared the stairs, out of the corner of her eye, she caught a glimpse of bright crimson. She looked over her shoulder and stumbled to a stop. A little girl with riotous red hair sat on the second step of the sweeping stairway, peering through the rails into the parlor. Hugging a rag doll close to her chest, she wore a white nightgown, her bare toes peeking out and curling around the edge of the first step. She was such a tiny thing.

Jessye felt as though a fist tightened around her heart. Her own daughter would probably resemble this child—only she would be sitting on the steps in a saloon, steps that led to rooms where gentlemen lived and women sometimes visited.

"Hello," Jessye said softly, unable to resist the temptation of speaking to the child.

The girl snapped her head around, her green eyes wide. She pressed a tiny finger to her lips. "Thhh. I ain't thupposed to be here."

Jessye walked quietly and sat on the third step, the skirt of her gown draping around her. If she were wearing britches, she would have had room to sit next to the girl. "You must be Mary Ellen."

Mary Ellen bounced her head up and down. "I like

to look at the pretty ladies." She peered through the railing a moment before turning her attention back to Jessye. "My mama is the prettiest."

"And you'll grow up to be as pretty as she is."

The girl shook her head. "No, I'm gonna look like the angel what brung me."

Jessye's heart gave a sudden lurch. "The angel that brought you?"

Mary Ellen bobbed her head. "Mama said an angel in San Antone brung me to her and Papa."

Jessye felt her throat tighten, her eyes sting. Coincidence. It was just coincidence. This child could not be—

"Your mama told me that you are going to be four."

The child bobbed her head. "I'm gonna have a cake with horses on it. Do you like horses?"

"Young lady, what are you doing?" a deep voice boomed.

Jessye uncharacteristically jumped. Mary Ellen popped up from the stairs and threw herself into her father's arms. An aching chasm widening in her chest, Jessye watched as David Robertson's arms tightened around the mite he held.

Mary Ellen pressed her cheek to his. "I wanted to dance."

"Sounded to me like you might be pestering Miss Kane," David said.

Jessye rose, her knees trembling as she gripped the banister of the stairs. "I assure you she wasn't pestering me. She's a delight."

David glanced at his daughter, and the love shining in his eyes told Jessye that he agreed. "One dance," he announced.

Mary Ellen squealed and squirmed out of his arms. She held the doll out to Jessye. Jessye took it, feeling the warmth of the child's touch within the fabric, a touch she might have had—

She watched as Mary Ellen placed her tiny feet on her father's shining boots. She heard the violins playing in the background as David Robertson waltzed his daughter around the foyer. When the music ended, he lifted his daughter into his arms. "Now, it's time for bed."

Mary Ellen snuggled her head against his shoulder and extended her hand. Jessye handed her the doll and watched as she tucked it between herself and her father.

"If you see my wife, tell her I'll be down in a few minutes," David said.

Jessye hoped her smile didn't appear as fake as it felt. Crossing her arms beneath her breasts, pressing them close against her, she tried to hold in the pain, the joy, the grief, all the emotions swirling through her like a tornado trapped within a house.

"He adores her," a soft voice whispered behind her.

Jessye swallowed the lump in her throat and blinked back the tears before turning to face Madeline. "She's a lovely child."

Madeline flicked her gaze to the stairs and back to Jessye. "We're very fortunate to have her. Our son had just died when we stopped by a mission near San Antone. A young woman had given birth, and circumstances were such that she thought it was in the child's best interest to give her to us."

Jessye was surprised to see tears glistening within Madeline's eyes.

"I don't know the woman's name or what became of her, but there isn't a day goes by that I don't thank her for having the courage to give up her child. I hope someday that she will know that we treasure the gift she gave us—and that her daughter is loved and happy."

Jessye's throat tightened. "I'm sure she knows that, Mrs. Robertson."

"You really must call me Madeline. Now if you'll excuse me, I'd best go rescue my husband. Knowing our daughter, Mary Ellen has no doubt convinced him that he has to sing her to sleep."

When Madeline disappeared at the top of the stairs, Jessye sought her escape. She found the door that led outside, shoved it open, and stepped into the warm night air.

A balcony surrounded the area. She walked to the far side and gripped the wrought iron railing. Tears leaked slowly through her closed eyes, trailing along her cheeks, pooling on either side of her lips.

"She's your daughter, isn't she?"

Harry's voice came through the darkness, stoked the pain flaming through her.

"No, she's not my daughter."

"After our dance, I wanted to talk with David because I thought I remembered hearing that he had a son, not a daughter. David told me how they came to have Mary Ellen. There's too much coincidence for her not to be yours."

Jessye spun around and pounded her fist into his chest. "She's not my daughter, you damn Englishman! I have no daughter because I gave her up." The tears increased, her shoulders slumped. "And it hurts, Harry. God, it hurts so damn bad."

He encircled her within his embrace. She wrapped her arms around him and gave his back one hard pounding just so he'd know it was anger driving her to accept his comfort—and nothing more. "It hurts in a bad way knowing what I gave up, and it hurts in a good way to see how much she is loved." She lifted her face to meet his gaze. "Did you see her?"

"Yes, I was standing just within the doorway. Your circumstances will change once we get these cattle up north. On the way back to Fortune, we could stop by here, and you could explain to David and Madeline that you want her back."

She shook her head. "Those people took her as their own. She became theirs. It wouldn't be fair to any of them to take her back now." She clenched her fingers around his jacket. "When I gave my baby up, I knew then that it was forever. But at seventeen, I just didn't realize that forever was an eternity."

His lips trailed over her face, gathering her tears. "You are the most remarkable woman I've ever known."

She felt anything but remarkable as her arms moved from around his back and eased up to entwine themselves around his neck. "She's so happy," she whispered.

"Yes."

"And loved."

"Definitely."

"I did the right thing, giving her up." She hated the doubt she heard reflected in her voice. She was grateful for all the Robertsons gave her daughter, but a part of her was unable to stop the resentment from building because she hadn't been able to give those things to her child.

Harrison cradled her cheek and gazed into her eyes, wishing he had the power to wipe away her doubts. But he knew he couldn't, because within the green depths, he saw the pain that still lingered. Knowing her daughter was loved by others had to ease the burden of her guilt, but it would never fully ease her pain.

He lowered his mouth to hers, tasting the salt of her tears. She whimpered, a soft sound that tore at his heart, a heart he'd never known he possessed until he'd met her. A woman whose strength had been forged by the fires of betrayal, she still possessed the innocence of a child. She should not be here, within his arms, because he was exactly what he claimed to be: a scoundrel.

And she didn't know how to play the game.

As her arms tightened around his neck, for one insane moment, he reveled in the fact that she did not know how to pretend love. Avarice had never been his weakness, but he was greedy now for the full taste of her. He teased her dampened lips with his tongue until they parted on a gentle sigh. He slipped his tongue into her mouth, savoring the lingering taste of wine. Easing his arm around her, he pressed her body flush against his.

His conscience felt as if it were being stretched on a rack, awaiting some henchman's assault. She needed comfort, not lust. His body aching with need, he realized one of them would suffer tonight.

Better it be him.

Pulling back, he met her gaze. "I think it's time we left."

She didn't protest when he took her hand and led her back into the house. He started up the wide, sweeping stairs, and she staggered to a stop.

"Where are we going?" she whispered harshly.

"To say goodnight . . . and good-bye." He saw the doubts flicker within her eyes, and he squeezed her hand. "Come on."

Wiping the tears from her cheeks, she nodded before walking up the two steps so they were even. He slipped his arm around her waist. "Just a quick peek," he said quietly.

"What if we get caught?"

He smiled devilishly. "Trust me. Slipping in and out of ladies' bedrooms is a skill I mastered long ago."

"Do they have a special school for scoundrels?"

He nodded. "I graduated at the top of my class."

"I don't doubt it," she said as they reached the landing.

He pressed his finger to his lips and led her along the hallway to a door that was partially open. A pale light spilled from the room. He pushed the door open further, and Jessye glided inside like a wraith. She glanced over her shoulder. "Come with me."

Nodding, he followed her inside the child's bedroom, filled with miniature furniture and dolls. Jessye neared the canopy bed and sank to her knees.

The child slept with her doll tucked close to her body. He watched as Jessye's gaze lit on the tiny girl, and she touched her daughter's hair. "Oh, Harry, she is so beautiful."

Something unfamiliar clogged his throat at the sight of her memorizing her daughter's features. How had he ever considered, even for a moment, that this woman had not loved her child? The depth of love reflected in her eyes was without equal. To be allowed to share this moment with her humbled him as nothing in his life ever had.

As Jessye began to rise, he helped her to her feet. Leaning over, she brushed a light kiss over the sleeping child's cheek. She walked quietly across the room, stopped in the doorway, glanced over her shoulder briefly, and stepped into the hallway. Harry followed, closing the door slightly.

Tears shimmering in her eyes, she leaned against the wall as though she needed something solid behind her to keep her upright.

"I suppose coming up here has been a blessing and a curse," he said.

She gave a brief, jerky nod. "I just need a minute."

He recognized from the jut of her chin that she would not welcome comfort from him now. How had he come to know her so well?

"You don't have to always be strong, Jessye."

"Yes, I do, because if I'm not, there is no way in hell I'm gonna be able to walk out of here and leave her behind."

He thought his fellow countrymen could take lessons from her on the best way to keep their chins up. He retrieved his handkerchief and handed it to her. "We'd best thank our hosts. Dawn comes early."

When she finished drying her eyes, he cradled her elbow and guided her down the stairs into the main parlor. David and Madeline stood at the entrance.

"We hate to leave good company, but I think it's time we gathered Kit—"

"He's already left," David said.

Harry didn't like hearing that bit of news, but he simply smiled. "Then we shall catch up with him at the hostelry." He took Madeline's hand and brought it to his lips. "Thank you for an enchanting evening." He shook David's hand before escorting Jessye out of the house into the night.

Once outside, she wrapped her arms around her middle.

"Are you going to be all right?" he asked.

She nodded. "It was just an evening I never expected."

"Your daughter is loved, happy, and safe. I would think a mother could wish for nothing more."

"Oh, Harry, you don't know all the things a mother can wish for, but thank you for those few moments that I will hold in my heart until the day I die."

He thought of all the expensive gifts he'd bestowed upon his mistresses over the years, and the appreciation he'd never received. How was it that this woman had the ability to make him feel worthy because of a gift that had cost him nothing?

❦ Chapter 11 ❧

Jessye stood outside the livery while Harry returned the carriage he'd rented to take them to the Robertsons'. She looked at the stars, and a peace settled over her that she hadn't known in over four years. She had kissed her daughter goodnight, touched her, inhaled her innocent fragrance, and knew she was safe in a world that was not always kind.

"Making a wish?" Harry asked as he came up behind her.

"I stopped wishing long ago."

"That's a shame," he said as he took her hand, slipped it around his arm, and escorted her toward the hostelry.

"You never struck me as a man who believed in wishes."

"I don't, but I always assumed women and children did."

The shadows and light from the lanterns played across his features as they passed several buildings. The constant shift in shading suited the way he only revealed small parts of himself before retreating behind that wall of self-interest, a barrier she now suspected shielded him from himself as much as from others.

She had deemed him lazy, but he worked as hard or harder than most of the men they'd hired.

She thought he placed his own wants first, and yet this evening he had made her feel cherished, as though he placed her above his desires.

She turned her attention toward the shadows hovering near the buildings. He could manipulate cards. Why not people? He had told her within the boundaries of business friendships did not exist. How far would he go to gain what he wanted?

He'd been blunt in Fortune about his wanting to bed her. Was Gerald right? Would Harry manipulate her heart simply to gain her body? A conquest to be left behind in ruin at dawn?

He shoved open the door to the hostelry, and she walked through, her skirt whispering over the floor. She knew she would forever remember this night.

They approached the front desk, and the sleeping clerk jerked awake. He reached into two separate boxes stacked behind him and handed Harry the keys to their rooms.

"Has Mr. Montgomery returned?" Harry asked.

"Nope."

"Where is the nearest gentleman's club—saloon— that is still open?"

"That would be Bret's place at the end of the road there." The clerk pointed straight ahead. "Just start walkin'. Cain't miss it."

"Thank you." Harry took Jessye's arm. "I'll escort you to your room."

"Are you worried about Kit?" she asked as they reached the stairs.

"Of course not. I'm not his keeper."

The briskness with which he spoke—as though he had no wish for her to know he was concerned about his friend—made her doubt his words. "He seemed upset talking about his brother's wife at dinner."

"I didn't notice."

Another brisk response. Interesting. Another lie? He stopped outside her room, unlocked the door, and handed her the key. "Goodnight."

He started to walk away.

"Harry?"

He faced her. Suddenly skittish for reasons she didn't understand, she closed her hand around the emerald teardrop. "I should give you back the necklace."

He shrugged. "Keep it. I have nothing suitable with which to wear it."

Her heart twisted at his attempt to make it seem as though the jewelry were nothing but a bauble. "I was thinking we could trade it for supplies."

"Don't worry about the supplies. Kit will work something out."

"With David Robertson?"

"If need be. Kit can talk an angel into sinning."

She tightened her fingers around the jewel. "I just feel guilty knowing the money could have been put to better use."

He furrowed his brow. "Better use? I took great pleasure in watching it sparkle tonight. In my mind, it was money well spent—and it was my money to spend. Now, if you'll excuse me, the night is still young and I am in the mood to prowl."

"It's after midnight."

"My favorite time of the evening. Goodnight, Jessye love. Sleep well."

He disappeared down the stairs. The scoundrel. She'd heard him ask about a saloon. She locked her door and hurried after him. She only wanted to peer quickly into the building, and if she ran into any trouble, Harry would be there.

Not that she expected trouble, but still it was comforting to know he would be near. Scowling, she walked through the lobby. She didn't like to rely on a man for comfort.

She stepped outside and saw Harry's silhouette. She'd spot that arrogant stride anywhere. She walked along the dirt street, grateful for the muffling of her footsteps. He had a purpose to his gait, and she was having a difficult time keeping up, damn his long legs.

The saloon come into sight, light spilling through the doorway. Harry veered down the alley between the saloon and the building next to it.

She quickened her pace, rounded the corner, and staggered to a stop. She watched Harry approach a slumped figure on the ground, slip his arms beneath the man, and lever him into a sitting position.

"Ah, 'arry, I knew you'd find me," Kit said, his words slurred.

"You're drunk. You'll have regrets come dawn."

"I have regrets now." He grabbed Harry's jacket and jerked him closer. "I'm in hell."

"I know," Harry said quietly.

"So are you. It used to be three of us—you, me, and Gray—in hell together. But I think Gray got out."

"Yes, I rather think he did."

"Lucky bastard." He released his hold on Harry. "Don't tell him I called him that. He despises being a bastard."

"I don't think his illegitimacy bothers him any longer, not since Abbie came to love him."

She heard a heart-wrenching sob.

"I would have gladly born her pain to spare her," Kit lamented, his voice rife with anguish.

"I know."

"What did Clarisse do to deserve such suffering?"

"She did nothing."

"I loved her. I still do. You can't understand that, can you? You who knows nothing of love. Who loved you? Ever? Not your father or your mother, and certainly not that jackanapes brother of yours."

"Love is for poets and fools."

"Then I gladly welcome the opportunity to be a fool."

Kit slid his gaze past Harry and gave her a crooked smile. "Tell him, Jessye. Tell him how grand love can be."

Her heart lurched at the command she could not obey.

Harry snapped his head around. "What in the bloody hell are you doing here?"

"I wanted to take a look at the saloon."

"Have you no sense, walking through town at night, alone?"

"Careful," Kit warned, sloppily patting Harry's shoulder. "One might think . . . you're testing the waters of love."

"Will you shut up? You're sloshed."

"Strong drink improves my vision. I see two of

everything." He slumped forward. "And I see Clarisse. So beauti . . . ful."

"Come along. We need to get you to the hostelry." Harry struggled to lift Kit.

"I'll help you," she said, stepping out of the shadows. "I can get his feet."

"Not necessary." Harry slung Kit over his shoulder and stood. "You can get the doors."

"You've done this before," she said softly.

"Many a night."

"You were right earlier when you said that I don't know you. When you asked the clerk where the nearest saloon was, I assumed you were going out to drink and gamble. But you were trying to find Kit, weren't you?"

"He is too much of a gentleman to empty David's liquor cabinet, but when he's in a mood such as this, he tends to stop at the first tavern he spots and drinks until he passes out. I didn't fancy the thought of him being robbed."

As they trudged toward the hostelry, she heard Kit snore and dared to ask what made no sense. "He was in love with his brother's wife?"

"His father arranged for Clarisse to marry the heir of Ravenleigh. The only time in his life he ever regretted not being born first was the day his brother got married."

"Did she love Kit?"

"*That* I do not know."

She licked her lips. "Why are you in hell, Harry?"

"You should never take to heart the ranting of a drunken man."

"I've worked in a saloon all my life. Men most

often speak the truth when they've had too much to drink."

"Unfortunately, I'm not in a position to take the cards from my pocket and risk having you cut to the high card."

"I don't want you to tell me because of the turn of a card. I want you to tell me because . . . because you want to."

"*That* will never happen."

"I trusted you with my secrets."

"It's not a matter of trust, but rather of shame. Now let's get this poor fool to bed."

"She's Mary Ellen's mother, isn't she?" Madeline's voice carried a hysterical edge to it.

Harrison sat in the Robertsons' drawing room, studying Madeline's pale face. Near dawn, when he'd returned to his room, he'd received the urgent message to come to their home. Now he was torn between revealing the truth and keeping the promise he'd made to Jessye to never bare her secret to anyone. He sighed deeply. "Yes."

"Oh, my God," Madeline whispered, reaching for David's hand and clutching it until her knuckles turned white. "Does she want her back?"

"Desperately."

"Dear God, no!" Madeline lunged to her feet and rushed to the window. David joined her and wrapped his arms around her.

In the soft light of dawn, Harrison saw the tears glistening along her cheeks as she pressed a fist to her lips. He slowly came to his feet. "But she won't take her from you."

Madeline swung around and looked at him, the hope in her eyes almost too painful to witness. Damn Gerald Milton for the bloody mess his lack of honor had caused.

"Are you sure?" Madeline asked.

"I'm positive. In her heart, you are the child's parents. Mary Ellen is your daughter. Jessye has no wish to put any of you through the hell she has endured."

"What of Mary Ellen's father?" David asked.

"He's dead." God, how Harrison wished that lie were true.

Madeline sank into a nearby chair, swiping the tears from her eyes. "So it was coincidence that our paths crossed again?"

He held out his hands imploringly. "I'm not a big believer in a higher power who guides our steps, but I can't deny that fate seems to have taken a hand here. Jessye has always feared she made a mistake, giving her daughter over to strangers. Last night, I think she found a measure of peace."

"I could not love Mary Ellen more had I given birth to her myself."

"That fact is evident, Madeline," he said quietly.

"But I also know what it is to give birth to a child and to lose that child." She rose regally, and he thought it a shame the woman wasn't British. "I need to speak with Jessye before you leave."

Standing in the mercantile, Jessye watched as Dan, Magpie, and Cookie carted supplies to the wagon waiting in front of the store. Kit had handed over a list to the owner and gone outside. His face had a greenish tint, and she doubted fresh air would make him feel much better.

He'd left her with instructions to purchase anything she thought they required, but his list was so complete that she couldn't think of anything else they needed.

She walked past the counter, trailing her fingers along the corner of the glass case. She stopped at the sight of a pair of dueling pistols displayed prominently in the front. Harry's pistols. So this was where he'd bartered them away.

The merchant was selling them for fifty dollars. She wondered how much Harry had actually gotten for them.

Kneeling, she pressed her hand to the glass and studied the one thing he'd ever treasured. What made them so precious to him?

She touched the money belt hidden beneath her clothes. Purchasing the pistols would leave them with no choice but to take on an investor. The profits would be split further, but she desperately wanted to give Harry back his pistols.

She rose and walked outside. Kit sat on a bench, his elbows resting on his thighs, his head buried in his hands. She strolled over and sat beside him.

"Kit—"

"Please don't talk so loudly," he rasped.

"I'm sorry. I know you don't feel well—"

"That is an understatement." Eyes closed, he leaned his head against the wall. "I have one foot in the grave."

She fought not to smile at the misery he'd brought upon himself. "I need to know how much money you need from me for the supplies we're purchasing here."

He waved his hand. "None."

She sat up straighter. "What do you mean, none? You're filling every nook and cranny in the supply wagon—"

"Harry gave me money."

"Where did he get that much money?"

"I've known Robin Hood too long to question his actions or to doubt his motives."

She furrowed her brow. "Robin Hood?"

He sliced his gaze to her. "Robin Hood is a legendary English thief who lived in Sherwood Forest. He robbed from the rich and gave to the poor. Harry has a penchant to rob from the arrogant."

"You're telling me he gives to the poor?"

"I met Harry while I was a student at Eton. His father provided him with a disgustingly large allowance. He had no need of money, and yet when we'd receive our allowances, he'd challenge several of us to various games of chance. He'd leave us with just enough money so we could get by—if we were very frugal—until our next allowance arrived."

"Is that why you became his friend? So he'd stop cheating you?"

"Not exactly. One night Gray and I realized he was manipulating the cards—no one was blessed with that much luck—so we decided to beat a confession out of him and force him to return our money to us. As we were on our way to his room, we saw him leave— and we followed. We followed him to an orphanage, where he placed a pouch on the doorstep. When he was out of sight, we retrieved the pouch."

"And found your money."

"Every shilling that had been lost to him."

Jessye shook her head slightly. "Why?"

"Wounded hearts are difficult to heal. Who am I to question Harry's motives when his deeds have a tendency to put my actions to shame? But I'll make you a wager. I will give you my share of the profits when we reach our destination if every man who now owes Harry money doesn't suddenly find Lady Luck smiling on him and his fortunes reversed so he ends up owing Harry little more than a pittance."

"I find it damn aggravating that I can't figure him out."

"You *want* him to be a scoundrel. It makes it so much easier to justify keeping your distance."

"I want to understand him. There are times when . . ." She looked at him imploringly. "Would my heart be safe with him?"

Kit sighed deeply and closed his eyes. "Probably not."

She surged to her feet, and he groaned. "Please—"

"I'm sorry," she said, truly meaning the words. Even though she worked in a saloon, she never understood why men drank to excess. She heard footsteps and glanced over her shoulder. Her heart slammed against her ribs.

Harry walked toward her. Beside him, Madeline Robertson looked much as she had last night—beautiful, confident—although she wore cotton instead of silk. Jessye rubbed her sweating palms over her woolen trousers, then jerked up her chin. What did she care how she looked? "Mornin'," she blurted before they'd stopped walking.

Madeline smiled warmly. "Miss Kane, I'd like to have a word with you."

Jessye nodded. Gerald had probably spilled his guts to them after she'd left last night, and the lady was appalled to discover the type of woman she'd had in her house.

Harry grabbed Kit's arm and dragged him to his feet. "Come along, Kit, I need to purchase a pair of dueling pistols, and I need your help to do it."

"You've never needed my help before," Kit grumbled as they disappeared into the store.

"You wanna sit?" Jessye asked bluntly, pointing to the bench.

"No, thank you. I won't be here long," Madeline said softly. "Last night, as I was drifting off to sleep, I realized where I'd seen you."

"We've never met," Jessye assured her.

"No, we haven't. But I've seen you. I've seen you within my daughter. Within her eyes, her smiles, the stubborn jut of her chin—"

"You're mistaken."

"Harry assures me that I'm not."

Jessye closed her eyes. Damn the man. She was going to make him regret ever being born.

"I couldn't sleep for fear that you'd take her from me, and here you are denying that she is yours."

Jessye opened her eyes, hating the tears she seemed unable to hold back. "She is not *my* daughter."

"No, she is mine, but you gave birth to her and placed her in my keeping. She is a gift I can never repay—"

"Just keep loving her and taking care of her, and we'll call it even."

Tears surfaced within Madeline's eyes. "Harry told me you were a remarkable woman, but then I knew that long ago." She reached behind her neck, unclasped a chain, and handed the locket to Jessye.

Jessye stared at the inscription on the golden oval: "A mother's love knows no boundaries."

"Inside, you'll find a portrait of our daughter and a lock of her hair. Know you are always welcome in our home."

Jessye glanced up. "Thanks for the invite, but I doubt I'll be taking you up on it. The two times I've given her up, it damn near killed me."

Madeline smiled softly with understanding. "I admire your strength, Miss Kane. May God bless you as you've blessed me."

Clutching the locket, Jessye watched Madeline Robertson walk away. Her daughter's mother. A strong woman in her own right. A woman who understood the depth of a mother's love.

❧ Chapter 12 ❧

*Harrison found the vast expanse of dark*ness calming. At night, the prairie revealed a beauty that it kept hidden through the day as they traveled mile after monotonous mile. The stars blanketed the sky with such brilliance that even a man as cynical as himself could not help but be awed.

In much the same manner that the woman who kept watch over the herd with him impressed him.

As he guided his horse around the outer circle of bedded-down cattle, he saw Jessye urging her horse toward him. Their standard nightly routine involved several guards watching the sleeping herd for a four-hour stretch.

A week had passed since they'd left Dallas. Tonight Jessye's watch coincided with his—a blessing and a curse. Since kissing her on the Robertsons' balcony, he had avoided her as much as possible, but his mind tortured him constantly. He remembered the feel of her body as though she were still pressed against him, the satiny texture of her flesh as though his fingers were still skimming over her shoulders, the shape of her lips and the sweet nectar of her mouth as though he were still kissing her. God, how he longed to kiss her again.

As soon as she came within sight, he couldn't keep his gaze from straying to her. Not that the cattle noticed. He'd heard the cowboys tell and retell horror stories of the stampedes they'd lived through, but these cattle seemed content to trudge tirelessly toward their destination. Harrison knew Texans had a tendency to exaggerate the truth, and he was beginning to believe that the stories he'd heard of men being pounded into the ground until the only thing visible was the butt of their gun were nothing more than tall tales.

Jessye's voice wafted over the herd as she sang one hymn after another, songs he recognized from his youth, when he'd sat on the hard wooden pew and listened to the threats of hell, which seemed so inconsequential when compared to his mother's devilish cruelties.

But Jessye . . . Jessye was an angel. He chuckled low. A stubborn, obstinate angel to be sure. And so damned courageous that he found he had no choice but to admire her, a thought that caused a tightening within his chest. He could honestly admit that he'd never admired a woman to the degree that he appreciated Jessye. And there were frightening moments when he feared that what he felt went beyond admiration, might possibly border on love.

But what did he know of love?

Never in his life had he wanted to bury himself inside a woman as much as he wanted to burrow within Jessye. The *want* was so strong that it was almost a *need*. And he'd never needed a woman. He'd always managed to maintain a distance—never revealing anything beyond the outer shell of what he was.

But with Jessye everything was different. She'd stripped away his defenses as easily as one might pull the petals from a rose . . . and therein resided the danger.

Because with her, he wanted more than the physical joining. He wanted to know her secrets, her fears, and her burdens. He wanted to see the joy on her face when they reached their destination, the cattle were sold, and the money was placed in her hand.

He wanted her happiness above all else.

And her happiness meant he could never have what he wanted, because he hadn't a clue as to how to give her love.

She neared, and the song she'd been singing fell into silence.

"We're extremely fortunate the cattle are of a religious nature and seem to find your hymns soothing," he said.

"Reckon you could sing them a lullaby," Jessye chided.

"I don't know any lullabies."

"I could teach you some."

"What would I do with them after the cattle are at market?" Except think of her whenever he heard one.

"Could sing them to your children."

"I shan't have children."

Removing her hat, she cocked her head at an angle that always made him feel as though she was studying his soul. "Don't you plan to ever get married?"

She sidled her horse next to his and halted it.

"I would not make a good husband. I do, however, make an excellent lover." Against his better judgment, he gripped her saddle horn, leaned over, cradled the back of her head with his other hand, and captured her mouth with his own. With a soft moan, she bent toward him, threading her fingers through the hair at the nape of his neck. His tongue delved deeply, mating with hers, conjuring up carnal images that made sitting in the saddle grow increasingly uncomfortable. He wanted desperately to lay her on a blanket beneath the stars.

Drawing back, he cupped her chin and stroked his thumb across her swollen lips.

"Too bad I'm not interested in taking on a lover," she whispered hoarsely.

"Then you should have shoved me away."

"Next time I'll shove you right off that horse," she warned.

"No you won't. You enjoy my kisses as much as I enjoy bestowing them upon you. If we urge our horses to walk a bit faster, we should be able to work in two more kisses before the North Star rises completely above the Big Dipper." He had been amazed to learn that few cowboys owned watches and that they used the position of the stars to determine the time of night. He smiled as she shook her head.

"Harry, you scoundrel. We move our horses too fast and we'll start a stampede."

"Ah, yes, the hell on hooves that the men constantly spin tales about. Our cattle are too docile."

"Don't underestimate them. Sometimes it takes nothing more than striking a match to send them running."

"And it takes nothing but a harmless kiss to send you running."

"Your kisses aren't harmless. They make me start thinking about turning down a trail that I know leads to heartache, and heartache is a town I've visited before. I don't much like the place."

"Then do us both a favor and see to it that our watches do not coincide in the future, because I find you increasingly difficult to resist."

"Because I'm the only woman out here." Jessye gave her horse a gentle kick in the side and urged it to follow the perimeter of the herd. She peered over her shoulder, caught sight of Harry, and somberness settled over her. The kisses he'd given her left no doubt that he was an excellent lover. She actually experienced moments when she thought she might be willing to settle for less than love just to know the full measure of his embrace, to lie with him on a blanket beneath the stars on a warm April night . . .

Maybe she would once they reached their destination, once she was holding the money in her hand that would proclaim her freedom and her independence. Wealth would make her strong, so she'd require nothing beyond herself—not even a man's love.

But the thought of giving herself to a man knowing that he didn't love her left her bereft. Could a physical union be truly magnificent when it lacked the emotions created by love?

She couldn't deny that her body craved Harry's touch. Unfortunately, her heart longed for him as well. He'd made it clear that he was a stranger to love, and she didn't know if she had the strength to introduce him to its magnificence, because to do so would leave her vulnerable.

And she just didn't know if she could truly survive another broken heart.

As he stared at the cattle swimming across the Red River, Harrison had a feeling that the past three weeks of tedious travel were thankfully about to end. The monotonous days that had characterized the trek north from Dallas left a man with too much time to think, and Harrison's thoughts often strayed to Jessye, memories of her sweet body pressed against his.

During the day, he had taken to traveling at the rear of the herd, where the dust kicked up by the cattle often served as a distraction, especially when he was overcome with a coughing fit. The worst moments came at night when it was his turn to circle the slumbering herd.

The lowing of the cattle reminded him too much of the loneliness gnawing at his soul. Bloody damned hell. If only his desires were limited to the physical, he would seek relief at the next town, but for the first time in his adult life, he craved something beyond the physical. He wanted a purity that held no deceptions, a closeness that went beyond touching.

He'd never felt so alone. Even Kit's friendship offered little solace.

"I hate crossin' rivers," Magpie said in a voice that reminded Harrison of a petulant child.

"We've crossed other rivers," Harrison pointed out.

"But none like the Red. Reckon I oughta be grateful that the water is somewhat low."

Harrison narrowed his gaze and focused his attention on the riders splashing into the water to keep the cattle from wandering. He estimated that three-fourths of the herd had already crossed. The remaining cattle were stretching their necks to keep their heads above water, and the undulating waves lapped at the thighs of the men. He cast a sideways glance at Magpie. "This is low?"

Magpie leaned forward, resting his arm on his saddle horn. "Yep. That driftwood tangled in the boughs of the trees lining the banks shows how high the water rose in the past. A flooded river is a cowboy's worst nightmare."

"I thought a stampede was a cowboy's worst nightmare."

Magpie nodded. "That, too."

Harrison looked across to the opposite bank, where Kit sat astride his horse, Jessye beside him. A shiver slithered up his back at the sight of the crude crosses visible just behind them. "What do those markers symbolize?"

"Graves," Magpie said somberly. "Most cowboys can't swim. One or two are bound to lose their grip on the saddle horn and drown."

"Do you swim?"

"Nope, that's why I hate fording a river." He released a bravado yell and kicked his horse's flanks.

"Bloody hell," Harrison grumbled as he followed, urging his horse down the steep bank into the choppy water, a brown that carried the hint of red, as though it reflected the blood of those who'd died within its depths. He tried to ignore the shadow of foreboding surrounding him as he contemplated the fact that they were not only crossing a river but they were also leaving the laws of Texas behind and trampling into Indian Territory.

The low bawling of the cattle increased in tempo. He heard the clack of horns hitting horns. The strength of the rushing water slamming against him surprised him. He feared it might be taking the cattle off guard as well. The orderly procession appeared to be reversing itself, the cattle turning as though they sought to return to the Texas border.

Magpie grabbed the back of his saddle and twisted his body around, concern etched in his features. "They're getting mired in the quicksand at the bank!"

"Mired at the bank?" Stunned, Harrison watched as the cattle milled around the riders and themselves, swimming in a circle, closing ranks until they looked like a raft of horns. "There's miles of bloody bank! Let's move them down."

Magpie nodded. He turned, then jerked back as a steer swung his head around, his lethal horns cutting across man and beast. In horror, Harrison watched Magpie's horse roll and heard Magpie's panicked yell as he lost his grip on the saddle horn and slipped backward into the river.

Hampered by the water and the circling beasts, Harrison made a feeble attempt to kick his horse into action. It released a high-pitched neigh and balked at going forward. Harrison saw Magpie's head bob up and the terror in his eyes just before he went back under.

He heard a crack of thunder that sounded like a gunshot. A steer flipped to its side, and a hole opened. He saw Magpie's hand reaching up. Gripping the saddle horn with one hand, Harrison slid into the water, wedged his way between his horse and the steers, and grabbed Magpie's flailing hand. Magpie broke through to the surface. Harrison jerked him toward the horse. "Climb on!"

Gasping for breath, Magpie shook his head.

"Damn it, man, I can swim!" Harrison roared over the din of frightened animals and rushing waters.

Relief swept over the younger man's face as he nodded and awkwardly scrambled onto the saddle. Harrison slapped his horse's rump, but the animal was penned in and only able to move forward at a snail's pace. Harrison grabbed the back of the saddle, but the wet leather and his slick hands prevented him from getting a firm grip. Thank God he *could* swim.

In ponds, lakes, and rivers where ample room allowed him to churn his arms and kick—but here nothing existed but the strong undercurrent and the press of large, warm bodies against his own. His drenched clothes weighed him down. Feeling the pull of a losing battle, he took one last gulping breath before the murky depths obliterated the light from the sun.

He tried to surface, but hooves, legs, and rounded bellies blocked his way. His world narrowed into an obscene prison, an oubliette so deep that its opening was not visible. His lungs burned, his throat tightened, and his chest threatened to crush against his spine.

Everything inside him screamed to breathe. The pressure built until he thought he would explode. The pain intensified, the panic heightened, the acceptance unavoidable. Escape was impossible.

The irony struck him hard. His father had sought to save him from the Thames only to have him drown in the Red River.

His last thought drifted to Jessye. He would never again gaze into her green eyes, see her smiles, or hear her sultry voice. Profound regret stabbed him as those eternal deprivations overshadowed the loss of his own life.

Jessye's scream shattered the air, quickly followed by rapid gunfire as Kit leveled his rifle and downed cattle, one after another. She felt powerless as she heard the pounding hooves.

"You're starting a stampede!" Dan Lincoln cried as he jerked his horse to a halt.

"Do you think I give a bloody damn?" Kit yelled as he reloaded and fired again. "Harry went under near those dead cattle. Gather the men and get him out."

"If he went under, he's dead."

Anger blazed in Kit's eyes as he grabbed Dan by the shirtfront and nearly hauled him out of the saddle. "Get the men down to the river while I clear a path." He released his hold and once again began to shoot cattle. Dan gave her a look that clearly implied Kit's attempt was futile. But he turned his horse and yelled for the men to get back to the river.

Her hands shaking badly, she reached for her own rifle.

"Jessye, get blankets from the supply wagon. Harry's going to need them," Kit ordered.

"I should stay—"

"You should go." He cast a somber gaze her way, and she knew his mind had accepted Dan's dire prediction. Only his heart refused to surrender hope. "You don't want to be here."

Tears burning her eyes, she nodded. He was right.

She didn't want to see Harry's limp body brought up from the river. "He'll need blankets."

She urged her horse into a hard gallop, the echo of gunfire behind her, the devastating thought screaming through her mind that Harry would need blankets, lots of them, whether he was alive—or dead.

It seemed like an eternity passed before she caught up to the supply wagon. "Cookie, I need blankets!" she yelled as she pulled up beside it.

"Damn it to hell. We have a drowning?" he asked.

"No, no, Harry . . . he just . . ." Her voice caught, her heart ached. "He—"

"Never mind, girl," he said as he reached through the opening in the canvas. "Just get the blankets to him and I'll head back that way myself."

Taking the bundle he offered, she wished she could stop trembling. She set her heels to her horse's flanks, hope warring with certainty. Kit had fired one shot when Magpie had gone in the water. His action had opened a hole large enough for Harry to slip through so he could rescue Magpie, but it had been impossible for Magpie to turn the horse when Harry lost his hold on the saddle. The obstinate cattle directed the path.

She neared the river. The cattle they'd kept on a tight, narrow trail were scattered to the winds. A lump rose in her throat at the sight of the men standing, a few kneeling near the river's bank. She drew her horse to a halt. The somberness was thicker than stew.

"He told me he could swim," Magpie cried. "He told me he could swim. I never would have gotten on his horse—"

"No one is blaming you, lad," Kit said. "He *can* swim."

She dismounted, her weak legs quivering so badly that she was surprised she could walk. She heard the horrid retching as she wended her way through the men to the front of the circle. Harry was on his knees, hands clenching his thighs, as he brought up his insides, gasping for breath. She'd never been so glad to see anything in her life.

As though sensing her presence from his kneeling position beside Harry, Kit glanced up. "Good." He signaled for her to join him.

She dropped to the ground and draped the blankets over Harry. He shook like a leaf during a storm, not that she was any steadier, but he looked as though he couldn't quite figure out how he'd come to be on land.

"He was unconscious when we pulled him out," Kit said quietly. "He took in a lot of water. Needs to rid himself of it."

"How long do you think he was unconscious?" she asked, dreading the answer. What if something had happened so he'd never again be right in the head? She'd heard stories of that happening to men.

"Haven't a clue. I had to pound his back—"

Harry stopped retching and sliced his gaze toward them. "Do you two . . ." He coughed. ". . . mind not discussing me . . ." He coughed again. ". . . as though I weren't here?"

Her relief that he was as ornery as ever was short-lived as a coughing fit seized him. Wrapping his arms around his middle, he moaned between coughs.

"You're gonna need to see the cook as soon as he gets here," she said.

Nodding, he drew in a ragged breath.

"We'll make camp nearby," Kit said as he stood

and cast a quick glance around the circle of men. "You can see about gathering up the cattle now."

"We're in Indian Territory," Dan said.

"Meaning?" Kit asked.

"I don't want any of the men riding alone."

"Fine. Do what you have to do to protect the men and get the cattle."

"What happens if the Injuns done got 'em?" someone asked.

"Negotiate to get them back, and if you can't, then leave them. Make no mistake. On this drive, the men come before the beasts."

Jessye had never seen so many mouths drop open.

"Now, get about it," Kit ordered. "I want to get out of this Indian Territory as soon as we can."

"Damn it, man! Take care!" Harry commanded.

"I'm tryin', but you're bruised and broken," Cookie snapped.

"I'm not broken," Harry grumbled.

"You got a couple of cracked ribs—"

"So take care that you don't damage them further."

Hunched beside the fire, unable to find the elusive warmth, Jessye watched as the cook tightly wound strips of cloth around Harry's ribs. She saw the shadow of bruises forming and knew by morning his back and sides would be black and blue.

"Have you given any thought as to how you're going to sit in a saddle come morning?" Kit asked.

"Probably in much the same manner that I'll sit in it during my night watch—gingerly."

"Take the night off," Kit suggested.

Moaning slightly as he shifted his body, Harry

shook his head. "I won't sleep anyway. Might as well be useful."

Carefully, he shrugged into his shirt and grimaced. Jessye was sure the action had caused him discomfort. Damn him for not being what she'd thought. She brought herself to her feet. "I got an announcement to make."

She felt all eyes come to rest on her. She reached into her pocket and pulled out a paper. She unfolded it until the absurd words were visible. "This is our agreement." Holding Harry's gaze, she tossed the contract into the fire. "From now on, the three of us are equal partners."

She spun on her heel and strode from the camp, fearful she'd reveal all her weaknesses if she stayed.

Harrison walked through the thick copse of trees, resenting the pain that shadowed each movement, resenting more that he'd taken no satisfaction in Jessye finally realizing that he was not bluffing. He had thought proving her wrong would bring him victory. Instead, her defeated mien left him with a measure of grief that he could not comprehend.

He found her standing at the edge of the river, staring at the waters, which reflected the moon in a kaleidoscope of ever changing images. Too much like life. Every time he thought he understood the game, someone changed the rules.

"Jessye?"

She spun around, the anger and tears in her eyes throwing him off guard.

"Damn you!" She pounded both fists against his chest and sent him staggering backward. He bit back a groan. "Damn you! What did you think you were doing this afternoon? Getting off your horse and going into the river to save Magpie. What were you thinking?" Advancing, she hit his shoulder. "Damn you!" She hit him again. "You don't even like him. Why in the hell would you risk dying for somebody you don't like?"

Within the moonlight, he saw the tears dampening her cheeks. "Oh God, Harry, I thought you were dead." She pressed her fists against her mouth and released a heart-wrenching sob. "I thought you were dead!"

He grabbed her arms, jerked her to him, and cradled her face between his hands, relishing the fact that he was able to do so. "I thought I was dead, too."

With a rapacious hunger, he captured her mouth, his tongue delving deeply, the need to reaffirm life clouding his judgment. If only she had hit him again, shoved him, kicked him, or bit his invading tongue—

Instead she welcomed him with a desperation that equaled his own. Her arms came around him, her hands pressing, touching as though to reassure herself that he was indeed alive and not a ghost. He welcomed the discomfort, for he had thought to never again feel a woman's touch, to hear her soft sighs, to inhale her sweet scent, to taste . . . to taste the salt of her tears.

They drove him beyond reason. When had any woman ever wept over him? Never. And that this strong, courageous woman would was enough to bring him to his knees.

His mouth still latched on to hers, he lifted her into his arms and carried her down to the warm earth. The

fragrance of wildflowers wafted around them. He
rocked back on his heels, and, holding her gaze, he
unbuttoned her shirt and bared her body to the moonlight, which glistened over her flesh, an ethereal caress. He dipped his head, took a puckered nipple into
his mouth, and suckled. Gasping, she arched against
him. He ran his hands over her silky skin and trailed
his lips across the valley between her breasts. "I want
to taste all of you, Jessye, all of you."

"Yes," she rasped, threading her fingers through his
hair.

If desperation weren't clawing at him, he might
have laughed at the realization that he'd never unfastened someone else's trousers. The urgency of his
needs, his desires caused his fingers to fumble with
the buttons. She moved his hands aside, finished the
task, and shed her clothes with fluid movements
etched in moonbeams that he thought he would remember for the remainder of his life.

She opened herself to him with no coyness. Her
honesty terrified him as much as the desire raging
through him. The cold scepter of death had touched
him today. He needed her, needed to feel the hot,
hungry passion of life.

Ravenous, he hovered over her, keeping his promise, tasting her mouth, her throat, her breasts, and her
most intimate of treasures. Gasping, moaning, she
writhed beneath him as though possessed by sensations too pleasurable to bear.

He tore open his own trousers, rose above her, and
sank into the hot, moist depths of her body. Her arms
came around him, her fingers digging into his buttocks
as she met his thrusts with wild abandon.

When she cried out, he captured her mouth, absorbing the full power of her release and matching it with his own.

Breathing heavily, he lay still, feeling the small tremors cascading through her body, the trembling of his own. The magnitude of what they'd just done slammed into him with the force of a battering ram.

In the river, as the blackness engulfed him, he'd thought his life was over. Only now did he realize that it had never fully begun. Emotions he'd long since buried fought to rise to the surface, just as he'd struggled this afternoon.

For reasons he dared not contemplate, terror ripped through him now with a greater ferocity. How could he fear losing what he did not possess—her heart?

A need to reaffirm life had motivated their actions. Nothing more. He could not allow it to be anything more. He would not give her the power to destroy him.

Yet she'd given him the power to hurt her. Regret surged through him. He'd never meant to harm her.

He lifted his head and met her gaze. He skimmed his fingers over her face. Incredibly lovely. He trailed his fingers along her collarbone. So dainty. She had discarded her clothes, but he had not completely removed his own. Even as an adult, bruises still shamed him, a visible sign of weakness. She deserved so much more, a man of better lineage.

He eased off her and righted his clothing before reaching for hers and handing them to her. He swallowed hard. "You can't go into camp looking as though you've just battled a wild animal. I'll get your bag."

He shoved to his feet and looked down on her, clutching her clothing to her breasts, staring at him through eyes mired with confusion. He spun on his heel and strode back to camp.

"How's Jessye?" Kit asked as Harrison neared the supply wagon.

"Shaken." He rummaged through the bags at the back until he found Jessye's.

"I'm not surprised. When you went under the water, her face . . . it might as well have been her drowning."

"Thank God, it wasn't." He snatched her bag and met Kit's gaze. "I doubt we'll return to camp tonight. I shall kill any man who speaks ill of her tomorrow."

"They all love her. I think they sought to spare her sorrow more than your life."

Harrison nodded, turned, and began to walk away.

"Does it hurt?" Kit asked in a low voice.

Harrison staggered to a stop. "The bruises will heal."

"I was referring to the pain in your chest where you have no doubt just discovered you have a heart like the rest of us."

"There is no pain," he lied.

"Then you don't deserve her."

Harrison stalked into the woods. He couldn't agree more.

Jessye sat on the bank, her knees drawn up against her chest, her arms wrapped tightly around her legs. How peaceful the river seemed. How deceptive.

She could not believe what she had allowed to happen between Harry and herself. Allowed? Wanted desperately. Needed urgently.

She'd felt powerless this afternoon, just as she had the night she'd given up her daughter.

She heard Harry's muted footsteps and braced herself for the confrontation. Oh, God, where had her restraint and self-preservation gone? What if she carried his child? She wrapped her fingers around the locket. She would never go through that hell again.

He hunkered down in front of her, placed her bag on the ground, and opened it. "Let me see if I can repair the damage," he said quietly.

Without looking at him, she snatched her belongings. "I can handle myself."

He reached for her shirt. She slapped his hands away. "What are you doing?"

"Your buttons are askew. I thought to set them straight."

She glanced down at the mess she'd made putting her clothes on. His finger touched her button. She jerked around. "Don't be nice to me, Harry."

"I'm not in the habit of making love to a woman and then treating her badly."

"Well, I got no habits when it comes to men except to avoid them. Gerald was the only one . . . this was different."

"In what way?"

She clutched the bag. How could she explain that although she'd experienced pleasure with Gerald, it had never been this earth-shattering? The efforts of an awkward, clumsy boy held no weight against those of an experienced man. The memories were sweet, but Gerald had never left her with this intense longing that she feared might never again be satisfied. Tonight, she'd reveled in Harry's power, strength, and knowledge. Ah, God, his knowledge: how to touch, how to move, how to reach through her body to unleash her heart and soul.

She cleared her throat. "Just different."

She didn't stop him this time as he straightened her buttons. When he finished, he skimmed his finger along her chin. "You'll hate me come morning," he said quietly.

She lifted her gaze to his. "I won't."

He gave her a sad smile. "The next day then. Or perhaps the day after that because I can't pay your price. I can't give you love."

She nodded, not surprised by his words. She wasn't the type men fell in love with, especially men like Harry: cultured and refined. A thoroughbred stallion standing next to a scrawny dog.

"Do you know why I always beat you at poker? Because your face reveals your every thought. And now your face tells me that I've hurt you."

"I never expected you to love me—"

"Expectation and hope are not the same thing."

"I never hoped it either."

"Good."

He started to rise. She grabbed his hand, and he stilled. "Would you mind staying just a bit longer? I don't want to go back to camp yet, but I don't really want to be alone. You don't have to talk—"

He pressed his finger to her lips. "Sometimes more is said with silence than with words." He settled against a tree and patted the ground between his spread legs. "Come here."

She hesitated a heartbeat before scrambling over his leg and pressing her back to his chest. He folded his arms around her, tucking them beneath her breasts. She rested her hands over his, reveling in the strength she felt there. She nestled her head into the crook of his shoulder.

The silence eased in around them, weaving camaraderie between them. She drew comfort from the sturdiness of his embrace. She watched a star fall from the sky and made a wish that her child would be spared all the mistakes her mother had made.

"Do you always cheat?" she asked quietly.

"Only when it's imperative that I win." He pressed his warm lips against the nape of her neck. "It was not my intent to cheat tonight, but I fear I may have."

She shook her head. "We were playing with the same deck, Harry."

He cradled her cheek and turned her head slightly, until their gazes met. "For whatever comfort this might bring you in the nights that follow, know this . . . when I thought death was a certainty, I chose a collection of memories that revolved around you to carry into the darkness with me."

Tears stung her eyes. She studied his face, and for one startling second, the wall vanished to reveal his vulnerabilities. He wasn't dealing her false flattery.

She drew comfort from his words and his actions, because she feared that whether he cheated or not, he had won her body, after slowly, methodically winning her heart.

❧ Chapter 13 ❧

The Indian Territory unfolded to reveal miles of undulating brown grass. As much as Harrison tried to appreciate the majestic expanse of never-ending land and blue sky, he had to readily admit that he was bored out of his wits. He thought he might actually welcome a hostile encounter with the fierce Comanche warriors he'd heard tales of.

Only twice had Indians actually approached the caravan and demanded payment for safe passage. Kit turned a few cattle over to them, and off they went.

Harrison no longer rode drag at the back of the herd but had moved to what the men referred to as a swing position, riding behind the point, within sight of Jessye. A foolish action, when he well imagined that any of the other men had more experience with weapons and could better protect her in case of an attack.

Still, he enjoyed having her within his sight. Especially when a steer decided to break ranks and trotted away from the main herd. He liked the way her bottom shifted in the saddle as she leaned low to guide her horse toward the errant creature and lure it back into formation. The way she angled her chin and smiled in triumph as they neared the herd.

Since they had made love, she never joined him on his watch, and he received no more stolen kisses. At night when he circled the slumbering herd, he found his conscience riding beside him.

He took every opportunity he could to avoid Jessye even though he loathed his cowardly retreat. Making love to her had been a mistake—tasting her fully had left him with an insatiable appetite that he feared only she could satisfy.

Dear God, even as he worked to avoid contact with her, he discovered that he wanted her more than he thought humanly possible. He wanted her smiles directed his way, her laughter to waltz around him, her smoky voice to whisper near his ear.

Even as he cursed the night they'd shared after crossing the Red River, he wished he'd savored the moments when she'd welcomed his body into hers. Fear had driven him that night.

His mind often drifted to the night when she'd delivered the baby, and later shared confidences with him. He longed for the intimacy that had shimmered between them even though they had not been touching. He was desperate for the deeper intimacy that touching would bring.

He was quite simply going insane.

His body aching and weary, Harrison crouched before the low embers of the campfire. He saw Jessye curled into a ball near the supply wagon, one hand tucked beneath her cheek, the other resting on her stomach. How easily she seemed to sleep, when he found it nearly impossible. With any luck, he might get two hours before the cook awakened everyone just before dawn.

Turning his head at a slight movement, he watched as Kit strolled across the camp and dropped beside him. "You were due back hours ago."

Harrison shrugged. "I took another watch."

"We'll be crossing into Kansas tomorrow."

"Thank God for that."

"Dan, Jessye, and I discussed it earlier. We thought it might be a good idea to send a couple of riders on ahead to determine if we'll meet any resistance from farmers or jayhawkers."

"Sounds like a solid plan."

"Jessye suggested that you and she go."

Harrison felt as though he'd been punched in the stomach. "You go with her." He surged to his feet and strode from the camp. He heard the muffled footsteps following him into the darkness.

"You've been avoiding her since we crossed the Red River. What happened that night, Harry?"

He staggered to a halt and spun around. "Nothing happened."

"You kissed her, didn't you? You kissed her and discovered she isn't like the cold bitches you've always bedded in the past."

Harry clenched his fists at his sides. God, if only that were all he'd done. "I suggest you head back to camp before you find yourself minus a few teeth."

"It won't change anything, you know. You can avoid her until hell freezes over, and it won't change what you're feeling. You can even watch her marry another, and it won't stop you from loving her."

"I don't love her," he ground out.

"In that case, you shouldn't mind escorting her tomorrow."

Harrison dropped back his head and gazed at the stars. The problem with having Kit for a friend was that the man was too discerning and too clever by half when it came to getting his way. "All right. I'll go with her."

"Good. You'll leave before dawn."

"I should be charming company after less than two hours' sleep."

"What does it matter? You aren't trying to impress her."

Kit walked away whistling a jolly tune that Harrison had often heard sung among the street vendors in the East End of London. He much preferred his friend melancholy.

Jessye cast a sideways glance at the man riding beside her. She'd avoided Harry for close to two weeks. The passion that had erupted between them had taken her by storm, and just like the forceful winds of a hurricane, it had left devastation in its wake.

She didn't regret what had happened that night, but she'd feared the hell that might follow. She'd given up one child. She knew she'd never give up another. She was older now, wiser, and more mature. She would have money even if she didn't have a husband.

She'd lain awake many a night, her hand resting on her stomach, alternately hoping she carried Harry's child, and praying that she didn't. Three days ago, much to her disappointment, her prayers had been answered.

Harry removed his hat, shifted in his saddle, and

faced her as squarely as he could. Lord, but she had missed him.

"How are you feeling?" he asked somberly as though testing waters.

"Fine."

He dropped his gaze to her stomach, and she watched his throat work as he swallowed. His eyes met hers. "Would you know by now if you weren't fine?"

"Trying to figure out whether or not you can stop avoiding me?"

"I'm attempting to determine whether or not I'm about to take a wife," he snapped.

She laughed. "Lord, Harry, I hope you ask her with a little more sweetness to your words or you're gonna get a no for sure."

"Damn it, Jessye!"

"You can stop worrying. I'm not carrying your child."

"Thank God for small miracles."

Her shattered heart cracked at the genuine relief reflected in his voice. "My thoughts exactly," she lied.

He settled his hat on his head, casting shadows over his face. "I would not have wanted you to suffer because of my actions that night."

"According to my recollection, the *actions* weren't one-sided."

"Still, knowing what I do of your past, I should have shown restraint. *That* is the reason I have avoided you. I did not want to place you in a situation you did not desire."

She furrowed her brow. "I don't understand. Avoiding me wouldn't have changed whether or not I was with child. That night happened because death nearly claimed you, and neither of us was thinking. It's not gonna happen again."

He pinned her with his gaze. "You think not? I want you with an intensity that borders on obsession."

Her stomach quivered, and the heat of his gaze almost had her melting like wax beneath the flame of a candle. "That's just . . . just 'cuz I'm the only woman out here."

"Dear God, you honestly believe that, don't you?"

"I know what kind of woman a man wants."

"And what kind of woman would that be?"

"Prim, proper, and pure."

"Ah, the three Ps. Is this something you were taught in school like the three Rs?"

"Life taught me that lesson."

"Life or Gerald Milton?"

"They're one and the same," she lashed out. "I don't even know why we're having this conversation."

"Because you questioned my avoidance of you, and I want you to understand that you play with fire when you find these absurd reasons to force me into your company."

The anger struck her like a bolt of lightning. "You arrogant ass! I'll admit I welcomed the opportunity to have a moment alone with you so I could let you know that you didn't get me with child, but you're the one who insisted I take this trek with you."

He looked as though she'd doused him with a bucket of cold water. "What? Are you insinuating that you didn't tell Kit that you wanted me to accompany you on this scouting expedition?"

"He told me that *you* wanted me to go with you."

"That bastard," he murmured in a tone that carried a sinister ring to it.

"Does that mean you didn't tell him you wanted me to come with you?"

"No, I did not. We've been had."

"Why would he do that?" she asked, confused.

"He has this overwhelming need to meddle in people's lives. We need to find a way to get even."

"We could send him snipe hunting," she suggested.

He shook his head. "We need something far worse than that."

She smiled at the anger receding from his voice, the camaraderie easing back into place. "I've missed your friendship, Harry."

Reaching out, he cradled her cheek with his roughened palm. "A friendship forged within the fires of hell can withstand the heat of anger."

"So you've said before," she reminded him.

He stroked his thumb over her lips, sending the warmth swirling through her. "I don't know if it can withstand the flames of passion," he said quietly.

"What happened that night won't happen again."

He moved his hand away from her face. "You keep telling yourself that, Jessye my love, and maybe you'll convince us both."

Shots rang out, shattering the calm, and her breath hitched. "Oh, God."

"Do you think it's an Indian attack?" he asked.

The cacophony of thunder continued. "I don't know."

"I suppose I should investigate."

Trepidation sliced through her. "Yeah, I reckon we should."

He jerked his head around. "I shall investigate. You'll stay here."

"The hell I will. If there's trouble, another gun might be needed."

"It sounds as if they have more than enough guns."

A deafening silence suddenly descended over the land.

"I don't like the sound of that," Harry said in a low voice.

Jessye kicked her horse into a gallop. She heard Harry's harsh curse, soon followed by the thunder of his horse's hooves.

"Approach with caution," he yelled once he caught up to her.

She nodded and slowed her horse. Her stomach roiled as the wind brought the stench of splattered blood, and her heart ached at the carnage that lay before her. Dead cattle littered the land. Wounded cattle bawled.

"Dear God, what happened?" Harry asked.

Jessye shook her head. "Makes no sense." She slipped her gun from her holster and checked the bullets.

"What are you doing?"

"Can't leave the ones that are alive to suffer." On horseback, she wended her way through the dead cattle until she reached the first steer slathered in blood but still alive. Her throat tightening, she aimed her gun and fired. The beast fell to its side, and a man jumped to his feet, his rifle raised.

"Whoa there!" Harry yelled. "We mean you no harm."

The man lowered his rifle and sank to his haunches.

Jessye followed Harry's lead as he made his way around the slain cattle. When they neared the man, they both dismounted. The man jerked his tear-stained face toward them, and sharp pain swept through Jessye.

The man was a boy who couldn't have been any older than sixteen. Beside him sat another boy, his shirt drenched in sweat, his eyes vacant, his arms wrapped around his drawn up legs as he rocked back and forth.

"What happened, lad?" Harry asked as he knelt beside them.

The older boy sniffed and rubbed his hand beneath his nose. "Jayhawkers."

Jessye slowly dropped to her knees beside the younger boy, desperately wanting to take him in her arms and console him, but fearful of his reaction after all he'd witnessed. "What are your names?"

"Tom. Tom Carter. This here's my kid brother Jake. Don't know how I'm gonna tell my ma 'bout all this."

"Where's the rest of your outfit?" Harry asked.

Tom glanced around. "It was only me, my brother, and fifty head of cattle. Just wanted to make enough money to get through the winter."

"These jayhawkers simply came through and started shooting?" Harry asked.

"Nah, sir. They asked for money first. Said we had to pay for safe passage. Told 'em we didn't have no money, and their leader shot our horses like they was nuthin'. Then they started killin' the cattle."

"But they didn't shoot you," Harry pointed out.

"Nah, sir. I'm supposed to spread the word that Texas cattle ain't welcome in Kansas. Only I ain't doin' nuthin' that damn bastard told me." He cast a sheepish glance at Jessye. "Forgive the language, ma'am."

"Nothing to forgive. I'd say you're pretty well calling the man what he was."

"What did the leader look like?" Harry asked.

Tom shrugged. "Just regular lookin', wore buckskin britches, but I'd know him if I see him. I see him again, though, I'm gonna kill him."

Jessye studied the soft cheek that looked as though it had never known the touch of a razor. The last thing this young man needed to do was seek revenge. She laid her hand on his shoulder. "Why don't you and your brother come back to camp with us? We've got a herd to get to market, and we could use experienced riders."

She watched the boy squeeze his eyes shut and swallow hard. "Gotta put the rest of these here steers out of their misery."

"I can help you with that chore," Harry said. He turned his attention to the younger boy. "Jake, is it?"

The boy blinked his large brown eyes and nodded.

"How old are you, lad?"

"Four . . . four . . . fourteen."

"I have a favor to ask of you," Harry said.

Jake's gaze darted warily between Harry and Jessye. "What?"

Harry tilted his head toward Jessye. "I fear all this carnage has upset my lady friend, here. I was hoping you might hold her while your brother and I do what needs to be done."

The boy looked at Jessye, his eyes reflecting a lost innocence. "I can do that."

He scooted over to her, and Jessye wrapped her arms around the trembling boy. He released a wrenching sob.

"Shh," Jessye cooed, rocking him gently as his tears drenched her shirt.

She watched Harry and Tom walk away to handle their ghastly chore. Her respect for Harry grew. He'd manipulated the boy right into the place where he needed to be, and he'd done it without stripping Jake of his pride.

"I'm not sure we should continue with this venture," Kit said.

Harrison studied the young boys sitting in front of the fire, a blanket draped around each of them. "Because of their experience this afternoon?"

"Because it seems no one is getting through to Sedalia. We met up with another group of men before dusk. It's not only jayhawkers, but farmers with rifles that are rebelling against anyone bringing the cattle through. For what these men will gain when we reach the end of the trail, I cannot in all good conscience place them in harm's way."

Harrison turned his attention to Jessye and quirked a brow. "What do you think?"

"I ain't much on quitting."

"You prefer to experience a few more afternoons like the one you had today?" Kit asked.

"That's unfair, Kit," Harrison snapped. He looked at Dan. "What are your thoughts?"

Dan shrugged. "The men knew the risks when they signed on. I ain't heard no grumbling."

Kit sighed heavily. "It's my understanding that this

vindictiveness runs rampant through the area. Perhaps it's somehow related to feelings stirred up during the war—"

"Then we head west," Harrison suggested calmly. "Around Kansas. If no one is getting the cattle to Sedalia anyway, then we're still likely to be the first ones to get them to the northern market."

"I wasn't aware of any trails that went around Kansas," Kit said.

"Far as I know, there aren't any," Dan informed him.

"So we'll blaze a new trail," Harrison said.

"Which will make the trek a bit more arduous," Kit said. "Not to mention longer."

"Then let's compromise. Map out a new route in case it's needed. Meanwhile, I will continue to scout ahead—"

"And risk being killed?"

Harrison shook his head in frustration. "Tom, how many men attacked you?"

Tom looked up as though still trying to determine what had happened and where he was. "Six. Seven."

Harrison met Kit's gaze. "Listen to me. They were two boys with fifty head of cattle. We're three thousand head and over two dozen men carting guns that they are not afraid to use. A half dozen men will not attempt to stop us."

"I don't share your confidence," Kit said.

"I don't like your idea of going alone," Jessye said.

Harrison gritted his teeth. "I am less likely to attract attention if I am alone."

"A woman and a man traveling are less—"

"But you are not dressed like a woman." He cursed himself at the pain that flashed in her eyes. "I simply meant that they are not going to realize you are a woman until they are close enough to see you clearly, and if they are that close, I don't want you there."

She angled her chin, and he knew he had no hope of winning the battle.

"I'm going." She spun on her heel and strode from the camp.

Kit chuckled. "I see you two kissed and made up."

Harrison glared at him. "You're going to pay dearly for that little prank you played."

Kit grinned. "Someday, Harry, you'll thank me."

As Jessye dismounted and led her horse to the small stream, she couldn't imagine why she'd insisted on accompanying Harry on this trek. The silence between them stretched tauter than a hangman's rope once the trapdoor had sprung open.

The sun had passed straight overhead a few hours before. Gauging distance was not her strong suit, but she suspected that they needed to head back soon if they wanted to make camp by nightfall.

"Today's journey makes me wonder if we aren't on a fool's errand," Harry murmured as he hunkered down at the water's edge.

She heard the displeasure in his voice. "I thought we all agreed it was best to have a look-see before we brought the cattle through."

"I'm not questioning the wisdom of caution. I'm only wondering why we haven't crossed paths with anyone."

"You suspect something?"

His hat shadowed his face, making it impossible to figure out what he might be thinking.

"Perhaps we should have brought a few cattle with us—something to stir up the dust and make some noise. Something to draw attention so we might discern what dangers our passing might arouse."

"Reckon we could do that tomorrow."

He swept his hat from his head, and his gaze came to rest on her. "If it increases our chance of running into danger, I'd rather someone else accompany me."

"It's all right for you to be in danger, but not me? I'm not some mealymouthed spinster who's afraid of her own shadow."

He unfolded his body. "I never insinuated that you were. Why must you take exception to any suggestion I make to protect you?"

"I don't need protection. I can take care of myself."

"Why do you persist in proving you're courageous? No one doubts that, least of all me. But a woman is susceptible to far greater dangers than men."

"I'm not weak, Harry!"

"I never said you were." He grabbed her arm and jerked her against him. Fire blazed within his eyes. "But neither are you completely safe."

He slashed his mouth across hers, demanding surrender. Instinct warned her to fight, but her heart urged her to yield. And yield she did, her body melting against his, her soft curves pressing against sturdy muscles that had hardened in the passing months of working with cattle.

With a guttural groan, he plunged his tongue into her mouth with a rapacious hunger. If he sought to frighten her, he failed miserably, because she knew he wouldn't harm her. Despite his words, with him she was safe.

He gentled the kiss, and his victory became hers, the outcome of the battle determined before it ever began. His strong hands tenderly cradled her face, tilting her head to accommodate his needs, to increase her pleasure. This kiss was more devastating than any that had come before it because now she knew what to expect, knew the difference between the kiss of a man and the kiss of a gangly, awkward boy. Harry's kiss was born of experience, hers of desperation. She cursed herself for wanting him as badly as she did, knowing he wasn't a man to share his heart.

He trailed his hot lips along her throat. "They say absence makes the heart grow fonder," he murmured. "I thought these weeks of exile would lessen the desire that plagues me." He lifted his head, met her gaze, and with his fingers, gently brushed the stray curling strands back from her face. "The gravest danger you face lies within me."

She combed her fingers up into his black hair. "I don't care."

He chuckled low. "You should."

His mouth covered hers, undemanding, without challenge. They were on even ground. She reveled in the knowledge as she slid her arms around his neck and raised up on the tips of her toes.

"Now, ain't that sweet," a deep voice mocked.

Jessye jerked back. Wearing buckskin britches and a fringed jacket, Gerald Milton sat astride a brown horse, six men behind him, guns drawn. "Gerald, what are you doing here?" she asked.

"First off, I'm here to get back the money your *fiancé* stole from me."

Harry stepped before her, using his arm to move

her behind him. "I did not steal any money."

One side of Gerald's mouth lifted in a sneer. "Nobody wins that many hands of poker without cheatin'."

Jessye stepped in front of Harry, her heart thundering. After her meeting with Madeline, she'd completely forgotten to ask Harry where he'd obtained money for supplies. "You played poker with him?"

"Be quiet," he insisted as he pushed her so she was once again behind him.

"Yep, he showed up a little after midnight. Ain't never seen a man shuffle a deck with one hand before."

"A skill my grandfather taught me. But I assure you I didn't cheat. I lost several hands."

"But you never lost one to me, which I found mighty interestin'. Now, I want my money back."

"I don't have it. We used the money to purchase supplies."

"Well now, that's just too bad."

Jessye watched with trepidation as Gerald gave a slight signal and his men dismounted.

"I tell you what we'll do," Gerald said. "We'll do a little swappin'. You just leave them supplies with your cattle. Me and my boys will gather them all up tomorrow."

"Are you implying that we turn our supplies and cattle over to you without a fight?" Harry asked.

"That's right."

"Expecting a snowstorm in hell, are you?"

Gerald's mouth grew hard. "Stretch him for me, boys."

Jessye watched in horror as the men descended on

Harry like a swarm of locusts. "No!" she screamed, hearing him grunt. She reached for her gun, but strong fingers closed around her wrist and stopped her from drawing.

"I wouldn't do that."

She jerked her gaze to Gerald. "Why are you doing this?"

"Gotta enforce the laws of Kansas. Your cattle ain't comin' through."

"You're as bad as the jayhawkers."

As he dragged her back, Gerald's laughter drowned the grunts and moans of Harry's struggles, his body blocked from her view. "We *are* the jayhawkers, darlin'."

"You killed all those cattle," she said, the surety nauseating her.

"Yeah, I sure hated doin' that, but example is the best teacher."

She bucked when her back hit the hard bark of a tree trunk, but his iron grip tightened around her. As Gerald pressed his body against hers to hold her in place, someone grabbed her arms, jerked them back, and tied her hands behind the tree. The rope bit into her wrists, the bark dug into her back. A cold shiver of revulsion slithered up her spine as he trailed his knuckles over her cheek.

"God, Jessye, I'd forgotten how spittin' mad you could get."

She took satisfaction in the feel of her booted foot making contact with his shin. Howling, he jumped back.

He narrowed his eyes into blue slits of rage. "You bitch."

Fighting the urge to cower, she angled her chin and slid her gaze past him. Her stomach roiled, and she slammed her eyes closed against the sight of Harry, trussed up like a steer about to be branded. His arms over his head, his hands and feet were bound, the rope stretched taut, the ends wound around the saddle horns of two skittish horses that the riders were having trouble controlling. She could only imagine the humiliation coursing through him.

The fight drained from her like water through a sieve. She opened her eyes and met Gerald's hard glare. She saw no remnants of the young man she'd loved. "Let him go."

Gerald smiled in triumph. "Be happy to." He sauntered over and stood slightly behind her, well out of reach of her foot. He fondled her breast, and she wanted to die of mortification.

"You send him and his friend back to Fortune—with nothin' but their lives. You and me will take the cattle north, and we'll split the profits." His breath was cold against her ear. "You can warm my bed at night just like you did all them years back."

"She's not giving you anything, you bloody bastard!"

Jessye jerked her gaze to Harry, and her breath backed up in her lungs. Although bound, he lay in magnificent defiance, his hands clenched, his muscles bulging, his emerald eyes filled with fury. She thought if he managed to gain his freedom, he'd break Gerald in half like a stale loaf of bread.

Chuckling, Gerald released Jessye and swaggered toward his other prisoner. "That so?" He brought his leg back and kicked Harry in the side. Jessye jerked

as Harry recoiled and grunted, but the ropes kept him
from curling into a ball.

"You're gonna head back into Texas," Gerald
growled.

She saw Harry's jaw clench. "I think not."

Jessye flinched when Gerald kicked him again.
"Gerald, stop it!" she cried.

Breathing heavily, Gerald stepped back. "Only if
he gives me his word that he'll walk back to Texas."

Jessye opened her mouth to tell Harry to say whatever he needed to in order to save his skin. This time
the cards weren't stacked in his favor, and she desperately wanted him to fold his hand.

"Not bloody likely," Harry said, his accent more
pronounced, more haughty.

Gerald took a menacing step toward him, but Harry
neither flinched nor cowered, which seemed to anger
Gerald more. "Fine," he ground out. "I'll fix it so you
can't walk anywhere."

Gerald mounted his horse and jerked back on the
reins, causing the horse to whinny and rear up. Terror
ripped through Jessye.

"Gerald, you can have the cattle," Jessye yelled.

Harry pinned her with his gaze. "He bloody well
cannot!"

"It's not worth it, Harry."

"We will not surrender the cattle," Harry ground
out, but in his eyes she recognized that he wasn't truly
referring to the cattle. He meant his own surrender—
and for the first time, she realized the true gravity of
the situation.

"You gonna give me the cattle, Jessye?" Gerald
asked.

Within Harry's eyes, she found not only her answer but also her strength. "No."

Gerald laughed. "Then I'll kill him."

"I'll rise up from the bowels of hell and drag you into Satan's realm to keep me company."

She'd never heard Harry's voice carry such vehemence, and she almost believed he meant every word he'd spoken. Gerald hesitated only a heartbeat before he reared his horse up and brought him down. She heard the sickening snap of a bone and Harry's strangled cry.

The horse whinnied and reared up. Its hooves churned the air before they slammed down on Harry's legs. Harry groaned. The two men sitting astride the horses to which the ropes were secured urged the animals back until they lifted Harry off the ground. The other men yelled and cheered.

Jessye closed her eyes and bowed her head. "Dear God." Tears stung her eyes as the cacophony of obscene noises grew hideous: the men's jeers, Harry's cries, the horses snorting and screaming, and Gerald's constant stream of curses. Nothing on God's green earth was worth this torment.

Silently, she repeated a litany of prayers, while her body shook and her chest ached. Dear God, they were going to kill him. She opened her mouth to surrender ... Cold metal touched her palm. She closed her hands around the pistol.

"Keep your head bowed," Kit ordered.

She felt the pressure of a knife sawing into the rope as it loosened its hold.

"Count to five. Shoot the man on the right horse

first and I'll take the one on the left so they don't pull Harry apart as they try to escape."

She heard the muffled footsteps as Kit moved away from her, to better his position.

One . . . two . . . three . . .

"Son of a bitch!" Gerald yelled. "You can go back to Texas in a pine box."

She snapped her head up. Gerald was aiming a rifle at Harry. "No!" she cried as she jerked her arms away from the tree. Gerald spun his horse around, and she fired the gun.

Crimson exploded over his chest, a stunned expression crossed his face before he crumpled and fell to the ground. Instantly, she turned her attention to the man who should have been her first target. She shot him and continued firing at any man who moved.

Caught in the throes of a nightmarish reality, she watched the tableaux unfold as though from a great distance, heard other guns fire, saw other men fall. She continued to squeeze the trigger until all that remained was an audible click in the deafening silence.

Kit's hand closed over hers. "It's over, Jessye."

Nodding, she dropped the gun and rushed across the clearing to Harry. She sank to the ground and gingerly placed his head in her lap while Kit cut the ropes that bound him. Sometime during the ordeal, he'd lost consciousness. A mercy.

Trembling uncontrollably, she glanced at Gerald. Blood continued to pool on his chest as he reached out a hand to her. She hesitated, but memories of a young man she'd loved caused her to carefully place Harry on the ground before inching over to Gerald.

He wrapped his shaking hand around hers, pulling her closer.

The anger and hatred faded from his eyes, and she was once again looking into eyes that had drawn her into the wonders of love.

He coughed, and his hold on her tightened. "Don't let me die alone."

Tears welling in her eyes, she wrapped her arms around him and drew him close. "Oh, Gerald—"

"Biggest mistake . . . ever made in my life . . . was leaving you," he rasped.

His hold loosened as his body went limp. She gazed into the lifeless blue eyes, remembering the laughter that had once danced within them. What had happened during the war to fill him with such hatred?

With tears streaming along her cheeks, she returned to Harry. Leaning over, she pressed a kiss to his forehead. "Stubborn, obstinate man. Don't you know when to fold a losing hand?" She looked at Kit, who was carefully examining Harry. "How bad?"

Shaking his head, Kit sighed deeply. "Bad."

"I never expected him to be so stubborn."

"You can ask him for the world, and he'll give it to you. Demand it of him, and he will fight until death rather than yield. I never should have allowed him to scout ahead. I should have taken that burden on myself."

"Would you have yielded?" she asked.

He solemnly met her gaze. "No, but then the pain would have been mine, not his."

She heard the thunder of hooves. Kit grabbed his rifle and surged to his feet. She closed her arms around Harry, as though that insignificant action could protect him from further harm.

Dan, Magpie, and Tom burst into the clearing and drew their horses up short. Kit lowered his rifle.

"We heard gunfire," Dan said as he dismounted.

"Jesus Christ," Magpie muttered. "These the jay-hawkers?"

"Damn right they are," Tom said. "That's the bastard that killed our cattle." He pointed at Gerald. "I say we leave him to the buzzards."

"We'll probably leave them all to the buzzards. Harry is badly injured. Tom, I want you to go get the cook," Kit ordered.

"Right away," Tom said. He swung into the saddle and urged his horse into a gallop.

Dan hunkered down beside Harry and cast a quick glance at Jessye before looking up at Kit. "The cook ain't gonna be able to take care of this mess."

"I know. But I didn't want that lad to see any more horror. I need you to help me determine where the nearest town is." Kit pulled the maps from inside his jacket.

Jessye glanced at Harry's bloodied britches, bent over, and pressed her cheek against his forehead. Kit was wrong. Even if Gerald had asked, Harry wouldn't have surrendered. The damn Englishman was more courageous than she'd ever given him credit for.

⚙ Chapter 14 ⚙

"*Well now, he ain't that bad off,*" Cookie said.

With Harry's head nestled within her lap, Jessye tried to take comfort in the man's words. A cook generally served as the doctor on a trail drive, but he wasn't really a man of medicine, so she knew she needed to take his diagnosis with a pound of salt.

Although the men had moved the dead jayhawkers out of the way, no one wanted to move Harry, fearing if they did so, they'd worsen his injuries.

"We do need to get him to a doctor," Cookie added.

Kit glared at the man. "Yes, that much I'd figured out on my own."

"With branches and rope, we can make a travois, put him on it, and have a horse pull—" Dan said.

"No," Kit said succinctly, leaving no question that his word was final. "What we are going to do is unload the supplies from the wagon—"

"Then how are we gonna carry the supplies?" Dan asked.

"We're not," Kit told him. "We are leaving the supplies and the cattle here. This cattle drive has ended.

We are going no farther. We are gathering the men and Harry and going back to Texas—"

"No," a choked voice commanded.

Jessye snapped her gaze to Harry's face, wondering how long he'd been conscious. His jaws were clenched, and only now did she feel the tenseness in his body as he fought back the pain.

Leaning near, Kit placed his hand on Harry's shoulder. "Listen to me, my friend. Lady Luck was smiling on you today, but it was a grim smile. Your right hip is smashed to hell. You have broken bones in both legs. You need to get to a physician—"

"You need . . . to get Jessye . . . and the cattle to market. Go around Kansas . . . like we discussed." His breathing labored, every word he spoke was strained.

"I'm not going," Jessye said quietly, stroking his cheek, feeling the tautness in his jaws.

"Yes, you will." Harry grabbed Kit's shirtfront and pulled him down, his knuckles turning white as he clenched the fabric. "Jessye invested all she had. She wants to . . . get the cattle to market . . . wants to hold the money in her hand. Take her."

"It's not worth it, damn it. Nothing is worth your life!"

He pulled Kit closer until Kit's ear was near his mouth. She heard the whisper, but not the words. Kit blanched. "Damn you, Harry. Don't ask this of me."

Harry nodded. "Follow Dan's advice. Have Magpie take me to a doctor. You take Jess . . ." His voice trailed off, and he relaxed within her lap.

"Damn you to hell, Bainbridge," Kit muttered. He surged to his feet and pointed a finger at Dan. "Load the men up with whatever supplies they can carry un-

til we have enough room in the wagon for Harry.
We'll purchase another wagon in the next town." He
stormed away as though hell's demons nipped at his
heels.

Carefully, Jessye moved Harry's head off her lap.
She rose and raced after Kit. "Kit!"

He staggered to a stop and spun around, the despair
reflected in his eyes astounding her.

"What did he whisper to you?"

"He said that you are his Clarisse."

She furrowed her brow. "What does that mean?"

"It means we take the cattle to market—at any
cost."

Biting back a groan, Harrison opened his eyes. Moonlight streamed in through an opening at the back of
the jostling wagon. He heard pots and pans clang.
Damn Kit for not doing as ordered. He struggled to
sit up, and small hands pressed him back down.

"You need to lie still," Jessye said softly.

"This is a wagon."

"We're not that far from a town. We'll purchase
another wagon there."

"The cattle?"

"Dan and the other men are moving them west."

"You should be with them . . . so you can hold that
money—"

"I'd rather hold you. The next few days are not
going to be pleasant."

"But the money—"

"Has lost its importance." She lifted his head
slightly. "Cookie had some whiskey. Drink it. It'll
dull the pain."

He doubted it, but for her peace of mind, he dutifully sipped from the cup she pressed to his lips. When he moved the cup away, she gently laid his head down on a mound of blankets. She combed her fingers through his hair.

"Oh, Harry, we should have given him the cattle."

"No."

"But your legs—"

"They'll mend."

"Kit said you'd rather die than give in."

He nodded slightly. His hip was a blazing inferno of pain. "Stubbornness was my mother's only gift to me," he said quietly. "After our initial trip to the cellar, I vowed I would never again say that I loved her. When I was eight, she sought to force the words from me. My family has this hideous castle. My mother loved it. It was as cold as her heart. When my father left for London, she took me to the dankest corner of the dungeon and locked me away. Every day she visited with a stale piece of bread and a cup of water. All I had to do was tell her that I loved her to gain my freedom. I would not speak to her at all."

"Dear God, but you must have a low opinion of mothers. To have had your mother treat you so cruelly, to know I gave my daughter away . . ."

He cradled her chin with his trembling palm and held her gaze. "What you did, you did out of love. Never compare your actions with my mother's. When my father returned and found me, I was near death. It was only then that he realized my mother was insane. He feared she might turn her wrath on the heir apparent, so he had her locked away in the tower."

"How awful for you—"

He stroked his thumb across her cheek. "Until I met you, I didn't know that a mother's love was capable of making such unselfish sacrifices as you made for your daughter."

Within the moonlight, he saw tears well within her eyes.

"I killed my daughter's father." She released a heart-wrenching sob. "Oh, Harry, God help me."

He cupped the back of her head and drew her close, until her face was nestled in the crook of his shoulder. "You don't need God's help, my love. You did the only thing you could do."

"The war changed him. He wasn't . . . he wasn't the young man I fell in love with."

His gut clenched at the thought of her loving someone else.

"I don't know what happened to him, why he changed—"

"Shh, Jessye, it doesn't matter."

"But he was my daughter's father."

"An honor he did not deserve."

"You might think differently if you'd known him before the war. I wish I'd told him the truth—that the baby had lived." She cradled the locket within her palm. "Mary Ellen is the best of us both. It's difficult to believe now, but in my heart, I know she was conceived in love."

She tilted her face slightly, and he saw the trail of tears glistening over her face. "Did you cheat when you played poker with him?"

"He owed you. By taking his money, I ensured that you would not have to split your profits with another investor."

Within the green depths of her eyes, he easily read the doubts plaguing her. Why did she have to be so damned honorable? "You have no need to feel guilty over actions I took."

"But if you hadn't cheated him—"

"Today would have ended no differently. I can tell when a man is bluffing. He would have killed me. He left you no recourse but to shoot him."

"How can you be so sure?"

Gently, he combed the wisps of hair back from her face. "How can you not be?"

She shook her head. "I just want enough money that I never have to depend on a man for anything again."

"And you shall have it, I promise."

"But at what cost, Harry? Now I'm a killer."

"Or a savior. Depends on your point of view. From where I lay, with a muzzle pointed at my head, I consider you a saint."

She gave him a quivering smile. "A tarnished saint."

"Untarnished saints are a bore."

She released a choked sob. "Oh, Harry, I'm supposed to comfort you, not have you comfort me."

"Then give me some more whiskey."

She did as he bid, and he drank greedily, hoping to drown the fear more than the pain—fear that he might never again walk.

It took them two days to find a doctor in a small town that didn't even have a name.

Jessye lifted Harry's head and poured more whiskey down his throat. God Almighty, she wanted to drink the whole blasted bottle herself.

Kit had gone to purchase another wagon and supplies. She didn't blame him. There was nothing for him to do here but watch his friend suffer. She knew he carried a burden of guilt already. Magpie had offered to travel back to Fortune with her and Harry, leaving Kit free to return to the herd once he was assured Harry would survive.

She felt the tremors running through Harry, the fever burning his body. If he survived what was to come, it would be a miracle, and she'd never known a miracle to pass her way.

She kept her gaze fastened on Harry's face rather than see the mangled condition of his legs as the doctor cut away his britches. She feared Harry might choke on the groans he fought to hold back. Why in the hell couldn't this doctor have morphine?

"The kindest thing would be to amputate these legs—"

"No!" Harry growled, struggling to sit up.

Jessye shoved him back down, her hand sliding over his sweat-slickened flesh, his breathing labored.

"You've got one broken bone in your left leg, two in your right, and this right hip is smashed to hell. I don't know how I'm gonna set it. You've got lacerations, bruises."

"Just do the best . . . you can," Harry ordered.

"Amputation is the best I can do."

"So I can become exactly what my father always thought I was—less than a whole man? I'd rather die."

"You will die if gangrene sets in," the doctor said.

"I'll stop the gangrene from settling in," Jessye said, her gaze holding Harry's. "You just set the bones."

"All you're doing is prolonging the inevitable," the doctor told her.

Jessye slammed her eyes closed. She never should have loaned him the money, never should have doubted his honor. She pressed her cheek against his, placing her mouth near his ear. "Maybe the doctor's right, Harry. This is like drawing to an inside straight."

"Have you ever drawn to an inside straight?" he asked, his voice raspy.

She lifted her face to meet his gaze. "No."

He gave her a tender smile. "I have. It's the sweetest victory, because the odds are so against you—and no one thinks you'll make it—no one believes in you . . ." His eyes glazed over with a pain that she thought went far deeper than the physical anguish he was experiencing. "You're holding the cards, but at least give me the chance to draw a winning hand."

"Damn you, Harry, the odds aren't in your favor."

"They never have been. That's why I cheat."

Damn him for making her smile at a moment like this. "At least finish off the whiskey to deaden some of the pain," she insisted as she held the bottle to his lips.

"His recovery will take months—"

"I'll see to his recovery," Jessye snapped, losing patience with the man, the entire situation. "Just set the bones and do what you can for his hip."

She brought the bottle away from Harry's lips.

"Shoot him if he cuts off my legs."

"I will."

"Good." Reaching out, he took her hand and gave it a squeeze. "Now, I want you to leave."

Horror swept through her. "I'm not leaving you."

"Love, I am about to show myself for the true coward I am. I'd rather you not witness that."

She threaded her fingers more tightly through his. "I'm not leaving."

She slipped her free hand beneath his head and leaned near, pillowing her bosom against his face. Staring at a knothole on the wall, she knew the moment the doctor began his work. Her body muffled Harry's strangled groan as he jerked and his hand squeezed hers unmercifully. Tears filled her eyes, her throat tightened. She pressed her lips to the top of his head.

His final anguished cry echoed through the room before he relaxed against her, lost in the oblivion of unconsciousness.

Only then did she allow her own sobs to drown out the obscene noises created by the doctor's efforts to save Harry's legs.

PART TWO

The Walk to Redemption

Chapter 15

Jessye heard the glass shatter, a common sound in a saloon, but she knew that none of tonight's drunkards had instigated the breakage. Dreading the necessary encounter, she hurried along the hallway, her heels clicking over the wooden floor.

She gave one brisk, hard knock to serve as a warning before flinging open the door. The mirror above her dresser was a cracked mosaic of distorted shapes. Without glancing at the man lying in what had at one time been her bed, she crossed the room, knelt, and picked up the broken figurine. The mother no longer held the child, and that image ripped through her heart—an intense reminder of her own sacrifice. She placed the child into the mother's arms, but they would never fit perfectly, as they had before.

Just as Harry's bones would never be perfect.

Wearily, she glanced over her shoulder, trying to look beyond the angry glare Harry cast her way. "Oh, Harry—"

"Send word to Gray that I want to see him."

231

Slowly, she rose to her feet. "It's after midnight. Only the debauched are still awake."

"Then he should be awake."

"I'm not fetching him. If you're lonely, then come into the saloon for a while—"

"How do you propose that I get there?"

"Magpie and I would help you."

"So everyone can bloody well see that I'm a cripple?"

"You are not a cripple!"

"I can't walk, damn it!" He averted his gaze and muttered. "I can't walk."

Her heart ached at the anguish in his voice, the limitations his encounter with Gerald had burdened him with. The bones in his legs had healed, but his hip remained as twisted as her mirror. He complained often, but never about the pain, although the agony he strove so hard to conceal revealed itself in the deepening of the lines that fanned out from his eyes.

Cradling the broken figurine in one hand, she walked to the bed and gripped the post. "That's my fault."

"I don't recall you being the madman who abused his horse in order to deliver painful blows to me because I had not dealt him honest cards," he ground out without looking at her.

"When we traveled back to Fortune, I kept you drunk so you wouldn't feel the pain. Maybe I should have had you on crutches so your legs wouldn't forget—"

"Oh, God, Jessye, they didn't forget. They are ruined! Mangled twigs." He sighed deeply. "Will you leave?"

"Will you please stop throwing things around my room?"

"It's the only thing I can do with any success— other than play cards. Send Magpie in."

"He can't afford to lose any more money to you." She walked to the bedside table and carefully placed the two broken pieces near the lamp. She touched the plate that still contained his supper. "You'll never gain your strength back if you don't eat." With a spoon, she scooped up some potatoes and turned to him. "Here, eat this."

With one swipe of his hand, he sent the spoon flying across the room. "I am not a child!"

Without warning, he grabbed her and jerked her onto the bed. She wanted to buck, but his strangled groan as he rolled on top of her kept her quiet. She wouldn't hurt him any more than she already had.

"I am especially not *your* child," he spat. "It's bad enough that I cannot stand up to piss like a man, that you have to bring me every damn thing that I need, but I will not now have you feeding me as though I were an infant. If you want a baby to coddle, I'll give you one, because that I can, by God, still do!"

Tangling his fingers into her hair, he brutally took possession of her mouth, his tongue delving deeply, as though to prove he had the ability to conquer.

Had it been any other man, she would have gouged out his eyes, brought the knee resting between his thighs up, and made him regret ever bringing her down to the mattress.

But she knew Harry too well. He never bluffed . . . but neither would he ever take a woman by force. She lay submissively below him, her hands balled on either side of her head, her mouth complacent, her tongue refusing to waltz with his.

She felt the tenseness of his body slowly unwind like a coiled rattler that had decided not to strike. He lifted his mouth from hers only briefly before placing the most tender of kisses on her cheek.

"You didn't deserve that," he said quietly.

She unfurled her fingers and placed her palm against his bearded jaw. He hadn't shaved since Kansas. "I never took you to be a man who would wallow in self-pity."

He lifted his head and met her gaze. "You wouldn't have to bear witness to my foul moods if you'd gone with Kit like I told you to."

That journey had not been an option. She'd been terrified of losing him, of hearing on the trail that he'd died. But he'd managed to survive—and she'd lost him anyway.

"I wish I knew how to help you."

"You can help me by leaving."

Tears burned her eyes, and she squeezed them shut to hold them back. In her heart, she knew he was lashing out at his condition, not at her personally. But knowledge seldom lessened the hurt.

She slid out from beneath him. "I'll send Magpie to clear away the broken glass."

"Why? It's not as though I'll cut my feet."

She chortled. "You know, Harry, sometimes I want to shake you every way but loose."

She marched toward the door.

"Send for Gray!"

"No!" She flung open the door, stepped into the hallway, and slammed the door shut. He was making her life a living hell . . . and she damned her heart for giving him the freedom to do it.

He'd always thought he possessed an intimate knowledge of hell. He'd been wrong. Hell was waking up and seeing pity reflected in the green eyes of spring.

The pity had been there in Kansas and had deepened with each passing day. He'd jerked Jessye onto the bed for one reason—to force the pity to retreat.

He'd rather see anger burning in her eyes. He'd wanted her to fight him—to lash out at him as though he was a whole man. Instead, she'd surrendered because the battle was so bloody uneven. He wasn't the man he'd been before Kansas, the man who'd begun to wonder if perhaps he possessed her heart. No, now he was the man she no longer challenged with her anger, her fire, or her passion for life. She never yelled at him. Everything was an "Oh, Harry" in a pitifully small voice, as though he were a child who'd done wrong and must be forgiven because he could do no better.

Whenever she walked into this room, misery accompanied her. Along with frustration and despair.

Sitting up, Harrison made his way to the edge of the bed. Using his hands, he eased his legs over the side. Thank God, his feet reached the floor. How he longed for the days when he'd gotten out of bed without conscious thought.

Bending over, he wrapped his hands around his left calf and slowly pushed his foot over the floor, pulled it back, pushed, pulled. He'd made the mistake of attempting to stand shortly after they'd returned to Fortune. Weakened from the trauma they'd sustained, his legs had buckled beneath him.

Or so the town physician had told him. Not that he completely trusted the man's knowledge. Time seemed a poor prescription.

Instinctively, Harry knew he needed to rebuild his muscles, an irritatingly slow process. But he would walk again. Even if he took only a few steps, he would, by God, walk.

The door swung open and he froze. He only worked his legs at night, after the saloon fell into silence, and no opportunity existed for anyone to witness his pitiful attempt to become a man once again.

Jonah Kane shuffled into the room, dragging a chair with him.

"What do you want, old man?" Harrison barked.

Jonah snapped up his head. "Jessye said you was looking for someone to play poker with."

"That was two hours ago."

"I was serving drinks till two minutes ago. Seen the light under your door, so I figured you was up." He shoved the chair across the room until it slammed against the bed. "Take a seat while I get a table."

"You expect me to move to the chair?"

"Iffen you want to play poker. I'd feel guilty takin' money from a man who couldn't even get out of bed."

"You won't take a penny from me, old man."

Jonah smiled. "Probably take me a good fifteen minutes to figure out which table I can fit through that door." He walked out, closing the door in his wake.

Harrison studied the chair. With a bit of patience and caution, he could grab the arms and lever himself into it. His only fear was that his legs would slide out from beneath him, and he'd land on the floor. Scrawny Jonah Kane would be unable to lift him off the floor. When he'd fallen before, to his humiliation, it had taken the efforts of Jessye and Magpie to get him into the bed.

Christ, the thought of a journey to a bloody chair had him shaking with trepidation. The distance between the chair and the bed was barely discernable. Taking a deep breath, he leaned forward to wrap his hands around the arms of the chair, swung over, and down. He hit the seat with a jarring thud that sent slivers of pain slicing through his hip.

But he was sitting, sitting in a chair in which he had placed himself. He reveled in the accomplishment. He glanced at the bed. Getting back into it wasn't going to be an easy task, but he'd worry about that when the time came.

He heard a tap on the door.

"Ready for me?" Jonah asked.

So now the man knocked?

"Yes."

Jonah opened the door and smiled. "Knew you could do it."

Cocky bugger. Harrison flexed his fingers while Jonah shoved a table into place. Harrison planned to take the old man for every penny he had. Jonah set two glasses, a bottle of whiskey, and a deck of cards between them. Then he grabbed a chair that Jessye kept near the window and pulled it to the table.

"I shall deal," Harrison informed him.

"Be my guest."

Harrison shuffled, finding comfort in the whisper of the cards. He slapped the deck on the table. "Cut."

Jonah tapped the top card. Harrison picked up the cards and began to deal.

"You're breakin' my daughter's heart."

Harrison stilled, his hand tightening on the deck until he could feel each remaining card cutting into his palm. "That is not my intent."

"Still, you're doin' it just the same. The only reason I ain't castrated you yet is 'cuz I figure you're in enough pain."

Harrison narrowed his eyes. "Did you come to lecture or play cards?"

"Play cards."

"Good, because I have no interest in lectures." He dealt the last card and studied each one he held. Two pair.

"It's eatin' her up thinkin' she's responsible for your legs bein' like they are."

Harrison set down his cards. "I have told her she is not to blame."

"Maybe you ain't told her in a voice that says you believe the words you're spittin' out."

"I do not hold her responsible for what happened. I cannot control what she thinks. I cannot control what she *does*! I told her to go with Kit. Her dream was to take the blasted cattle to market and hold that money in her hand. She was supposed to follow it."

"Maybe her dream changed betwixt the time you left here and the time you got to Kansas. You asked her of late what her dream is?"

He hadn't asked anything of her since Kansas. They no longer shared conversations or secrets. He couldn't stand the way she looked at him, as though he'd never walk again.

"Are you playing or talking?" Harrison asked.

"Playin'." Jonah tossed a quarter into the pot.

Harrison tossed one in as well. "How many cards do you want?"

"None."

Harrison snapped his gaze to Jonah. "None?"

"I see your hearin' ain't impaired none."

"You're holding nothing, and you're not going to try to get something better?"

"How do you know I got nuthin'?"

"I dealt the cards."

Jonah rubbed one of his gnarled fingers across his chin. "And you know what you give me, do you?"

"I know that your cards cannot beat mine."

"What's the point in playin' if you always win?"

"What is the point in playing if you always lose?"

Jonah shoved his chair back and stood. "Time for me to get these weary bones to bed."

"But we haven't finished the game."

"I have. You done told me that you beat me."

"But I haven't shown you my cards."

"I'm takin' your word for it."

Leaning back in the chair, Harrison sighed. "You didn't come in here to play poker."

"Nope, came in here to get you out of the goddamn bed." He cackled. "Bet Jessye five dollars I could do it."

"You sorry son of a—"

Jonah held up a finger. "Watch what you say, boy. This bein' my saloon, I'd hate to have to kick you out on your ass."

"Jessye wouldn't allow it."

"Probably not, so I'm gonna leave you with a bit

of advice since you know cards so well. Life is just like 'em. Winning ain't in holding a good hand, but in playin' a poor one well."

"Hear tell you moved from the bed to a chair last night."

Harrison glared as Dr. Hickerson poked and prodded his useless legs. The man's gray hair stuck out at odd angles, reminding him of the quills on an enraged porcupine.

Stilling his hands, the physician looked at Harrison with a challenge clearly reflected in his brown eyes. "That true?"

Harrison gritted his teeth. "Are my minute accomplishments to now serve as fodder for the town gossips?"

"I doubt Jessye mentioned it to anyone else. And I wouldn't call it a minute accomplishment."

"I didn't use my legs. I simply swung into the chair like an ape traveling from branch to branch."

"Shouldn't be so hard on yourself." He squinted. "Are you moving your legs around like I told you?"

"Yes, but I can't see that it's making a damn bit of difference."

He smiled triumphantly. "I can. You'll be using those crutches before long."

Harrison didn't bother to look at the wooden monstrosities leaning against the wall beside the bed. He despised the things and the thought of using them. "How much longer before I can walk like a man?"

Dr. Hickerson unfolded his body, his bones creaking. "That's up to you."

"Damn it, man, that's all you ever say. Can't you

give me something a bit more substantial?"

"You want me to tell you that you're going to start walking tomorrow or next week or next month, and I can't do that because I don't know. If you had come to me with that many broken bones, I would have amputated your legs, so I don't know everything I should to help you walk again. I know it's frustrating, but it's going to take time." He opened his black bag and brought out a jar. "I made some salve that you can work into your legs when your muscles start cramping."

Harrison took the jar and set it on the bed. He would have preferred to sling it across the room, but his legs ached more often than not, and they always felt so damned tired. He even felt exhausted, which made no sense, when he did nothing all day. He'd been less weary herding cattle.

Dr. Hickerson picked up one piece of the broken figurine. "What happened here?"

"It offended me."

Glancing at the mirror, the doctor shook his head. He touched a finger to his brow. "The healing has got to start here before it can start there." He pointed to Harrison's legs.

"There is nothing wrong with my head."

"Except visiting you is about as refreshing as being burned at the stake." He grabbed the crutches and laid them against the bed. "Try using them."

Despair swept through Harrison. "I have tried."

"I don't know how to help him." Jessye lay on her back, the warm, gently flowing water of the river soothing her as she stared through the canopy of leaves above.

"These Englishmen are a proud lot."

Jessye watched Abigail Rhodes dip her three-month-old son Colton in the water. "I guess you'd be an expert on that, being married to one and all."

Abbie smiled. "I don't think any woman ever becomes an expert on men. Just when you think you've got them figured out, they do something you'd never expect." Her smile withered away. "But I do know whenever Grayson visits Harry, he comes home, grabs a hoe, and beats at the ground like there's no tomorrow."

Jessye straightened. The water wasn't deep in the center of the river, and when her toes settled against the silt at the bottom, the water lapped at her waist.

Colton released an excited screech, and Jessye watched his feet kick the water, sending droplets flying. Abbie laughed joyfully.

"Abbie, can you come here a moment?" Grayson yelled.

Jessye dunked into the water until it covered her shoulders. She saw Grayson peering through the brush at the edge of the river, around the bend where he'd taken the other three children to swim as though sensing that Jessye needed to talk with Abbie woman to woman. Yet even knowing that his gaze wasn't fastened on her, she blushed furiously.

"Will you hold Colton?" Abbie asked.

"Sure." Jessye took the child, keeping her eye on him as Abbie waded through the water. "Wonder what your pa wants?"

Colton slapped his fists against the water. His feet

made contact with her chest. He gave an unexpected shove that nearly forced her to lose her grip on him. "You're a strong fella, aren't you?"

She crooked her leg and raised it until his tiny feet could find purchase. Careful to keep his head above the water, she watched him bob as he bent his knees.

"Having fun?" Abbie asked as she returned.

"Yep. What did Grayson want?"

Abbie smiled. "A kiss."

Jessye felt the heat warm her face more than the summer sun. "I'm sorry. I'm imposing—"

"Don't be silly. We come to the river to swim almost every afternoon. Grayson insists we play an hour each day. Funny. Before we were married, it seemed like I didn't have enough hours in the day to get the work done, and now . . . well, I reckon some of my priorities changed."

"You look younger," Jessye told her, then grimaced because the compliment sounded more like an insult.

Abbie's smile grew. "I think it's the laughter, or maybe it's just the smiles." She shrugged. "I only know he makes me happy."

Jessye felt the tiny feet walking along her leg as Colton reached for his mother. "He's walking here!"

"It's the water. Holds him up so he thinks he's a big boy." Abbie tickled him before playfully snatching him away from Jessye.

Jessye furrowed her brow. "So he's not walking?"

"No, it'll be months before he's walking on the ground." She blew air against his belly. He kicked frantically at the water. "But he can kick."

"You say you come every day?"

"Mmm-hm. I think that's why he has such strong

legs. I don't remember my other children having a kick this strong."

Jessye flopped back, arms outstretched, and the water lifted her to the surface. She'd never noticed how easy it was to move in the river. She jerked upright. "Abbie, I got a big favor to ask of your husband."

And she prayed Harry would forgive her.

❧ Chapter 16 ❧

"*Are you out of your mind?*" Harrison asked, staring at Grayson Rhodes. "Accompany you and your family on a picnic?"

"My son is three months old, and you've yet to see him."

Harrison waved his arm magnanimously through the air. "So bring him to my prison. I'm allowed visitors."

"Self-pity doesn't become you, Harry."

He watched with increasing dread as Grayson jerked aside the curtains and the morning sunlight spilled into the room. "It's a beautiful day, the sun is shining—"

"It's August. It's hot."

Grayson turned. "All the more reason to go outside where you can at least sit in the shade or feel a bit of breeze. It's unbearably stuffy in here."

"In case you've failed to notice, I've lost the use of my legs."

"I'll carry you."

Harrison slammed his eyes closed. "As though I were a child—"

"As though you were the closest thing to a brother that I've ever known."

Harrison's throat tightened as he opened his eyes. "I can't, Gray."

Grayson crossed the room in long, easy strides that Harrison hated himself for envying.

"I placed the wagon behind the saloon. We'll go out the back door. No one will see. When we ride out of town, people will have no idea how you came to sit on the bench seat. Besides, it'll be well worth your efforts. Abbie has prepared the tastiest picnic."

"This isn't one of those large community affairs she's fond of, is it?"

"No. Just my family on our land, a pretty little spot by the river."

Harrison scratched his beard. He'd allowed it to grow back. In defiance, he supposed. Whatever closeness had developed with Jessye he'd severed with his surly attitude. "Do your children know about my . . . condition?"

He nodded. "It won't matter one whit to them."

"How can you be so sure?"

"Because they're children."

"Children taunted you for being a bastard."

"Not young children. It's only as we grow older and more cynical that we hurt others in an attempt to turn attention away from our own faults."

Within the pit of his gut, Harrison knew he was making a mistake, but it wasn't the first, and he seriously doubted it would be the last. "All right, I'll go on one condition."

"And that would be?"

God, he hated asking, despised the dependency.

"That you bring me some hot water so I can wash up. I'm a bit rank."

Grayson smiled. "You always were one for understatement."

Harrison had tried sitting with his back against a tree, but the pressure on his hip was more than he could bear. It hadn't healed properly, but he knew nothing could be done now but to accept it.

So he'd stretched out on the quilt, on his left side, raised up on an elbow. He'd never expected to envy the illegitimate son of a duke. In his mind, he had no doubt that Grayson was happy. Abbie obviously adored his friend, as did the children from her first marriage.

Her daughter, Lydia, greatly resembled her mother. At nine, her oldest son, Johnny, looked much like his father, but he lacked his father's serious nature. The youngest boy, Micah, was six. He had his father's dark hair but his mother's violet eyes, enlarged by the spectacles he wore until he resembled an owl. Micah squatted in front of him, his gaze intense as though he could see into Harrison's sordid soul.

"You and me are the same," he croaked after a while, in a voice that had always reminded Harrison of a frog.

"In what way, lad?"

He blinked his eyes. "I cain't hardly see, and you cain't hardly walk."

Harrison's stomach tightened. He couldn't walk at all. After the doctor had left two days before, he'd tried again to use the crutches within the privacy of his room. He'd fallen flat on his face. His only comfort had come from the fact that he'd regained enough strength in his arms that he could pull himself into bed. Reaching out, he touched the rim of the boy's spectacles. "But these help you see, do they not?"

The lad bobbed his head, the locks of dark brown hair flapping against his forehead. "I bet somethin' could help you walk."

"I don't think so, lad."

"Uh-huh." He jumped up and ran off to join his brother at the edge of the river, where he stood with a fishing pole in his hand beside Grayson.

"Children have such faith, don't they?"

Harrison jerked his head around at the familiar smoky voice. The horse snorted as Jessye dismounted. "What are you doing here?" he asked.

Shrugging, she threaded the reins through the branches of a nearby bush before plopping down beside him. "I was out riding and thought I'd stop by."

He resented like the devil that he couldn't even sit up without making a gruesome spectacle of himself. "Gray told me this was a secluded spot."

She nodded, her gaze on the river. "I was out here yesterday. Went swimming with Abbie."

"Well, Abbie returned to the house right after we ate lunch. She took the baby and Lydia with her. So if you want to see her, that's where you need to go."

Jessye began plucking up blades of grass. "I didn't come to see her." She gave him a sideways glance. "Yesterday, I played in the river with Colton, and his little legs were kicking. He can't walk, but in the water . . ." She dropped her gaze. "I thought if you went swimming, maybe your legs would remember—"

He started laughing, long and hard.

"It's not funny. You haven't used your legs in months, and it occurred to me that you just needed to start over, from the beginning, learn to crawl—"

He abruptly stopped his laughter. "Oh, I can crawl, Jessye, on my belly like a slug creeping out from beneath a rock at night." He jerked his gaze toward the river. "Gray!"

But all he saw was the water lapping at the shore. Grayson and the boys were gone. Suspicion lurked and knowledge dawned. He snapped his gaze back to Jessye. "Bloody damned hell! You arranged this."

She nodded. "Don't be mad at them. I didn't know how else to get you out here. I knew you wouldn't come if I asked."

Impotent rage surged through him. "So now I am to be a prisoner here until Gray returns and hauls me—like a sack of potatoes—to your room at the back of the saloon? I can't even live in my old room because it's at the top of the stairs. Have you no idea of the humiliation I feel at being dependent—"

"I do know, damn you! I do know and that's why I'm trying so hard to help you. Do you think I would have given up my daughter if I'd been independent? If I'd had money or a man's name? I know the humiliation of not being able to control my destiny—and I know the strength required to take that first step to never again be dependent upon anyone or anything but yourself." Tears flooded her lovely green eyes and spilled over onto her cheeks. "Let me help you, Harry."

With his thumb, he captured her tear. "It's not the same."

"It's not that different. Why do you think I invested

in the cattle venture? Why do you think I risked my reputation and my life? Because I never want to be dependent on anyone again."

She reached out and then drew back, as though fearing his rejection. She clasped her hands tightly within her lap.

Clenching his teeth against the pain, he struggled to sit up. He scooted back until he could roll onto his left hip and lean against the tree. "You were supposed to go with Kit." It was an inane comment, with no bearing on the argument at hand.

"I couldn't leave you."

"Why?"

She shook her head and studied her hands. "Don't look to me to give you a reason to walk. That's got to be within you."

"You don't think I *want* to walk?"

"I think you're scared. You want to walk so badly that it's frightening, almost paralyzing. As long as you don't try, there's always the possibility that you might walk. But you're afraid that if you try and fall, it'll mean that you'll never walk. When all it means is that you fell and need to try again. If you don't try, I dadgum guarantee that you never will walk."

"Fine words from someone who doesn't trust any man to be honorable simply because one man wasn't."

"You're right." With a sigh, she jumped to her feet. "Spend your life lying in the shade. I'm gonna swim in the sun."

He watched her run the short distance to the water's edge. A smile tugged at the corner of his mouth as she hopped up and down, tugging off her boots. She pulled her shirt over her head, and his breath caught at the sight of her white chemise. She draped the shirt over a nearby bush. *Take off the chemise,* a little voice inside his head dared her.

But she left it in place and jerked off her trousers. Christ, he would have traded his soul to the devil to have the ability to go after her. The skimpy undergarments left little to his imagination. Ah, to see her in the sunlight instead of the shadows of the night . . .

He glanced around quickly. If Grayson were hiding behind some bushes watching, he'd have to kill him. But all he saw were a couple of squirrels, some mockingbirds, and butterflies fluttering low to the ground.

He turned his attention back to Jessye. She waded out a few steps before crouching and diving into the water. Graceful, so incredibly graceful. She came up to the surface, rolled to her back, and spread her arms out. He saw her small feet kick against the current.

"Come on, Harry! The water's warm," she called out.

And his body was fevered with need. He didn't have the best view in the world, but he could tell the soaked material was plastered against her skin. Her face was turned toward the sun, away from him. Even if her eyes were open, she'd be unable to see him.

A short distance away from him, a tree stood nearer to the bank. He lay on the ground. Ignoring the pain in his side, he stretched out his arms and pulled himself forward, inch by agonizing inch. He was taken off-guard by the sense of accomplishment that filled him as he reached the tree and worked his way into a sitting position, hoping she hadn't noticed the journey he'd taken.

God, he nearly laughed, as though he were playing hide-and-seek as a child might.

She twisted in the water, her gaze falling on him, her smile bright. "Come on in, Harry."

"I'd drown."

"Colton didn't drown."

"Yes, well, I'm certain someone held the lad while he was in the water."

She stopped floating and began to bob in the water, her arms moving in a constant circle. "I'll hold you."

His stomach knotted at the smoky allure of her voice, the images that flashed through his mind. He almost shouted for her to close her eyes so she wouldn't see his ungainly entrance into the river.

But pride held him back. Pride and fear. Fear that he would indeed drown—or have to be rescued. To discover that not only could he not walk but he also could no longer swim—

She released a quick screech and went beneath the water.

"Jessye!" He stretched up as much as he was able—and couldn't see her. Frantically, he scanned the river. "Gray! Gray!" Damn the man for leaving. He'd hoped he was at least within shouting distance.

Jessye popped back up to the surface and just as quickly went under. Terror seized him. "Jessye!" Nothing. He fell to his stomach, raised up on his elbows, and dragged himself to the water's edge. "Bloody damned hell!"

He sat up and pulled off his boots, his gaze trained on the river. "Jessye!"

Still nothing. No bubbles, no arms, no legs, no light green eyes. Ah, Christ, if she'd drowned because he hadn't been able to move fast enough—

He took a deep breath and slid into the water. He kept his head above the surface. The scent of the river, mud, fish, and plants filled his nostrils. "Jessye!"

He heard the huge splash as she came up from the depths of the river. Relief surged through him, quickly followed by suspicion. He furrowed his brow. The depths of the river. With only his arms, he'd pulled himself to its center and his knees skimmed the bottom. "It's not deep."

She shook her head. "No, it's not."

"I thought you were drowning," he said sharply.

"I figured you might." She lifted a shoulder, having the grace to look slightly ashamed. "I reckon I cheated." She waded toward him. "But I just thought if I could get you in the water, you'd see that you could move your legs here like you can't out there, and if we could get your legs to work again—"

"I didn't kick to get out here. I only used my arms."

"How about now?"

"I'm on my knees."

"Does it hurt?"

Her question took him off-guard. The water moved gently around him. He wasn't truly on his knees. He kept afloat by moving his arms, but the pressure on his hip was less than it had been in a long time. "I can't stand."

"You don't need to. But you can float, and little by little, your legs will start working again."

Her eyes held such hope that she almost had him believing her words. "What if they don't?"

"What have you lost? You're out of the bed, out of

your room, outside. The sun is shining and the birds are singing—"

He skimmed his finger along the curve of her chemise. "And you are very nearly naked." He raised a brow. "There might be some advantages to this endeavor."

"Let's take off your shirt."

Although he was surrounded by water, his mouth went dry as she unbuttoned his shirt. When she pulled the shirt over his head, he lifted his arms and sank beneath the surface, experiencing a heartbeat of panic before he felt her arm go around him and bring him back up.

She smiled brightly when he dragged his hand down his face to get the water out of his eyes.

"Keep yourself afloat while I hang this up to dry," she ordered.

"What about my trousers?"

"I think you'd best keep them on." She trudged toward the bank.

"I've no objection to you removing all your clothes," he called after her.

She laughed as she draped his shirt over a bush before gliding back to him.

"So how is this supposed to work?" he asked.

He watched the doubts flicker within her eyes.

"I don't know. I sorta thought you could float on your back and I would hold you. Maybe after a time your legs would remember what to do. They need to regain their strength before you can walk." She cradled his cheek. "It might not work at all. We have to expect that it won't, I reckon, so we're not terribly disappointed if it doesn't."

He didn't want to acknowledge the spark of hope burning inside his chest. He took her hand, turned it slightly, and pressed a kiss to the heart of her palm. "All right. Let's give it a go."

She trudged behind him. "Just lean back."

He did as she ordered, but his legs didn't want to cooperate. Maybe they never would.

Her arms came around him, and he settled his head against her shoulder. His legs began to move with the current, a gentle motion, more movement than they'd experienced in months. They were cheating, really. Manipulating legs that refused to yield. Perhaps . . .

"I've been a real bastard these past few months. Why are you so forgiving and willing to help me?" he asked.

"Purely selfish reasons. I want my bedroom back."

With the sun shining on his face, he smiled at her lie and wondered at her true reasons.

Jessye bent backward, trying to ease the ache out of her lower back. She usually took a nap in the afternoon to help her get through the grueling night of serving drinks and food to men, but this afternoon had been spent in the river. She'd been shocked when she'd removed Harry's shirt to see how thin he'd become. She didn't know why she'd expected otherwise. He only left the bed when Grayson came to visit and give him his bath.

Washing the last of the glasses, she smiled. Today had been a success. Harry's legs hadn't moved with the strength or agility of Colton's, but she'd caught a slight movement now and again, and Harry had actually teased her a time or two. He'd been loathe to leave the river when Grayson and his family had returned in the late afternoon.

She dried her hands on the towel. Her heart had nearly broken when Grayson had carried Harry back to his bed—his prison, he called it. He'd forbidden her to write his father, so, as much as she despised the role, she was his keeper more than his friend.

She walked out of the kitchen into the hallway that led past the room that had once been hers. Now she slept in Harry's old room at the top of the stairs, but his room was stark and bare . . . unlike hers, which carried mementos of her youth. Sometimes, she feared he would come to know her better by staying there, better than she knew herself, while she learned nothing more about him than what she already knew. Somewhere along the trail between Fortune and Kansas, she'd fallen in love with him.

Yet despite his attention, his kisses, the secrets they'd shared in the night, and the passion, she knew he would never truly love her. On the trail, she was the only woman within hundreds of miles; and now she was still the only woman within his reach—and an unsophisticated female at that.

She stopped by the door that led into his room, resisting the urge to open it slightly and peer inside, to catch a glimpse of him sleeping. She'd often watched him on the trail. In sleep, he appeared almost innocent. What a cheating illusion that was.

A low, muted groan shimmered against the door. She pressed her hand and her ear to the oak. She heard a strangled cry. She shoved open the door, her heart leaping into her throat.

Harry's legs were curled beneath him. Reaching

back, he snatched the covers over himself, but not before she saw what she thought was a swollen knot on his calf. He jerked the corner of the pillow out of his mouth. "Get out!"

She stepped into the room. "Has this happened before?"

"Get out!" he growled. "And shut the damn door."

"I'm gonna get the doctor." She turned.

"No!"

She swung back around. "Harry, you're in pain. He might be able to do something—"

He waved his hand frantically in the air. "In the drawer here by the bed there's a jar. Get it."

She rushed across the room, jerked open the drawer, and pulled out the jar. "What is it?"

He snatched it from her. "Some sort of liniment. Now go."

She watched him struggle to twist the lid with a trembling hand. She took the jar from him and opened it. A pungent odor rose up and stung her eyes. "What is this?"

"Something to ease"—he groaned—"the pain. Now get out of here." He moved the sheet aside until a portion of his leg was visible. With his fingers, he scooped out some of the salve and began to rub it on his calf.

"Will you leave?" he muttered.

"No." She dipped her fingers in the jar. "What do I do?"

"Jessye—"

"Harry."

He sighed deeply. "Just work it in."

She eased the sheet aside, exposing his thin legs.

Little wonder he couldn't walk. She remembered the way his trousers had stretched across his thighs whenever he'd crouched in front of her, the way it had felt to have his strong thighs wedged between hers. She rubbed her hands briskly together to spread the salve and create warmth. Gingerly, she laid her hands on his knotted calf.

He moaned low. She glanced over her shoulder to see that his eyes were squeezed shut. He'd stuffed the corner of the pillow back into his mouth. She increased the pressure on the knot, rubbing gently until she felt it give way and relax. "Everything's going to be all right, Harry. It was a stupid idea to go swimming."

"Do tell."

Nodding, she gathered more salve, warmed her hands, and located the next hardened knot. She worked her fingers around the knot. Strange. She'd made love to him and never seen his bare legs. She should have insisted he remove all his clothes that night.

She moved to the next set of rebellious muscles. "I just thought if Colton could walk in the water, so could you. I'm so sorry. This isn't what I wanted for you."

She continued to massage the small knots and larger ones, kneading, rubbing, hard pressure, light. She had no idea if she was helping or hurting, but since his moans were lessening, she could only hope she was easing the pain without causing further damage to his legs. The minutes passed slowly as she hammered at each knotted muscle until it gave in to her ministrations.

Her hands ached and her back was stiff when she finally kneaded her fingers over each of his legs from ankle to upper thigh, searching for obstinate muscles. She didn't find any.

Still, it wouldn't hurt to search again. Even though his legs were thin, she still enjoyed the feel of his skin, the dark, wiry hair on his legs tickling her palms. She took her hands on a journey up each leg and back down, her fingers slowly circling until she began to imagine him doing the same for her. Only she would want his hands covering her entire body.

"I think you'd best stop," he said in a strangled voice.

Jessye jerked her gaze to his. The molten heat within his eyes was enough to send tendrils of desire weaving through her. Her mouth went dry. "Are you . . . still hurting?"

He lifted one corner of his mouth into a cocky grin that made her heart soar. How long had it been since she'd seen him smile?

"Where I'm feeling discomfort, I doubt you'd want to rub."

Grateful he still lay on his stomach, she darted her gaze to his hips, bare flesh separated from her sight by only a sheet. Reaching up, she pulled the thin material over his legs, when she was tempted to toss it completely aside. Daring to sit on the edge of the bed, she laid her palm against his bearded cheek. "Your muscles bunching up painfully like this has happened before," she said quietly.

"Not to this extent. The physician gave me the salve, and usually I can manage just fine on my own." He sighed deeply. "Tonight the pain caught me unaware, worse than it had ever been before."

She combed her fingers through his hair. "Why didn't you call for me?"

"The pain would have gone away eventually."

"Why do you have to be so damn proud? Why won't you let me help you?"

Despair showed deep in his eyes. "It . . . shames me for you to see me like this."

"Oh, Harry," she whispered, brushing her lips over his temple. "What do you think I see? I see a man who nearly drowned trying to save another; a man who refused to yield even though he knew it meant death; a man who held me when I was filled with sorrow and made me feel courageous when I wasn't. You haven't changed in my eyes. You've only changed in your own."

"I can't walk."

"But you will again someday."

"You honestly believe that?"

She nodded and smiled tenderly. "Even if you have to cheat to do it."

Her gaze drifted to the figurine on the bedside table. The mother was once again holding the child, a jagged crack, now mended, joining them. "You fixed it," she whispered, reaching out.

He folded his fingers over hers. "Don't touch it. I'm not certain it's dry yet, and even if it were, I'm not certain it's strong enough to withstand handling." He brought her fingers to his mouth and skimmed his lips over her knuckles, sending streams of warmth flowing through her. "Thank you for trying to fix me."

Tears scalded her eyes.

"I would not have blamed you for leaving me to suffer alone. I have not been . . . pleasant these past few months."

Her fingers curled and tightened around his. "I just wish I knew what to do to help—"

"Take me swimming again tomorrow."

Her eyes widened, and she pulled her hand free of his. "I don't think that's such a good idea. Look what you just went through."

He rolled to his side, carefully keeping the sheet in place. "I have lain here for weeks and watched my legs dwindle away, feeling little, not knowing how to stop the deterioration." He rose up on an elbow, his eyes glittering with hope. "Tonight, at long last, I felt something—"

"Pain!" she snapped, rising to her feet.

"Rebellion. A boy grows into a man by rebelling. It's a painful process. God knows I barely survived it."

"You can't compare your legs to a child—"

He met her gaze. "I think you were right about swimming. The movements were slight, but they were there. I didn't want to give them up. That's why I wouldn't leave the water until dusk. I shan't make that mistake again, but I do want to go back to the river . . . with you."

With you. Those words wrapped around her heart even though deep down she knew she was the logical choice. She was free during the day, while everyone else had farms to manage or cattle to gather and graze.

She gave a brisk nod. "All right. We'll go in the afternoon."

A slow, sensual smile eased over his face. "I will walk again, Jessye."

"I know."

Then he would no doubt walk out of the saloon and never glance back.

❧ Chapter 17 ❧

*Harrison glared at the rain pounding un-*mercifully against the window. Forked lightning threatened to strike the ground, and thunder boomed.

In the past fortnight, he'd grown accustomed to swimming in the afternoon, actually anticipated the time he spent with Jessye. Through her eyes, he experienced moments when he no longer felt like a cripple, when he honestly believed he might walk again.

He shifted in the soft velvet chair. How like a woman to adorn a room with pretty, but uncomfortable, furniture.

He heard the knock, considered not answering, but knew his silence wouldn't keep her out. "Come in."

The door opened and Jessye walked in. Her gaze darted from the bed to the window, her eyes widening. "You walked."

He returned his attention to the raging storm. "I crawled."

"How did you pull yourself into the chair?"

"As ungainly as a longhorn getting up from the ground."

He listened to her gentle footsteps, which were cautious, as though she sensed his foul mood rivaled that of the weather.

"You might consider leaving this room. Go into the saloon, play some poker—"

"I have no wish to be seen as I am."

"You are so infuriatingly stubborn."

The frustration in her voice nearly made him smile. "A trait I learned from you."

"I was never *this* stubborn."

"Have you heard from Kit?" he asked, wanting, needing to veer the subject away from himself.

"No."

"Shouldn't he have reached Chicago by now?"

She sat on the edge of the windowsill and peered at the storm. "He took a route no one had ever driven cattle over before. No telling how long it might take or what he might run into."

"I shall find a way to see that you are at least re-imbursed the money you invested."

Her lips curled upward as she met his gaze. "I knew the risks. If we met with success, I'd be independent. You don't owe me if we don't meet with success."

Still, he didn't like the idea that she might end up with the short end of the stick. She'd had enough short sticks in her life. Today, her mood reflected the rain: melancholy, wistful. God, he missed the fire that had once emanated from her. Their last encounter with Gerald Milton had broken his bones, but he feared it had broken her spirit.

"What do you see beyond the rain?" he asked quietly.

She shook her head and glanced at her hands.

"Something's bothering you."

She raised a shoulder until it touched her chin. "I was at the mercantile earlier. I saw a porcelain doll. It had red hair." She darted him a glance. "I've never seen a doll with red hair. Almost purchased it."

"Why didn't you? Surely, the saloon makes some profit."

She relaxed her shoulder, placed her finger on the pane, and followed a solitary drop of rain as it made its journey like a tear searching for its comrades. "We've got a bit of money set aside, and Pa wouldn't have minded if I used a little on something for me. Just don't know what I would have done with a doll."

"You could have sent it to Mary Ellen."

She worked her teeth back and forth over her lower lip. "I thought about that . . ." She shook her head. "It's best just to let her go."

"But you haven't. You told me that you wake up every morning thinking of her—"

"It's worse now." She turned slightly, grabbed a chain, and pulled a locket out from behind her collar. "Madeline gave me this." She opened the locket. "Now, every morning I look at my baby and wonder . . ." He saw the tears well in her eyes before she returned her attention to the rain. "God, I wish this rain would stop. Makes me sad when I got no reason to be."

The woman was an artist at changing subjects when she no longer wished to discuss them. He rubbed his thighs. His legs had a strange, impatient feel about them, as though they knew they were going to be denied a trip to the river. "How long do you think this storm will last?"

She sighed deeply. "Too long for us to swim. Besides, September is here, and the weather will get cool soon. We're gonna have to figure something else out." She snapped her locket closed and slipped it into hiding. She dropped to the floor, folded her legs beneath her, and placed his foot in her lap.

"What are you doing?" he demanded.

She pressed her palms to the sole of his foot. "I think it's important that your legs do some moving every day. Push against my hands."

He stretched out his leg, her palms offering support and only the barest of resistance. When he'd reached his limit, she moved his leg back into place until his knee was bent.

"Again," she ordered, her gaze focused on his leg, while his was riveted to her face.

What had ever made him think—even for the barest of moments—that her features were not spectacular? Their time in the sun had added freckles to her nose and the curve of her cheeks. But her defiant chin had refused to be conquered. He knew from their swims that her shoulders had attracted freckles as well, and he was actually grateful that she'd never removed her chemise, for beneath the fabric her skin would be flawless and know only the kiss of his lips and not that of the sun.

She moved his leg forward and back, forward and back, and he imagined his tongue imitating the same motions within her mouth, circling, swirling, tasting, thrusting . . . his body inside hers—

He dropped his foot to the floor, trying to control his breathing. His thoughts could wander, while his body could not. Why would any woman want a man who was not whole? How often he regretted that he hadn't pursued her more aggressively on the trail, that he hadn't made love to her more than once while he was whole, while he'd possessed . . . everything.

He studied the storm without and felt the tempest building within. He could control neither.

"Let me work your other leg," she said.

"I truly don't believe this little exercise will help."

"It can't hurt."

"I need to be alone."

"Do you need me to get you—"

"I don't need anything but solitude."

The guilt gnawed at him as she rose gracefully to her feet. She did not deserve to witness the dark cloud hovering over him.

"I'll send Magpie in after a while to help you get back into bed—"

"I can get myself into bed, thank you."

"You've done this before?" she asked, bewilderment in her voice.

"Often, since we've begun swimming." He dared to glance at her and give her a self-deprecating smile. "Usually late at night when I can't sleep. This is the first time I've been caught. I shall avoid afternoon excursions in the future."

"I always knock before I come in."

He heard the pain in her voice and cursed his callousness, but damn it, he had no desire for her to see his slow, awkward journey from bed to chair. "For which I'm eternally grateful."

She turned quietly to leave.

"Jessye?"

She turned back to him, the sadness still in her eyes.

"Purchase the doll and send it to Mary Ellen as a friend."

"I don't know if I have the strength to be her friend when I want to be her mother."

"You never stopped being her mother."

"That's why it's so hard. I don't want to hurt her, and I'm afraid I will." She walked from the room, leaving behind an audible click as she closed the door.

"Bloody hell!" He scooted the chair back in short, spasmodic jerks. He pressed his foot against the wall, wishing he had the power to kick a hole in the blasted thing, wishing his legs had the strength to carry him to Jessye so he could end this incessant longing that he feared might forever be left unfulfilled.

He bent and straightened his leg, bent and straightened, over and over. The exercise wasn't nearly as enjoyable as when his foot was cradled within her lap, but neither did it conjure up carnal images that he feared might make him go as mad as his mother.

"What in God's name are you doing?" Harrison asked as he sat on the edge of the bed. He found it increasingly easier to sit as long as he remembered to roll to his left side first instead of his right, so the ache in his hip was lessened.

"Making you a walkway," Grayson told him as he nailed a short post into the floor.

"Jessye will snatch that golden hair right off your head—"

"It was her idea. It came to her a couple of nights ago when she used the banister to pull herself up the stairs after a particularly tiring evening of working in the saloon. She thought if you had a couple of banisters to support your weight that perhaps you could walk from the bed to the chair by the window."

"She's entirely too optimistic. I can't even stand."

Grayson shrugged as he reached for another post. "Which is the reason I'm doing this. Nothing wrong with your arms. You can use the railing so they lift some of the weight off your legs." He stopped hammering and glanced at Harrison. "It's going to take a while. It's not going to be easy. I wouldn't have taken time from my crops to do it if I didn't think the idea had some merit."

A tightening in his chest, Harrison looked at the sanded and polished wood, a true measure of friendship—so incredibly difficult to accept. "I'm supposed to trust that this walkway, as you call it, is going to support my weight? When did you become a carpenter?"

Grayson flashed a grin. "When I became a farmer. You'd be surprised by all the things I've learned to do."

"And you enjoy it."

"Having the ability to provide for my family is satisfying, Harry."

"Westland's children seem to have accepted you easily enough."

Grayson went back to hammering. "The war took him away when they were still babies. They hardly knew him."

"But when he returned—"

"The land always came first with him. That's where we differ." Grayson met and held his gaze. "Abbie and the children come first with me. Nothing will change that."

"Good God, who would have thought that you'd change your roguish ways and become such an adamant family man?"

"Certainly not me."

Harrison ran his hand over the post closest to him. "I'm happy for you, Gray. I know you went through hell for a while."

"Abbie says the hottest fires forge the strongest metals." He smiled. "She thought I was in need of some reshaping."

"I thought you were perfectly fine as you were."

"That's because you're a scoundrel."

Harrison chuckled. It had been a while since he'd felt like a scoundrel. At moments, he missed it terribly.

He watched the care Grayson took with his task and hated that he could do nothing more than sit idly by while the project neared completion. He'd always felt closer to Kit than to Grayson. Still, Grayson was a friend, and a trusted one at that, who might hold answers to unfathomable questions. "When did you know that you loved Abbie?"

Grayson ran his hand along the smooth finish of the polished wood, one of two railings that ran from the window to the bed, supported by beams at short intervals. "When I realized that I would gladly walk into hell to see that she was happy." He came to a stop in front of Harrison. "And that I would stay there for eternity if need be."

Gripping the banisters, Harry took one painstakingly slow step after another. The more weight he shifted from his arms to his legs, the more lethargically he moved.

When he reached the window, he bowed his head and released a deep, shuddering breath. He was making progress. At least now he could stand at the window, as long as he maintained a hold on the banisters.

Clumsily, he turned and made the monotonous journey to the bed. God, how he wished he'd appreciated the miles he'd ridden on a horse. Taken pleasure in the sunset. Danced. At least he had the memories of one dance with Jessye within his arms.

He sat on the edge of the bed and stared at the crutches leaning against the mattress. They would give him the freedom to leave the room whenever he wanted.

He still needed practice, and he knew it would be a long while before he allowed anyone to witness his awkward attempts, but there was no better time than the present to begin. The saloon was quiet, and if he were very careful and moved very slowly, he might be able to pour himself a glass of whiskey—and no one would know.

No matter how many ways Jessye looked at the ledgers, she couldn't change the numbers. Her father had a bad habit of purchasing more stock than was needed so their cash reserves were always low. She couldn't bring herself to chastise him. He'd only say, "We'll need it all some day, girl."

Perhaps before the war, before over half the men in the town had died on a bloody battlefield miles from home.

It also didn't help matters that her father had a bad

habit of extending credit. "Can't turn away a man down on his luck," he'd say. "Just a nip to help him through the night."

The nip often turned into a bottle or two.

She'd grown accustomed to her father's generosity over the years. She loved him, faults and all. Still, she'd be relieved when they heard something from Kit. She desperately wanted her investment to pay off.

Yawning, she closed the ledger, leaned back in the chair, and rubbed the nape of her neck. Two o'clock in the morning was much too late to go to bed, but the night just didn't contain enough hours.

The office door opened, and she smiled sleepily at her father. "Thought you'd gone to bed."

"I got distracted. Do you know where the papers are that say I own this building?"

"They're here in the desk."

"Can I see them?"

She reached into the top drawer, shuffled some papers, and brought forth the deed to the saloon. He took the document from her, looked it over, and nodded. He picked up her pen and the bottle of ink. "I need you to come with me and bear witness."

The hairs on the back of her neck prickled. "Bear witness to what?"

He turned on his heel and walked from the room. She jumped up from the chair and rushed after him. "Pa, what have you done?"

She hurried down the hallway, past Harry's room, the faint notion registering in her mind that his door was ajar. She staggered to a stop at the doorway that led into the saloon. Harry sat at a table near the bar.

Unshaven, his clothes wrinkled, he didn't look happy to see her.

Cards were strewn over the table, and coins were stacked in front of him. Not a lot of money, but enough to make her heart pound unmercifully against her ribs.

"Come here, daughter."

As though in a dream, she walked toward the table, fearing the answer to a question she couldn't bring herself to ask. With intense green eyes, Harry watched her as her father dipped the pen into the inkwell and scrawled his name across the bottom of the paper. Her father glanced over his shoulder. "I need you to sign as a witness."

"Exactly what am I signing?" she asked.

"Signing ownership of the saloon over to Harry. He won it fair and square. I had three aces, but he drew to an inside straight."

"An inside straight," she whispered, her knees threatening to buckle beneath her. "How could you do this?"

Harry narrowed his gaze, and she felt as though he'd sliced into her heart. "It was a fair game."

"A fair game. What do you know about fairness, Harry? You manipulate cards. You manipulate people. I did all that I could to help you walk again, and the first time that you shuffle in here, you take my father's saloon? The only thing that means anything to him?" Shaking her head, she backed up a step. "I won't sign it. I won't give you my father's saloon."

"Jessye—" her father began.

"No, Pa, I won't do it. He's a scoundrel and a cheat—"

"Girl, you watch your words. Once spoken, they can't be unspoken. I knew what I was doin' when I put the saloon in the pot. I gave my word, and a true Texan never goes back on his word." He dipped the pen back into the ink. "Come and sign it as a witness."

"Only the ownership changes," Harry said. "You and your father can continue to work and live here—"

"Now, aren't you a kind and generous man." She snatched the pen from her father's hand and scratched her name across the bottom of the deed, nearly tearing into the paper with her anger. "Because I've got no choice, I'll work here until Kit returns with my share of the profits. Then my father and I are getting as far away from you as we can."

She turned on her heel and headed for the stairs.

"Jessye!"

She spun around and glared at Harry. If he'd been wearing a smug smile, she might have returned and scratched out those beautiful green eyes of his. Instead his eyes held a measure of regret.

"Meet with me at ten in the morning to discuss a few changes I'd like to make."

"Go to hell."

She heard his low laughter as she climbed the stairs, realizing too late the absurdity of her words, sending a man to a place where he no doubt already lived.

He owned the saloon! Using the railings, Harrison walked to the window more with his arms than his legs. Using one hand for leverage, he leaned against the polished wood, reached up quickly, jerked the curtain aside, and regained his balance.

Between the time Jonah Kane went to retrieve the documents and returned with the papers scrunched in his gnarled hands, Harrison had told himself a thousand times that he would cancel the debt, laugh the poker game off as a late night's entertainment, and be content.

But in the end, hope had been greater than decency, for here at last was a reason to crawl out of bed in the morning. Here at last was a chance to be a whole man, even if he didn't have a whole body.

He looked at the black void sprinkled with diamonds of light and was acutely reminded of the nights on the trail, nights with Jessye, when he had tasted her lips, touched her flesh, inhaled her delicate fragrance. She had been relegated to being his nurse, was the one responsible for finding ways to help him walk again. She looked at him with a defiant angle to her chin, but pity in her eyes.

But not tonight. By God, not tonight. Anger had flared within her eyes, passionate anger, and he had reveled in the sight. She would pity him no more, even though the price would be her hatred.

His hands tightened around the banister, his bones pushing against flesh. He despised the pity. His father had looked at him with sympathy when they'd found him in the dungeon. His father had sought to make amends. Anything Harrison wanted, he got. He had tested his father's limits and discovered none existed.

He feared the same might be true of Jessye. What would she give him out of pity?

Better to have her hatred, her anger—he could stand tall against those.

But pity had the power to bring him to his knees.

He would make the saloon prosper, he would make it all that he envisioned it could be, and when Kit returned with her share of the profits, he would sell the saloon to her—at a fair price. A price steep enough so she would not doubt his motives, but low enough that he could live the next few weeks with only a niggling of guilt.

Pulling her hair back unmercifully, Jessye secured it with a tight knot at the back of her head. She'd thrown water on her eyes most of the morning to ease the swelling after crying for much of the night. She loathed the tears, but she'd shed more since knowing Harrison Bainbridge than at any other time in her life.

He had betrayed her, her kindness, and her father. She should have followed his edict and gone with Kit. Nothing on the trail could have hurt her more than the stunt he'd pulled last night: taking from her father the one thing that mattered most to him.

She tugged on the bodice of her dress, straightened her shoulders, and angled her chin before jerking open her door and stepping into the hallway. Only her father's quiet insistence made her now walk down the stairs to keep her appointed meeting with Harry.

But she wouldn't go to his room. If he wanted to meet with her, it would be in the saloon. He could use the crutches he'd mastered to get there.

She hit the last step, grabbed the banister, swung around, and froze, her foot dangling over the floor. Harry sat at the same table he'd occupied last night. But he was not the man who had cheated her father. He was the man she'd fallen in love with in Dallas. His beard was gone, revealing a face that was leaner than before, but still composed of strong lines and sharp edges. He had trimmed his hair, and the black locks teased the collar of his black jacket, while just above his red brocade vest, a black cravat made itself at home against his throat.

As though suddenly aware of her perusal, he snapped his head up, capturing and holding her gaze with those emerald eyes that always intrigued her. Gone was the anger and the self-loathing that had filled them these many months. Instead, she saw impatience and barely restrained anticipation. Her heart flipped over and filled with gladness, as though he'd never betrayed her.

He raised a hand and wiggled his fingers. "Come on, Jessye my love, we have lots to accomplish today."

Jessye my love. She knew he didn't give any credence to the last word, but he hadn't spoken it since he'd lain on a table in a doctor's home and taken a journey into hell. The word curled around her like a vine. With legs as unsteady as a newborn filly's, she walked toward him.

As she neared, his eyes darkened. "You'll forgive me for not standing, I'm sure."

She nodded mutely as she sat in a chair across from him. The crutches were behind him, almost hidden by the breadth of his shoulders. She suddenly realized that although he didn't carry the weight on him that he had before Kansas, he wasn't as thin as he'd been when they first returned to Fortune. Working to strengthen his legs seemed to have strengthened his upper body as well.

"You cleaned up," she rasped with a throat dryer

than the dust kicked up by a herd of cattle.

He raised a brow as though amused. "Magpie turned out to be quite a skilled valet."

"You never had him cleaning you up before."

"I decided it was time. Besides, can't have the owner looking like death warmed over. Might make gents think twice before coming in to purchase a drink." Harrison realized the mistake of his wording as her expression changed from one of awe to bitterness.

"Ah, yes, the owner." She leaned back in the chair and crossed her arms beneath her breasts, glaring at him as though he were one of the ticks that the longhorn cattle infamously carried into Kansas.

He damned his reckless tongue as he pulled aside the papers on which he'd made notations through the night, unable to sleep as ideas swirled through his head. He'd cursed Kit a thousand times for not being here to help him work out the details, but he thought all things considered that his plan was a fine one. Whether or not it would impress Jessye remained to be seen—although, judging by the angle of her jaw, he had a feeling she was in no mood to be either receptive or impressed. He cleared his throat, thinking it would be easier to face a band of jayhawkers than Jessye when she was miffed.

"First of all, we need to give the saloon a name," he told her.

"A name?" she echoed as though he'd lost his wits.

Looking up from his notations, he resisted the urge to reach out and smooth the furrow between her delicate brows. "Yes, this town decidedly lacks imagination. You stroll down the street and see signs that merely say, Mercantile, Livery, Blacksmith, Saloon. In England, everything has a name. White's. The Wild Boar. The Black Swan. You see, so much more appealing to the senses . . . a name, that is."

"I reckon you could call it Bainbridge's, you bein' the owner and all," she said caustically.

"I was thinking of something a bit more enticing. The Texas Lady, perhaps—"

"Harry, do you know what this place means to my pa?" She folded her arms on the table and leaned forward, her eyes imploring him to understand. So much for his thinking pity alone had the power to bring him to his knees. "It means everything to him."

"He invited *me* to play poker, and I was not the one who put the saloon in the pot," he pointed out in his own defense.

"Even if I give you the benefit of the doubt and think you didn't cheat, you know cards well enough that I figure you knew what he was holding, knew your hand beat his. You could have folded."

"Not really. He paid to see my hand. Honor dictated that we carry the game through to the end."

"You Englishmen have a strange understanding of honor."

"You are simply viewing last night's game through anger."

"Damn right I am, because I know you cheat."

"I did not cheat—"

"Then you sure are packin' a heavy load of luck."

She shoved her chair back and surged to her feet. Nearly throwing himself across the table, he grabbed her wrist. "We are not finished here."

"I made you a full partner in our cattle venture—"

"As I recall, I had to earn that honor."

She jerked her wrist free of his hold and easily stepped beyond his reach. Seething at his limitations, he settled back in his chair, trying to mask his frustration.

"He's earned the honor with years of sweat and toil," she spat.

"And he willingly gave it all away last night. I refuse to feel guilty because I held a more valuable hand. He could have walked away."

"So can I."

Swearing soundly, he watched her march up the stairs. So much for his notion that he could become a whole man in spirit, if not in body. She left him feeling very much like the scoundrel he'd once been and resenting like the devil that *he* could not walk away.

❧ Chapter 18 ❧

Pacing in her room, Jessye tried to block out the pounding of hammers hitting nails, crashes, banging, and ripe swearing ascending the stairs. Curiosity was killing her.

The knock on her door brought her to a halt. "Come in."

The door opened slightly, and her father peered inside, his grizzled features wary. "Ain't you comin' down to help?"

"No, Pa, I'm not."

"Now, Jessye, you can't stay mad. He won fair and square."

She shook her head in disgust. "You don't know him like I do, Pa."

"Know him better than you think. 'Sides, I'm still pourin' the drinks, and you're servin' 'em. Nothin's changed."

Everything had changed. Why was he blind to that fact?

"Now, come on, girl. The only thing worse than a lousy winner is a poor loser."

"I am not a poor loser," she pointed out, even as she sulked on her way to the door.

Smiling broadly, he closed the door behind her and patted her shoulder. "You'll see. Everything is gonna be fine."

She seriously doubted that, but she didn't want to hurt him any more than he was already hurt, and railing at him over playing cards with Harry would do little good now. She was nearly halfway down the stairs when the sight before her nearly caused her to lose her footing.

Grayson Rhodes stood atop a ladder hanging her crystal chandelier, an extravagance she'd indulged in shortly after the war ended. Her breath backed up in her lungs when he almost toppled before regaining his balance.

"Bloody hell, Gray. Take care. Jessye will have my head if you break that thing," Harry shouted.

"Jessye will have your head now," she informed him as she hurried down the remaining stairs and skirted around the banister.

And she would have, if he hadn't had a sleeping Colton nestled on his shoulder. The sight of Harry holding a child melted her anger. She quickly squeezed and opened her eyes to stop the tears that would put her feelings to shame. She angled her chin and planted her hands on her hips.

Harry raised a hand imploringly. "It's only a temporary measure, Jessye, just until Kit returns with our money and I can order another one. Right now, all we really have to offer is spit and polish, but . . . we just needed something special for tonight. Something to hint at the grandness I envision—"

"Bloody hell!" a voice croaked, a voice she recognized as belonging to Abbie's youngest son.

Jessye spun around to see Abbie and Micah struggling to right a can of whitewash. They had brushes in their hands, and uneven splotches marred the wall.

Abbie smiled with gratitude. "I'm so glad you're finally here. We can really use the help. I don't know how we'll get all these walls painted by tonight."

Stunned, Jessye could do little more than stare.

"How's this look, Mr. Bainbridge?"

Jessye turned and saw Johnny holding up a long plank of wood. With charcoal, he'd inscribed Texas Lady. On either side of the words, he'd drawn a lily.

"Looks good, lad, but take care in painting it," Harry instructed.

The boy puffed out his small chest and looked at Jessye. "I got to do the letterin' on account I got good penmanship. Pa said so."

She glanced up at Grayson to see him smiling at the boy with so much love and pride reflected in his eyes that it was difficult to remember Johnny wasn't his by blood.

"Come on, daughter, make yourself useful," her father scolded.

Along with Abbie's daughter, he was rubbing the counter with a rosin that made it shine.

"We can see our faces," Lydia said, beaming at Jessye's father as though he'd worked a miracle.

Laughing, he tweaked the girl's nose before returning to his task.

Jessye marched to the table, where Harry sat overlooking everyone's efforts. "What are you doing?" she demanded.

"Trying to increase profits." He raised a brow. "I looked the books over last night. This enterprise is not a very profitable one."

"We get by."

"If you were content with that, you never would have agreed to risk your savings on our cattle venture."

Colton made a tiny mewling sound, and Harry began to rub his back. An irritatingly distracting thing for him to do. His hand nearly swallowed the child's back, and she remembered the night he'd stroked her after they'd crossed the Red River. "That still doesn't explain what you're doing."

"This place is depressing. A man comes in here, orders a whiskey, and spends much of the night nursing that one drink and wishing things were different. The somberness of this establishment gives him no reason to order another drink, so we're going to liven it up a bit."

"With whitewashed walls, a sign"—she leaned forward until they were nearly nose to nose—"and my treasured chandelier?"

"And faro."

She jerked back. "Faro?"

"Do you play?"

"No, but I've heard of it."

He smiled devilishly, and her heart flipped over. "Gray is going to make us a faro table, perhaps two if I make it worth his while. There's money to be made with faro, more so than poker. We're going to order a higher grade of whiskey than this rotgut your father serves." He held up a hand. "No offense intended, but you know I'm right. We're going to offer the men a bit of culture and a chance to hand their money over to us."

She heaved a sigh. "Culture? Harry, the men of Fortune are farmers who need their money to purchase seed and tools—"

"I'm not referring to the men of Fortune. I'm talking about cattlemen. In spite of the hardships we endured, I believe cattle will one day be a booming business in this state. Cattle to the south of us will need to be moved north. It makes sense that they would follow the nearby Brazos River. We simply need to give the cattle drivers a reason to route the herds through this town. We won't make great profits all year long, but for a short time, we shall reap the rewards."

"And just how are you planning to let all these cattlemen know about your saloon?"

"I would think the answer was obvious. Magpie. Word of mouth. He's searching for cattle, crossing paths with others searching for cattle." He waved his hand magnanimously through the air. "Let's give them something to talk about. The Texas Lady shall become a legend before we're finished."

She rolled her eyes. "Oh, Harry, I thought I was a dreamer."

"You are, my love. Who do you think taught me?"

Damn him! He was appealing to all her soft spots. How could she stay angry with a scoundrel who spewed forth such sweet words?

"Hey, Mr. Bainbridge, I'm done with the sign," Johnny announced proudly, edging his way past Jessye to shove the plank in front of Harry's face.

Harry pressed his finger to the boy's arm and gently

moved it back. "Excellent, Johnny. I couldn't have done a better job myself." He leaned over so he could see around the boy. "Gray, help Johnny and Jessye hang the sign outside, will you?"

"Certainly." Grayson strode over and took Colton from Harry. "I think the whole family should see this." He hesitated. "Did you want—"

"No, no," Harry murmured. "Have too many details left to go over. Can't leave anything to chance."

"Right," Grayson said quietly, and Jessye saw sympathy in his eyes. "Chin up and all that rubbish."

"Right. Now get everyone out to watch you. I could use a few moments of quiet to ponder some of the remaining tasks. Jessye, go with him and see that he hangs it straight. I don't trust him with a hammer and nail."

"But you trusted him with my chandelier," she pointed out.

He smiled. "Touché. But be a good sport and oversee the hanging of the sign. For Johnny's sake. He's quite proud of it."

How could she refuse to give a child his moment in the sun? Yes, sir, Harrison Bainbridge was a manipulator, a cheater if she ever saw one.

By the time she stepped onto the boardwalk outside the saloon, nails were already in place, and Grayson held the ladder steady while Johnny reached up to hang the sign. She took several steps back to get a good look at the boy's efforts. Her gaze fell on the window, and she peered through it to see Harry.

He sat rigidly, his head bent, one hand gripping the table, while the other rubbed his right hip and thigh.

"Move away from the window, Jessye," Grayson said quietly.

She snapped her attention to him.

"Pity doesn't sit well with him," he said, his voice low.

She walked to the railing, wrapped her fingers around the coarse wood, and stared at the dusty street. "I don't pity him. I just hate to see him suffering."

"He's making progress."

She glanced up at him. "I haven't seen him walk using those crutches—"

"I don't imagine you will. He's a crafty fellow and too proud for his own good."

"He was already sitting at that table when I came down this morning—"

"And he'll probably be sitting there when you go to bed tonight."

"He needs to move around some."

"What he needs is to feel that he has some control over something. I have no doubt that you're angry at the manner in which he came to own this establishment, but for his sake, try and put your anger aside . . . at least for a while."

Putting her anger aside was damn near impossible as she glared at the gaudy dress he'd had someone sew for her. She couldn't deny that in the three weeks that he'd owned the saloon, business had been brisk.

She wasn't surprised that he had plans to set himself up as the faro dealer as soon as Grayson finished making the table. She had little doubt that his enterprise would make considerable money. A shame he hadn't thought of it before he became obsessed with herding cattle.

She touched the dress as though it were a snake. It looked more like a corset with a skirt that might graze her calves. She thought if she sneezed, her breasts, small as they were, would pop right out of the thing. The man was loco if he thought she was going to wear that as she served drinks.

She snatched it off the bed and headed down the stairs. Harry sat at his usual table, a young man she'd never seen sitting across from him, leaning forward slightly as though listening intently. The man's black craggy hair was in dire need of a haircut.

She tromped to the table. Harry slid his unnerving gaze to her while the young man snapped his head around. She almost staggered back with the shock of seeing such old eyes on a young face. She should be accustomed to seeing the wary look in the men returning from the war, but it always caught her off-guard.

The young man jumped to his feet, knocking over the chair. With one hand buried deep within the pocket of his jacket, he righted the chair with the other before looking at her as though he wished he'd died on some godforsaken battlefield.

"Jessye, this is William Vaughn."

She smiled warmly, hoping to put him at ease. "Mr. Vaughn."

"B . . . Billy. My friends call me Billy."

"Billy then."

"He's going to work for us, cleaning the saloon."

She smiled with gratitude at the young man. "I can certainly use the help."

"He's not going to help you," Harry explained. "He shall do all the cleaning. Your obligations to the Texas Lady end at midnight after we've sent the last drunkard out the door and closed it behind him."

She jerked her gaze to Harry. All her life, except for the time she'd herded cattle, she'd scrubbed, cleaned, and polished the saloon. She knew its surfaces as well as she knew the feel of her own skin. "I've always cleaned the saloon."

"And you've done a remarkable job, but it's taking a toll on you now that we are attracting more customers. You're losing weight and look exhausted."

She couldn't tell him that she looked tired because she wasn't sleeping well at night. She tossed and turned with thoughts of him, hating him one moment, loving him the next. Loving him weighed heavily on her mind, because her head warned her that she should despise him. "I appreciate the consideration."

"As well you should," he told her smugly, and she balled her hands around the green dress to stop them from slapping him.

He nodded toward Billy. "You'll find an empty room at the top of the stairs, last door on your left."

"Yes, sir. I appreciate it. You won't be sorry." Billy turned to leave.

"William," Harry snapped. The man glanced over his shoulder. "The first time I find you drunk is the last night you work for me."

Billy nodded. "Yes, sir."

Jessye watched him walk up the stairs. "Can we really afford to hire him?"

"I'm only paying him a dollar a day plus room and

board. He struck me as a man who did more than
squat in the shade."

She returned her gaze to Harry. "You've never forgiven me for saying that, have you?" She thrust the
dress at him. "Is that the reason for this?"

He gave the dress a passing glance as though it
were of no consequence. "The dress will entice men
to stay longer, purchase a few more drinks, and will
no doubt result in them slipping you an extra coin or
two—which you are welcome to keep."

Her jaws clenched until her teeth ached. "You're
generous to a fault, Harry. I am *not* wearing this indecent dress."

He arched a dark brow. "Some would say that you
were dressed indecently while we trailed cattle."

"At least I had everything of importance covered."

He chuckled. "Ah, yes, and it was nicely covered.
Do you realize that I knew the exact shape of your
rounded bottom before I ever held it?"

If her mouth hadn't gone suddenly dry, she thought
she might have spit at him. "And now you want to
gawk at my bosom? Well, I ain't gonna wear it." She
spun on her heel.

"You *will* wear it," he said with a deadly calm that
sent icy chills rippling up her spine.

She swung around.

"You will wear it," he repeated, "because I own the
saloon and you work for me. So you will do as I say
or you and your father will find yourselves on the
street."

She clutched the dress, her fingers digging through
the fabric into her palms. "I always knew you were a
scoundrel, but I never realized until now that you
were such a pitifully small man."

Chapter 19

*T*he pitifully small man tipped the bottle, poured himself another glass of whiskey, and cursed his brilliant ideas.

He'd been right. Tonight the saloon was packed—men stood, backs against the walls, because every chair was occupied. Barely keeping pace with the customers' demands, Jessye looked like a rag doll, ready to fall into a heap at any moment. He'd need to hire another serving girl, perhaps two.

Men were doing what they'd never before done as she served their drinks: trailed their fingers over her bare arm, slapped her on the rump, leered at the small swells of her breasts revealed by the low cut of the dress.

The rage surged through him because he'd placed her in this embarrassing predicament and was in no position to protect her. What in God's name had possessed his mind when he'd ordered the damn thing?

He'd wanted control, to feel like a man again, whole and complete.

Instead, he felt like cow dung.

The last thing he'd ever wanted was to harm her,

but since the encounter with Milton, he'd taken all his frustration out on her . . . he'd tried to force her into hating him because he thought only then would he stop loving her.

He squeezed his eyes closed. Oh, God, he wanted her, but how could he expect her to accept him: a man crippled of body and, more, crippled of heart?

Opening his eyes, he grabbed the bottle and slammed it against the wall, spewing liquor and glass. The saloon fell into an eerie hush, and all eyes turned on him. At least they no longer were focused on her breasts.

Her brow furrowed, she rushed over, and the pain of regret stabbed him deeply.

"Harry, what are you doing?" She sank to the floor and picked up shards of glass.

"Leave that for Billy," he ordered. "Bring me another bottle of whiskey, then go change out of that damnably annoying dress."

Defiance and victory shot into her eyes as she slowly rose. "Thought you wanted me to wear this dress."

"I changed my mind." He arched a brow. "That is not a prerogative limited to women, you know."

He watched her raging battle: defying him, against running upstairs to rip off the hated garment.

"Please," he offered with genuine contriteness, "go change into something better suited to your . . . temperament."

As though recognizing that she may have won more than a battle, she gave a slight nod. She went to the bar, grabbed a bottle of whiskey, and returned it to his table before stomping up the stairs.

*   *   *

With a weary sigh, Jessye closed the saloon doors and
locked them. Habit forced her to place the key into
her skirt pocket. Tightening her fingers around the
metal, she withdrew it, charged across the saloon, and
tossed it onto the table where Harry sat. She pivoted.

"Sit down," he commanded.

She spun around. "Harry, I'm tired and I got cleaning to do."

"Billy will handle the cleaning."

As though waiting for a summons, the young man
emerged from the back, one hand stuffed in his coat
pocket as he carried a bucket of water. "Thought I'd
get the floor done first, then them dishes."

"Whatever works best for you," Harry said. "Now,
Jessye, sit."

"I'm not a dog to follow commands—"

He sighed in exasperation. "Please."

She angled her chin. "Pretty please?"

She watched his jaw tighten. "Pretty please with
sugar on it."

She dragged back a chair and plopped down, relishing the small victory.

Leaning over, he grabbed her calf. She jerked free,
suspicion lurking. "What do you think you're doing?"

"I am going to remove your shoes and rub your
feet. As much as you ran around tonight, they must
hurt."

The man was gifted with understatement, but the
impropriety . . .

She glanced over her shoulder at Billy, who was
on his knees scrubbing tobacco juice stains from the
floor.

"He's too busy to notice," Harry said quietly.

"I oughta show him how it's done. He's gonna be here all night. He needs to scrub the floor with both hands—"

"I rather imagine he would if he had two hands to use."

She snapped her gaze to his. "I thought—"

He shook his head. "He prefers to keep his lack of a hand hidden so it appears he has it shoved in his pocket. In truth, he left it on some battlefield. This bloody war your country fought seems to have left few men whole."

An image of Gerald Milton flashed through her mind.

"Don't think of Milton—"

"How did you know?"

"The sadness, the regret that touches your eyes. Did you purchase the doll?"

She nodded. "Haven't found the gumption to mail it yet."

"You will in time."

"I'm just not sure it's the right thing to do. Madeline invited me to visit them anytime, but I told her I couldn't. It about killed me to say good-bye."

Harry leaned forward. "When you said good-bye before, in both cases, you thought it was forever. You've been handed a gift, Jessye my love. The chance to say good-bye, knowing another day will come when you can again say hello."

The temptation to visit her daughter was greater than anything she'd ever experienced. Just a time or two. To watch her grow, to see her happy. Harry was right. She had been handed a gift. She'd given her daughter over to strangers, and two Englishmen had crossed an ocean, and their paths had brought her past back into the present. Fate was an intertwined tapestry that she should accept rather than question. She nodded. "I'll send the doll and see what happens."

"Good." He patted his thigh. "Now, give me your feet. You've rubbed more than mine. Let me return the favor by easing your hurt."

The heat suffused her face as she studied him carefully. "Give me your word that your hands won't wander above my ankles."

He placed a hand over his heart. "You wound me with your distrust—"

"Your word."

He smiled slightly. "You have it."

Lifting her feet, she carefully placed them in his lap, grateful she sat to his left. She didn't know if his right hip could bear the weight. She watched, mesmerized, as his deft fingers untied the laces to her shoes and slipped them off. When those fingers kneaded the soles of her feet, she thought she might turn into a pool of hot wax and slide to the floor. Closing her eyes, she dropped her head back. "This is gonna go a long way toward earning my forgiveness."

"What do you have to forgive me for?"

She squinted at him. "Stealing the saloon, making me wear that gawdawful dress."

He grimaced. "Regarding that dress ... I'm going to say something to you that I have never said to anyone else in my entire life."

She angled her head thoughtfully, waiting expectantly. She watched him swallow.

"I apologize profusely for treating you badly." The raspy words sounded as though he'd pushed them through clenched teeth. He pressed his fingers into her feet, then relaxed.

"Why did you do it?" she asked.

"Stupidity. Arrogance. A gamble."

"What were you gambling on?"

"That you would leave."

"Who did you make the wager with?"

"My heart."

Her chest tightened as he looked away, but his fingers never ceased their movements. She imagined his tender kneading making its way up her calf, to her thigh . . . she had been no stranger to pleasures of the flesh, but Harry had taught her things she'd never dared to dream.

She heard the shuffling gait and tried to pull her feet from Harry's lap. With a wicked glint in his eyes, he held fast. Her father stepped out from the back.

"Books are done. We had a hell of a night."

Harry nodded. "Gray should have the faro table finished in another week or so. Business should improve considerably once we get it set up."

"Well, I always knew the old girl would do good," he murmured, patting Jessye's shoulder. She watched him amble slowly toward the stairs and climb them as though he carried the weight of the world on his shoulders.

She jerked her feet from Harry's lap before he could grab her ankles. "I'll forgive you for the dress, but never for taking the saloon from him." She started to rise.

"Care to win it back?" he asked, his offer a low, seductive caress.

She sank into the chair. "What?"

He shuffled a deck of cards, his gaze holding hers. "A small game of chance, and I'll give you the opportunity to win back the saloon."

Her heart pounded as she scrutinized him. "You're gonna put the saloon in the pot?"

He slapped the deck onto the table, right in its center. "Yes. Two cuts of the deck. You first. Me second. High card takes the stakes."

"So if I cut to the higher card, I get the saloon back?"

"That's right."

"And if you cut to the high card?"

"You spend the night in my bed."

Blood rushed through her head, pounding between her temples. She grew hot on the outside, cold on the inside. She desperately wanted to tell him to go to hell, but the haunting memories of the years her father had struggled to keep this place going, the look on his face the night he signed the papers over, the regret in his eyes tonight—

"You'll cheat."

He rolled up his sleeves and held out his hands, palms up, fingers splayed. "How can I cheat when I'm not holding the deck? You don't even have to show me your card until after I've cut for my card."

Her mouth went dry, her gaze darting between him and the deck. She'd lost her virtue at the age of seventeen. Its value was nothing. But her body. She'd given it to Gerald out of love. To Harry once out of desperate feelings that confused her even now.

That he would consider making this offer made her feel sordid and dirty. A saloon in exchange for her body. It was more than soiled doves were offered. And in the end, she knew it wasn't the saloon she wanted, but her father's pride.

She snatched up a portion of the deck, pressed the cards to her chest, and slowly angled them to reveal the top card. A jack of hearts.

"I assume you're accepting the terms of the wager?" Harry asked.

She glared at him. "Just cut to a card."

With a smooth fluid flick of the wrist, he tossed the top card onto the table. A queen.

Her heart sank to the floor as she fought to draw in a breath and set her cards on the table face up.

"I realize you might have some concerns over your reputation. You need not come to my room until after Billy retires."

She stood, shaking so badly that she was surprised her teeth stayed rooted. "You're so considerate."

She spun on her heel.

"Jessye?"

She glanced over her shoulder.

"Be sure to wear your softest nightgown."

Jessye stared at the door that led into Harry's room, a room that had once been hers. Strange how she no longer considered it her room.

Pride had forced her to bathe, brush her hair to a sheen, and slip into her cotton nightgown. She would endure the night, but derive no pleasure from it, and in the end, in some warped manner, she'd be able to claim the victory as hers.

She'd prayed that Billy would take all night to finish cleaning the saloon, but she'd heard him enter his room shortly after she'd entered hers. Instinctively, she knew Harry had sent him to bed without finishing up his duties. He'd probably justified excusing him early because it was his first night to work.

It would be her last. Tomorrow she would leave. Kit could send the money from the cattle drive to her. Meanwhile, she'd survive on the pittance she had and be glad of it.

She took a deep, unsteady breath, hating the jitters that cascaded through her. She rapped lightly on the door.

Harry's low, deep voice bid her to enter.

She opened the door. Harry sat on the edge of the bed wearing nothing but trousers, his bare feet enhancing the intimacy of seeing his chest bare. Her toes curled against the floor.

He gripped one of the bed's four posters and slowly, painstakingly, pulled himself to his feet. His knuckles turned white, and she saw within the harsh lines of his face what it cost him to remain standing, the shame he felt because he could not come to her. She would have to go to him.

Her heart melted.

She quietly closed the door and padded across the room. She watched his throat work as he swallowed. With his free hand, he cradled her cheek with such tenderness that she thought she might weep. His gaze swept across her face like a lover's caress.

"Do you remember the exact words of the wager?" he asked quietly.

She furrowed her brow. "I'm to spend the night in your bed."

His thumb stroked the corner of her mouth. "Listen carefully to the words, Jessye, for they are the key to your deliverance. Spend the night in my bed. That is *all* that we wagered. I expect nothing more." He held her gaze. "Nothing more."

Her stomach felt as though a noose had just been loosened. "You mean you just want me to sleep in your bed?"

He gave her a devilish grin. "What I *want* does not enter into the wager. You need not touch me. You need not invite me to touch you. Although I shall no doubt attempt to persuade you that you want more than a night simply lying in my bed."

She knew it would take little to persuade her.

Releasing a groan, he closed his eyes and sank to the bed. She dropped to her knees and placed her hand against his right hip. "You're in pain. Do you want me to get the salve and work it in—"

"No," he growled. He took her chin between his thumb and forefinger and lifted her gaze to his. "For tonight, I do not want you to view me as a cripple."

Her heart very nearly shattered. "Harry, you're not—"

He pressed his finger to her lips, silencing her words. "Get into bed."

She glanced past him to the head of the bed, where he'd turned down the covers. She wondered at the effort he must have exerted to make the bed appear welcoming. She rose, walked a short distance away from where he sat, and slipped between the sheets. She scooted over, making room for him to join her.

She became aware of an edginess about him, a wariness, and she wondered if he was as nervous with tonight's arrangement as she was. "I'd forgotten how comfortable my bed is," she said softly, hoping to ease the tension.

"I never intended to kick you out of your bed."

"You didn't. I offered."

"I doubt climbing stairs will ever again . . . be my forté, but hopefully, soon, I shall be able to take up lodging somewhere else."

"I don't mind you being here as long as you aren't breaking my things."

"What about your heart?"

Her breath backed up in her lungs. "What?"

"Do you ever worry that I'll break your heart?"

"No," she lied. "You know my heart shattered long ago. It can't be mended as easily as broken china."

"Do you think it can be mended at all?"

"I don't know. Shouldn't you be getting into bed?"

"Turn down the lamp," he said quietly, apparently finding the floor more interesting than the woman in his bed. She didn't want to think of all the women with whom he might have been intimate. The first time she'd set eyes on him, his handsome features had very nearly struck her dumb. The odd thing was that even though she knew him better now, his features still had the same effect on her.

She rolled over and lowered the flame until its muted glow allowed the shadows to flow into the room. Harry became little more than a silhouette sitting on the edge of the bed. He lifted the covers, and in the darkness, she still detected the awkwardness of his movements as he maneuvered to get beneath the sheet. He had yet to remove his britches, and she imagined how ungainly he might appear as he did so.

If only she knew how to convince him that none of that mattered. If only . . .

Harrison lay in the bed, straining to hear her breathing and inhaling her faint lily fragrance. She'd worn her hair down, brushed until it shone like a liquid flame. He desperately wanted to plow his fingers through it. With any luck, she'd drift off to sleep shortly, and he'd have the opportunity to touch it, perhaps to stroke it across his mouth.

"Harry?" she whispered, as though someone else were in the room to overhear them.

"Mmm?" He continued to stare at the ceiling, fearing that if he glanced at her, his restraint would snap like a brittle twig.

"This is really all you want, for me to *sleep* in your bed?"

"That was the wager."

"You risked losing the saloon just to have me sleep in your bed?"

"Why does that strike you as so odd?"

"I don't know. I just always thought men—"

"How many men have you slept with?"

Silence stretched between them before she finally confessed, "I've told you before. There was that night with you. And of course, the nights with Gerald."

Both had certainly taken her on a journey through hell.

" 'Course, I didn't really sleep with Gerald. We'd just sneak away for a few minutes—"

"A few minutes?" He rolled his head to the side to look at her. A mistake. Even though she was little more than a shadowy waif, he wanted to touch her.

"We were young, eager."

He smiled at her indignation, and he thought if he hadn't asked her to turn down the flame in the lamp, he would see her blushing and angling that cute chin of hers.

"But still, a few moments? Where did you sneak away to?"

"The loft in the livery or maybe we'd just go out beneath the stars—"

"On the ground? The man was a true romantic."

"You'd never take a woman on the ground?"

He grimaced at the challenging reminder of the night they'd shared. He would take her anywhere he could have her. "You're right. You deserved better from me that night."

"How many women have you bedded?"

"Not nearly enough."

She laughed, a soft, gentle sound that rolled through him.

"Harry, you scoundrel, you'll have me confessing everything and you won't reveal anything."

He rolled onto his side, wincing at the pain that the sudden movement caused. "What do you want to know?"

She shifted so she was facing him. How easy it would be to simply reach out—

"Why did your father send you here?"

He scoffed. "I thought we were going to discuss my paramours—"

"Truth be told, I figure you had too many to keep count."

"Three," he said quietly. "The first was blond. The

second had hair the shade of a raven's wing. And the third"—he took a curling lock of her hair between his thumb and forefinger and brought it to his lips—"had glorious red hair."

He took satisfaction in hearing her breath hitch.

"You're telling me you've only bedded two other women?"

"The wooing and courting takes more effort than squatting in the shade. I prefer to expend my energies in other pursuits."

"Gambling."

"It is a passion, at times an obsession. And when Lady Luck does not smile upon me, it is a dangerous endeavor. I owed some very unsavory men a great deal of money. Rather than discover his second son drowned in the Thames, my father offered to pay off my debts if I agreed to come here."

She rose up on an elbow, stirring up her sweet fragrance. He inhaled deeply, savoring the scent.

"But you cheat—"

"You suspect that I cheat. You have yet to prove it. Besides, a gentleman may gamble away his allowance in a number of ways: horses, boxing—"

"You struck me as being smarter than that."

"Smarter, but not necessarily wiser. I sought to bring shame upon my family's name as my family had brought shame to me. I expected my father to disown me." He glanced past her to the shadowed corner. "Instead he sought to save me."

She cradled his cheek, and he felt the callused pads of her palm and fingers. "You know what your problem is, Harry? You don't understand your own worth."

He held his breath as she blocked the pale light of the low, flickering flame, coming nearer, closer, until her lips touched his as gently as a butterfly lights upon a petal. Once. Twice. Her fingers pressed harder against his face as her mouth settled over his.

Groaning deeply, he plowed his hands into her hair, cupping the back of her head, while his tongue taunted and teased until she parted her lips, giving him full access to her mouth. She whimpered softly, and the curve of her breasts brushed against his bare chest.

He pulled her back, angling her head so that the shadows ebbed away to reveal the pale green of her eyes. "Take care, my love, for I will call your bluff."

"If only I were bluffing . . ."

The wistfulness in her voice served as a siren song stronger than he'd ever heard. Her mouth returned to his with urgency. Their tongues parried, upping the stakes. Regrets would no doubt be the price they both paid, but he had long ago learned to live with regrets.

Jessye wasn't sure when she realized that simply sleeping in his bed wasn't what she wanted, but she knew it with a frightening certainty. She was setting herself up for heartache, and even as she damned herself for doing it, she welcomed the sensation of his fingers skimming along her throat, her collarbone, until they reached the first button of her nightgown. She braced herself over him, each button easily giving way as his hand slowly journeyed to her waist, to the last button.

Only then did he withdraw from the kiss, his breathing labored, his gaze intent. He cradled her face, his thumb tenderly stroking her cheek. "I'll give you one more opportunity to fold."

She placed her hand flat on his bare chest, right above his pounding heart. If only it were in the pot . . . wishful thinking that made no difference to her decision because she'd given him her heart long ago, on a star-filled night. She lifted her gaze to his. "I'm not folding."

"Sit up," he rasped in a voice that sounded strangled with emotions.

She did as he bid, tucking her feet beneath her, watching his eyes as they slowly roamed the length of her, warming each place they touched. He lifted his hands to the parted material of her gown. More slowly than she thought possible, he moved the material off her shoulders. The gown skimmed along her back until it pooled at her hips.

"Dear God, but you are more lovely than I imagined," he said in a low, reverent voice. "I could not see you clearly before."

He trailed his finger along the curve of a breast, sending warmth spiraling through her. "No freckles," he murmured as he rose up on an elbow. "I shall be the envy of the sun."

He folded his hand around the nape of her neck, bringing her closer. He kissed her lips, the sensitive underside of her jaw, her throat. His mouth was hot and moist, gentle but demanding, demanding that her body respond—as though it had a choice.

He moved his hands down, bracing her ribs on either side as his mouth took a leisurely sojourn over the swells of her breasts. Unexpected heat shot through her, melting her limbs, her bones, her very soul until she felt like the molten wax of a candle, giving way so the fire could continue to consume.

It had been too long since she'd felt this way . . . no, no, she'd never felt this way, as though each second were an eternity. His tongue circled her nipple, and her breathing became shallow, need and desires unfurling. His fingers dug into her flesh as his mouth latched onto her nipple and he suckled.

She released a tiny cry and arched back. She threaded her fingers through his hair. "Harry . . ."

He rolled her to her back and pulled her gown past her feet, exposing her full body to his perusal. Nothing before had prepared her for the patience this man bestowed upon her now.

His mouth captured hers, hungrily tasting and devouring as though his patience had come to an end, but he swept his hand over her body as though in no hurry, as though he sought to memorize with touch what he was unable to see clearly within the faint light hovering at the edge of the bed.

She pressed her hands to his chest, felt the quivering of his muscles, and only then realized the strain he attempted to hide. Gently, she shoved against him, guiding him to his back. "You're cheatin', Harry," she whispered near his ear before nipping it.

"How so, love?"

"Making me show my hand without revealing yours." She moved the sheet aside. He grabbed it and jerked it back into place.

"I'll do it," he said, his voice strained.

Her heart ached as she pressed a kiss to the center of his chest. "That's no fun."

His hand came up to cradle her head. "Then douse the flame completely."

She lifted her face to his. "No."

She slid her hand beneath the sheet and unfastened his britches. She felt his gaze boring into her as she eased the trousers past his hips, his thighs, his calves, his feet, and slung them off the bed. She sat back on her heels, giving herself the luxury of looking at him as he had looked at her. His hands were clenched into tight fists at his sides.

"I know my legs—"

She met his gaze squarely and smiled warmly. "Oh, I'm admiring a great deal more than your legs." She laid her hand on his flat stomach. "You are fine looking."

"You are blind."

She'd often heard that love was—and now she knew it to be true. She kissed his misshapen hip and trailed her mouth along his body until it met his lips. "Maybe."

She felt the rumble of his chest against her breasts as he groaned, clasping her to him as though she were a lifeline in a turbulent sea. The patience was gone, replaced by an almost desperate need to possess her. He shifted them both until she was again on her back, and he was nestled snuggly between her thighs. His mouth possessed hers with an undeniable urgency. She raised her knees, and he slid inside her with one long, sure stroke.

Nothing had prepared her for this moment of rightness. It no longer mattered that his heart was not hers to heal, for he had somehow managed to piece hers back together.

He rocked against her, increasing her pleasure even as she heard his strangled grunts.

Without warning, he withdrew and rolled off her, gasping for breath.

"Harry—"

"Shh." He pressed her face into the nook of his shoulder.

"You're in pain."

"We can do this another way." With his hand, he cupped her intimately, his fingers caressing as he sought her mouth.

Even as the sensations mounted, she held back, sliding her mouth from his and pressing her lips to his damp throat. "No."

She eased him back. Raining kisses over his face, she whispered, "I want you, Harry."

She straddled his hips. "I want everything you can give me."

"I wish to God I could offer you more."

"Why pray for more when I'm content with what you have?" She lifted her hips and slowly sank down, sheathing him like a glove. She ran her hands up and down his chest as she rocked back and forth.

He released a guttural sound, his gaze latched onto her as his hands molded her breasts and his fingers taunted. Sensations spiraled and coiled within her. She felt his body tensing.

The pleasure mounted, peaked, and she stood at the precipice, hovering.

He splayed his fingers across her back, drew her down until her curves were pressed against the hardened planes of his body. He flipped her over, and his final driving thrusts sent her flying over the precipice.

With a harsh moan, he arched his back and stilled. His arms quivered as he lowered himself. She felt the whisper of a kiss across her temple before he rolled off her and drew her into the curve of his dew-coated body.

Lethargically, she lay there, one hand curled against his chest, trapped between their bodies, while the other gently rubbed his hip.

"Does this get better with experience or age?" she asked.

"A little of both I should imagine." He cradled her face and turned it up slightly. "Was it better for you?"

She gave him a tired smile. "Much."

He gave her the devilish grin that so easily melted her heart. "Of course, in your case, it could simply be because we took more than a few moments."

"Was it better for you?"

His smile eased away. "Incredibly so, and it shouldn't have been."

Her fingers tensed on his hip. "Because you were in pain."

"Perhaps we should put this experience to the test and see if it remains . . . better."

Jessye awoke to the gray light of dawn easing through the curtains. Her bare backside was pressed against the curve of Harry's stomach. They had put the experience to the test several more times throughout the night—and it was always better.

She now knew his body almost as well as she knew her own. Guilt should have gnawed at her. Instead sadness swelled within her. She would never again have a night like this, for although their bodies had spoken volumes, neither of them had voiced declarations of love.

She eased toward the edge of the bed. Harry's hold on her tightened.

"Where are you going?" he asked lazily.

"The night's over."

To her profound regret, he loosened his hold.

"A pity."

She squeezed her eyes shut against the threatening tears. She moved away from him, snatched up her nightgown, and slid it over her head. Fearing her heart was reflected in her eyes, she rose and walked to the door, but she felt his gaze following her movements.

"Jessye?"

She glanced over her shoulder. He sat in the bed, the sheet draped up to his waist, his hair standing up on one side, almost making her smile, his face solemn.

He bunched his fists around the sheet. "I give you my word, as God is my witness, that I did not cheat your father the night I won the saloon."

Relief swamped her, and for reasons she couldn't explain, she believed him now as she'd never believed him before. She gave a curt nod, tears burning the back of her throat. She put her hand on the knob, took a deep breath, and looked back at him. "What about last night? Did you cheat when we cut the deck?"

She saw the battle raging across his features before remorse settled within his eyes. "Yes."

She fought back the tears and swallowed to push down the lump that had risen in her throat. She angled her chin defiantly. "Hell, Harry, I'd be flattered if I weren't the only woman you have access to."

With as much dignity as she could muster, she jerked open the door, walked through it, and slammed it in her wake. She heard him call her name, but she continued down the hallway, her shattering heart drowning the echo of his voice.

❧ Chapter 20 ❧

She should be bloody well flattered, Harrison thought as he jerked up a pillow and brought his arm back to throw it at the door.

Her scent wafted around him. He lowered his arm and buried his face in the pillow, the pillow she'd lain on through the night. Her fragrance had seeped into the feathers, into his memory.

And memories were probably all he would have for the remainder of his life. A thousand times through the night he'd considered telling her that he loved her, but the words had clogged his throat.

He would rather die than hear her laughter if he revealed his heart. He had always valued the rewards of risk, and when he thought of all he might gain if he risked his heart . . .

He pulled the pillow away and glanced at the rumpled sheets where she had lain. Last night had been the sweetest of his life, and the most passionate. He had known it would be so.

Ignoring the throbbing pain in his hip, he swung his legs off the bed and sat brooding. He should have told her the truth, but her eyes had held such hope that he was a better man than he was.

Her faith in him was a burden he could not carry.

Jessye knew she should have flopped onto her bed and fallen into a deep sleep, but she was restless, feeling like a caged animal searching for a way to get beyond the iron bars. She'd been awake most of the night, sleeping only during small snatches of time. She'd hated the moments when she'd failed to stay awake. If Harry wasn't making love to her, he was talking in a resonant voice that had served to arouse her passions as much as his hands and mouth.

He was a master with his hands. Little wonder he could manipulate cards. He'd certainly manipulated her: heart, body, and soul.

As much as she wanted to hate him for it, she couldn't. She would carry the memories of last night with her until the day she died, knowing her final thoughts would be of him.

Her maudlin mood broke when she stepped into the kitchen. She narrowed her eyes at the mess she beheld. Harry *had* sent Billy to bed early—before he'd cleaned a single thing. Why had she expected less?

She heated the water and began washing the glasses, grateful for the distraction. Busy hands and all that. She smiled at the thought; it sounded too much like Harry.

She heard the shuffling gait and glanced over her shoulder.

"Gawd Almighty!" her father exclaimed as he glanced around the room with a critical eye. "Looks like a damned tornado come through here."

"I think Harry excused Billy early, it being his first night and all."

"Sounds like somethin' Harry would do. Not doin' things when they should be done just makes you have to work that much harder later on. Some men never learn that."

She watched as her father slipped his head through the neck of his apron and tied it behind him. "You wash and I'll dry," he offered.

She nodded slightly and handed him a glass. She watched his wrinkled, gnarled hands efficiently wipe the glass just as he'd so often wiped away her sorrows. She felt the tears welling. "I love you, Pa."

"I love you, too." He touched his roughened knuckle to her cheek. "What's wrong, girl?"

"I just needed to hear the words."

He studied her as he had when she was a child reluctant to confess a wrongdoing. "You look tired, daughter."

"I didn't sleep much last night. I . . . I . . ." She turned her attention to the murky tub of water. "Harry told me that he didn't cheat you the night he won the saloon."

"And you stayed up ponderin' that fact, feelin' guilty for distrusting him? Why didn't you just ask me? I coulda told you he didn't cheat."

She smiled warmly at him. "Now how would you know whether or not he cheated?"

"On account I was the one that did the cheatin'."

Her heart slammed against her ribs. "What?"

He grinned with pride. "Yep. Used to be good at it when I was young, but your ma made me promise when I married her that I'd stop, and I kept that promise. I haven't cheated in years. I was grateful to see I hadn't lost the knack for turnin' a card."

Shaking her head, she laughed. "Pa, you're supposed to cheat to ensure that you win."

His grin eased away and his eyes reflected wisdom. "You cheat when it's worth it in order to gain somethin' better."

She widened her eyes. "But, Pa, you lost!"

"What did I lose, Jessye? A building? Wood and glass. And what did I win? My old daughter back. He was hurtin' you, girl, and you were lettin' him do it. Wouldn't tell him to go to hell, not until he owned this saloon. Then you were standing up to him again."

"Are you saying you lost this saloon on purpose so I'd tell him—"

"So you'd stop looking at him like he was a cripple. So he'd stop feeling like one. I gave him a reason to crawl out of bed in the morning. A man needs that. And look at what he's done with the place. We're making more money now than we ever have."

"He needs it, and you don't?"

He cupped her chin. "I have your love, Jessye girl. That's all I need. Probably all he needs as well."

She stared at him. "Are you saying I should love him?"

"Don't you already?"

She jerked her chin free of his hold. "I'm trying not to. He's a scoundrel, Pa. He knows nothing about loving. Why last night, he—" The heat suffused her face, hotter than the water she was using to clean the glasses. She couldn't tell him the truth about last night.

"He what?"

"He just cheated me is all."

Her father narrowed his eyes. "Do I need to be gettin' out my shotgun?"

"No, Pa. I knew the risks when I sat down to play him."

He leaned near. "I could teach you what I know of cheatin'—"

She smiled lovingly. "No, I think we got enough cheaters in this here saloon."

Using the crutches for leverage and balance, Harrison slid his hand over the faro table. "Looks good, Gray."

"I thought you'd be pleased."

"I'm more than pleased. A share of the profits will go to you."

"Then you'd best find an exceptional dealer."

"I plan to handle that myself."

Gray raised a brow. "Indeed? What do you know of faro?"

Since the night Jessye had spent in his bed, Harrison had fought to move beyond the shadows. Although his movements were still awkward, and he was dependent on the crutches, he knew his legs were growing stronger. But his hip. He feared it would never again have the strength to support the whole of his weight.

"I know the rules and I know that it will be a challenge. I need a challenge."

The front door opened. Jessye stepped through and staggered to a stop, her eyes widening as she stared at him. He had avoided allowing her to see him as he truly was, always making certain he was at his table before she came downstairs for the day, never leaving before she retired for the night.

The excitement over the faro table had made him careless. He straightened himself as much as possible. "I thought you were seeing to supplies."

She closed her mouth and the door. "I was." She held out an envelope. "But you had this waiting at the post office."

"What is it?"

"I think it's from Kit."

"Well, then bring it over. Let's have a look."

Despite her aloofness in the two weeks since their clandestine meeting, he could not prevent his gaze from caressing her as she strolled across the room. She was so incredibly lovely. He took the envelope from her, removed the parchment, and unfolded it.

"What does it say?" Gray asked.

He scowled at his friend. "Give me a moment to read it." He had no idea what personal things Kit may have included.

Dear Harry,

We finally reached Chicago. Tell Jessye that her investment will be returned tenfold.

I plan to travel to Fortune at a leisurely pace, seeking out other opportunities for wealth. I suggest you keep your eyes and ears open. Driving cattle is too damn lonely and too much work. I shall leave it to the men who find it satisfying to endure suffering and hardship. There seems to be an overabundance of the fellows.

Look for me to arrive before Christmas.

Kit

Harry glanced up from the letter and met Jessye's gaze. "He says your investment will be returned tenfold."

She leaned forward, her eyes wide with disbelief. "Tenfold? You mean ten-times?"

"That's what he says, and Kit has never been one to lie."

She sank back against the wall as though all the breath had been knocked from her. "Tenfold. My God. I can go anywhere, do anything. Independent. I'll be completely independent."

Harrison felt as though someone had just bludgeoned him. When Kit returned, she would carry out her promise. She would leave. He darted a look at Gray. "Will you excuse us for a moment?"

"I need to head home, anyway, but one more thing before I go." He reached behind him, grabbed a cane with a hooked handle, and extended it toward Harrison. "I made this for you."

Harrison wished Grayson had presented it to him before Jessye had arrived. It was bad enough that she'd seen him on crutches. He didn't want her to think he might never progress beyond a cane. But the workmanship on Gray's gift was remarkable. "It's a very handsome . . . piece of work. Thank you."

"I just wanted it to be there when you were ready for it."

"I do appreciate it."

Gray nodded. "Let me know how the table works out."

"I will." He watched Gray walk through the door before returning his attention to Jessye.

She moved forward and braced her hands on the table, concern clearly reflected in her eyes. "Kit said more than that. He has some bad news."

"No, no bad news. However, he doesn't plan to rush back."

She smiled brightly, closing her fists and pressing them to her chest as though she needed to hold all the good news close. "It doesn't matter. Just knowing that it's coming—"

"Jessye . . ."

Her smile withered away. "What's wrong?"

He cleared his throat. "The night that you came to my room. I took no precautions to ensure that I did not get you with child. I realize it's only been a little over two weeks, probably too soon to know for sure—"

She waved a hand in the air. "I took precautions."

He was caught off guard not only by her words, but also by the disappointment reeling through him. "What?"

"After you kissed me in Dallas, I figured sooner or later I'd weaken. After you put Kit to bed, I went out and talked with some soiled doves—"

"You went out alone at night!"

"Will you calm down. I survived."

"Only by the grace of God. Have you any idea what might have happened?"

"Yes! I could have gone through the hell of havin' to give up another baby. So I had *those* women tell me a couple of things that I could do to make sure I didn't get with child." She lifted a shoulder. "That evening on the trail after you almost drowned, I was caught unaware, but the night I came to your room, I came prepared. I'm never going through the hell of giving up my baby again."

"I would have married you."

A corner of her mouth curved up into a knowing smile. "I appreciate the sentiment, Harry, but you can't stay faithful to the top card on the deck if you think the one on the bottom is better looking."

He watched her stroll away, the pain in his hip insignificant when compared to the anguish in his heart.

Harrison studied his reflection in the mirror. He thought he looked quite dapper. When he wasn't sitting at the faro table, he practiced walking in his room with the cane Gray had made for him. He'd fallen more than once, bruising his pride more than his body.

But tonight he'd bathed, shaved, trimmed his hair, and put on his starched white shirt, red brocade vest, black waistcoat, and trousers.

A bloody shame no one would see him.

But he wanted his first excursion into the saloon to be late at night, after everyone had gone to bed. He still wasn't pleased with the speed of his walk, but shuffling across the small bedroom had grown tedious. He needed to push a little harder, a greater distance.

He heard the tinkle of glasses, pots, and pans fall into silence. He held his breath, listening for Billy's footsteps echoing along the hallway. Jessye would have already retired. Her father as well. Billy was the last for the night.

He met his gaze in the mirror. "Let's see how you do, old boy."

Squaring his shoulders, he leaned heavily on the cane, and with minute steps made his way to the door. Quietly, he opened it and peered into the hall. All was clear.

He moved into the hallway, trying to ignore the horrid sound of one foot dragging after the other. Still, he no longer heard the *clomp, clomp* of one crutch hitting the floor before another. The cane was quieter, but it did not provide the support to which he'd become accustomed. Sweat beaded his forehead, and he strained to breathe as though he were running instead of moving at a snail's pace. He wouldn't make it to the faro table on the far side of the saloon tonight, but by God, he would not stop until he'd at least reached his table at the back of the saloon.

He turned the corner. The table came into sight.

"Harry!"

He jerked his head around and froze. Jessye stood at the bar, her mouth agape.

"Harry, you're walking."

"I wouldn't go that far."

She smiled with absolute pleasure. "I would. Sit down. Let's celebrate." She leaned over the bar and grabbed a bottle of whiskey and two glasses.

Pride had him taking larger steps than was wise. Near the table, he teetered, grabbed the chair for support, and practically toppled onto the seat, the jarring motion sending shards of pain through his hip. "I'd intended this exercise to be done in private, not before an audience," he grumbled as he righted himself.

"Ah, Harry, when will you realize that I don't care

that you're not as graceful as you once were." She sat
and poured whiskey into the glasses.

He narrowed his eyes. "You've been drinking already."

"Just one. Maybe two. All right. Three. I couldn't
sleep. Thought it would help." She smiled brightly.
"When do you think Kit will get here?"

"I haven't a clue. He mentioned something about
trying to arrive before Christmas," he murmured,
bringing the glass to his lips. Whenever it was, he
feared it would be too soon. He watched the delicateness of her throat as she tipped back her head and
sipped on the amber brew. How he longed to press
his lips to the pulse that jumped there.

She set down her glass. He reached over, grabbed
the bottle, and refilled her glass. "You probably
couldn't sleep because your hair is pulled back into
that taut braid. Why don't you loosen it?"

She gave him a knowing smirk. "The next thing
you'll tell me is that my nightgown is too tight."

"That's probably true. You seem to sleep well
enough when you aren't wearing it."

The red crept into her face like sun bursting over
the horizon. "You're no gentleman."

"I never claimed to be."

"And I reckon I ain't no lady."

"On the contrary." He took her braid and unraveled
the strands. "You are the finest lady I've ever had the
pleasure to know."

"Don't tease me."

"I am not teasing. I speak naught but the truth. You
are courageous, Jessye. I know of no other woman
who could have stood up to the trials of the past year

as you have. You even suffered through my foul moods."

"And now you're walking." She tossed back her drink, and her eyes widened. "Oh, that burns."

He took but a sip from his own before refilling hers.

"What are you going to do with your share of the money?" she asked.

"Order another faro table, perhaps. And you?"

She sighed dreamily. "I don't know. Go somewhere and start over, I reckon."

His stomach tightened. "Where do you think you might go?"

"Ain't got a clue. Someplace where dreams are big." She sliced her gaze over to him. "What kind of dreams do you have?"

"My dreams usually revolve around a woman wearing very little clothing."

Laughing, she took another swallow of whiskey, and he realized she was well on her way to getting drunk. Otherwise, she would have scolded him profusely.

"You gotta dream bigger than that, Harry. If you could do anything, be anything that you wanted to be . . . anything at all . . . what would you do?"

"I would make you happy."

She smiled crookedly and lifted her glass. "I am happy." She downed the remaining whiskey.

"Not truly happy."

" 'Course I am."

"No, you pretend . . . much better than I do." He leaned forward. "What is your heart's desire?"

"To get away from here and buy my pa a saloon."

He cradled her cheek and held her gaze. *"Your* heart's desire, Jessye."

Tears sprang to her eyes, and she shook her head.

"A daughter, perhaps," he answered for her. "And a man who would stand beside you."

"Don't do this to me, Harry."

"Is that your heart's desire?" he insisted.

"Yes!" She jerked away from him, poured whiskey into the glass, and gulped it in one swallow. "But I can't have it. Can't ever have it. Men like their women pure and docile. I'm not either one of those blasted things."

"So don't tell him about your past transgressions."

She furrowed her brow, hope filling her eyes. "Wouldn't he be able to tell on our wedding night?"

He swirled the liquid in his glass. "I don't know. I've never bedded a woman who had no experience."

She sank back in the chair, despair sending the hope into oblivion. "Even if he couldn't tell, having a lie like that between us would eat at me. You can't build a marriage on a foundation that ain't strong enough to carry truths."

He smiled. "You get philosophical when you're drunk."

A corner of her mouth tipped up, and her eyes glittered with amusement. "Yeah." She placed her elbows on the table and leaned toward him. "What's your heart's desire?"

"You'll be disappointed if I tell you."

"No, I won't." With her finger, she drew an X over her chest.

"My heart's desire is to have another night with you in my bed."

She scrunched up her luscious mouth. "That's such a small thing to want."

"Not if you live for the moment as I do." He withdrew a deck of cards from his pocket and placed it on the table. "Care to make a wager on heart's desires?"

Jessye laughed. Damn the scoundrel! His plan all along had been to lure her back into his bed, and she was drunk enough not to care. Besides, memories of that night were worth reliving. Why not take another night of memories with her before she left? "Sure, Harry. Why not? But you shuffle them cards first."

"Certainly."

She watched his deft fingers cut and shuffle, over and over. She wished she could figure out how he cheated. He set the cards down. "Cut."

She reached for the cards, then drew her hand back. Her thoughts were getting fuzzy. Too much whiskey. "Now what exactly are we wagering?"

"Hearts' desires."

"Right." She pointed her finger at him. "If you get the high card, I spend the night in your bed . . . and if I get the high card . . ." She furrowed her brow. "I don't spend the night in your bed?"

"If you draw the high card, I shall marry you and give you the daughter you want."

Hope spiraled and fell. She chuckled. "Harry, now I know for sure that you cheat. You'd never wager something like that." God, it was a sin for him to sit there looking so incredibly handsome. Another night in his arms would be no hardship.

"What the hell," she muttered as she reached out

and cut the deck. She turned up the bottom card in her hand. A four.

She smiled at him. "There's no point in you even turning up a card."

"Now, Jessye, I don't want you to later accuse me of taking unfair advantage. We must carry this through to the end."

She watched as he wiggled his fingers over the remaining deck. He picked up half the cards and turned them to reveal a two. "Damnation," he muttered.

She stared, blinked, her mind befuddled. "I must have misunderstood—"

"No, my love, you won."

"I won. You and me are gettin' hitched?"

"It appears so, although I would prefer to wait until Kit returns so he can stand as my best man."

She nodded mutely, wondering where her breath had gone. Her body felt like molasses. She really shouldn't drink. It made it impossible to think clearly. "I . . . I was gonna move—"

"So now you can stay."

"What . . . what will I do with all the money that Kit's bringing me?"

"Decorate a nursery?"

She squeezed her eyes closed. "I'm getting dizzy."

She felt his hand cradle her shoulder. "You should go to bed."

She looked at him. "Yeah, yeah I should." But she sure wasn't going to sleep now. "Harr—"

He placed his finger on her lips. "I hate to ask, but it seems I drank more than I should, and I'm a bit dizzy myself. Can you help me back to my room?"

"Sure." She scooted the chair back and walked to

his side. She needed time to think, to sort through what had happened.

He struggled to his feet, using the table for support. Then he wrapped an arm around her shoulders. "Small steps," he ordered.

She concentrated on the tiny steps, one foot in front of the other, because her mind simply could not accept the magnitude of what she'd just done. Never in a million years had she expected to win.

And why did she feel as though she'd lost?

Because he'd never mentioned love.

The turn of a card had determined her fate . . . not the love of a man.

⚜ Chapter 21 ⚜

*Jessye struggled to open her eyes. Her tem-*ples were throbbing, her neck was stiff. After escorting Harry to his room, she'd sought solace and understanding in another glass of whiskey and then another.

All the whiskey only made it impossible for her to think, and now it would make it impossible for her to get out of bed without heaving up her insides.

She squinted against the sunlight easing through the curtains. Last night's events blurred into distorted memories. She remembered cutting cards, and somewhere in the recesses of her mind, she thought she was getting married.

What an absurd notion! She was certain Harry would wake up this morning and laugh the whole episode off.

She cringed as someone banged on her door. She tossed the covers aside, eased her feet to the floor, and padded across the room. She opened the door and peered into the hallway. "What?"

Billy's cheeks reddened as he averted his gaze. She

clutched the opening of her nightgown. "What did you need?"

"Uh, nothin', uh, well, Mr. Bainbridge needs you."

"He'll have to wait." She started to close the door.

"He's been waitin' out back."

She halted and stared at him. "Out back?"

"Yes, ma'am. He had me go to the livery first thing this morning and rent a buggy. He went out for awhile. Then he came back and told me I was to come up here and get you." He leaned over, his gaze darting around the hallway as though he needed to impart a secret. "He can't walk up stairs."

She leaned against the doorframe. "How *did* you come to work here?"

He straightened. "He hired me."

She massaged her aching temple. "I know that, but how did you meet?"

He looked away, the red creeping back into his face. "Oh, that. Well, one night, he came outside to take a . . . uh, to answer nature's call . . . and tripped over me. I was drunker than a skunk, feeling sorry for myself on account of losing my hand in the war. Lord, he chewed me up one side and down the other for not appreciating what I did have. Took him a good twenty minutes to get back on his feet. Wouldn't let me help him none. Told me when I was ready to stop feeling sorry for myself, I could work for him. Took me a couple of days to do that." He looked at her and grinned. "Anyway, he wants to take you for a buggy ride, and I was supposed to come up and get you."

Jessye grimaced. "Could you have a cup of strong black coffee waiting for me down there?"

"Yes, ma'am."

She closed the door. Damn Harry for being compassionate. Damn him for being kind, understanding, and all the things she didn't want him to be—all the things that made her love him more than she thought humanly possible.

When she finished changing from her nightgown into a faded dress, she walked down the stairs, took the coffee from Billy, and went out back. Harry stood beside the buggy, leaning on his cane.

"What took you so bloody long?" he asked.

She flinched. "I had to get dressed."

He limped toward her. "Are you ill?"

She glared at him. "How can you be so jolly after we drank so much whiskey?"

"Ah, I see. The fresh air will do you good then. Come on, get in." He took her arm and led her to the buggy.

"Where are we going?"

"I have something to show you."

"Harry, I really don't know if I can take a buggy ride. Can't you just tell me?"

"You really need to see it, but we can do this later if you prefer."

She heard the disappointment in his voice. She needed to talk to him anyway, to set things straight. Might as well do it after he showed her whatever it was he needed to show her. "Let's go," she said as she clambered into the buggy.

She downed the black brew as he limped around the horses.

"What do you think of that bank of clouds over there?" he asked.

She glanced away from him and studied the billowing white formations as she felt the buggy rock. Damn his pride for not wanting her to see him get onto his seat. She waited until the carriage stilled before looking at him. "It's lovely."

"I thought so."

He picked up the reins and gave the horses a gentle slap on the backside. They started forward. Jessye closed her eyes, hoping the world would stop spinning before they arrived at their destination.

"What do you think?" Harry asked as he led her to the middle of the clearing.

Jessye glanced around as the cool autumn winds stirred the leaves and plucked them from the trees that bordered three sides. Before her, the land stretched into eternity. She shuddered.

"Are you cold?" he asked.

She nodded. "I didn't realize cooler weather had moved in."

He shed his jacket and handed it to her. "Put this around your shoulders."

"I'm not going to take your jacket so you can be cold."

"This is summer weather in England."

She draped his jacket over her shoulders and drew it closely around her. His scent wafted around her, and the warmth from his body soaked into her flesh.

"So what do you think?" he repeated.

At a loss, she looked around again before facing him. "What do I think about what?"

He arced his arm in a grand gesture. "The land. I know it's a bit dreary now with the leaves falling, but I should think come spring that it will be majestic.

There is a river nearby so water should be no problem. I thought in that area where there are no trees that perhaps we could have a pond."

Her heart slammed against her ribs. "Harry, what are we doing here?"

"I assumed you wouldn't want your daughters raised in a saloon. I thought this might be a nice spot to build a home, but if you don't like it—"

Stepping back, she held up a hand. "Harry, last night is fuzzy. What exactly did we do?"

"I made wild, passionate love to you—"

"No, that I would have remembered."

He smiled wickedly. "So moments with me are memorable, are they?"

She sighed in frustration. "I know we had a wager—"

"And you won. We are to be married, and I'm to give you a daughter. Perhaps in time, a son. Although he was not part of the wager, I thought you might not object—"

"Harry, you don't plan marriage and children around cards and wagers—"

"But we did, and a man must stand by his debts."

"You don't get married because of debts."

"I would agree if we were not so well suited to each other."

"Well suited? Have you got any idea how often you make me mad?"

"And you make me equally angry, but it does not change the way I feel about you."

"Which is what exactly?"

He took a step back and cleared his throat. "I beg your pardon?"

"Exactly how do you feel about me?"

"I admire you, adore you actually. Do you not like me?"

"I like you fine, but a marriage is supposed to be built—"

"On a foundation of trust. I remember you told me last night. So have you something you wish to confess?"

She stared at him, wishing her mind would clear up. "What?"

"You said last night that there could be no secrets between you and the man you were to marry so I thought I should give you the opportunity to tell me if you have any other secrets."

"I've already bared my soul to you. There's nothing else to confess."

"So now, I must bare mine."

Her heart hammered as he glanced down, and she saw his grip on the cane tighten.

"You asked me once why I was in hell." He lifted his gaze to hers. "My second mistress was named Margarite. She was a beauty, colder than the first—"

"You don't have to tell me."

"I do because my mother was not the only one who taught me that a mother's love did not extend to me, and I'm not certain you believe me to be an honorable man where women are concerned."

Harry shifted his stance, and she saw the strain in his face. "Do you want to sit somewhere?" she murmured.

"No, some things are better said standing." He glanced away and cleared his throat. "Margarite discovered that she carried my child. I offered her the protection of my name."

Jessye's chest tightened. "You were gonna marry her?"

"Yes." He met her gaze, and the agony she saw reflected in his eyes almost brought her to her knees. "But it seems, she wanted neither me nor my child. I found her on a blood-soaked bed. She had tried to rid herself of the babe and paid with her life."

She took a tentative step toward him. "Oh, Harry, I'm so sorry."

"The fault was mine, Jessye."

"You can't blame yourself because she did that."

"I can, I did, and I still do." He balled his hand into a fist and pressed it against his chest. "Because we never talked, you see. I did not know what her dreams were and what they were not. What we shared was not real, but I embraced it because it felt safe. I thought there was no risk, and I was wrong. I began to gamble recklessly, my debts amounting to unreasonable excesses." He laughed mirthlessly. "I think I rather hoped someone would drown me in the Thames because I could think of no other way to escape the guilt. I do not wish to bring it into our marriage, but I thought you should be aware that it is there."

Her throat tightened as she absorbed the true extent of his guilt and pain. How could she tell him at this moment that she wouldn't marry him? She wrapped her arms around him and pressed a kiss against his neck. "For what it's worth, Harry, I decided after we crossed the Red River that nothing on God's green earth would force me to give up your child if I found out I was lucky enough to be carrying her."

He slipped his arm around her and held her close. "Thank you for that."

Tears stung her eyes, and she tightened her hold on him. "I appreciate that you trusted me enough to bare your soul."

Unfortunately, she didn't think he'd given her his heart.

"Kit! By God, it's about time!" Harry cried.

Jessye spun around to see Kit embrace Harry in a hearty hug. "Missed me, did you?" he asked.

"You don't know the half of it," Harry said cheerily, stepping back, balancing himself with the cane. She could not believe the progress he'd made in the three weeks since they'd cut cards. They'd even taken strolls through the town, but she could always tell when he tired, for he leaned on her more heavily.

It was the middle of the afternoon. Only a few men sat in the saloon, gawking. Kit dropped the saddlebags from his shoulder and held out his arms, tilting his head toward her. "Jessye?"

She practically skipped across the saloon. He took her in his arms and swung her around. "You're rich, sweetheart!"

"So I hear."

He placed her smoothly on her feet. He grabbed his bags. "Let's celebrate."

"Billy, bring us a bottle of whiskey and three glasses," Harry ordered as he led the way to his table in the back.

He pulled out a chair for her, waiting patiently as she sat. She thought she might never grow accustomed to all the courtesies he bestowed upon her since that fateful night. He'd even had a dress sewn for her as though he truly expected them to get married.

He took his seat and wrapped his warm fingers around her cold hand. She watched as Kit opened his bag, pulled out two brown packets, and placed one in front of her, one in front of Harry.

She worked her hand free of Harry's and trailed her fingers over the coarse paper.

"Five thousand," Kit said quietly. "I won't be offended if you feel a need to count it."

She shook her head and pressed her fingers to her lips. "I don't believe it. Even after Harry got your letter, I didn't believe it."

Kit looked at Harry. "Of course, yours is a bit less."

Jessye sat up straighter. "I said we were equal partners—"

"I divided the money equally—"

"Kit," Harry snapped.

Kit smiled. "But Harry had instructed me to take from his share whatever fifty cattle were worth and give the money to Tom and Jake. The lads were quite taken with your generosity."

As was Jessye. She studied Harry, wondering if she'd ever understand the man. "I thought we'd all agreed that we weren't taking on any charity cases."

"The lads' situation seemed to warrant a breaking of the rules. I thought it bad enough that they had to deliver heart-wrenching news to their mother with only a hundred dollars in their pockets." He shifted uncomfortably in his chair. "It was not generosity that prompted my request, but fairness."

"You need not defend your actions," Kit said.

"I realize that, although I would appreciate a bit

more discretion on your part in the future when I ask a favor."

"Ah, yes, we wouldn't want Jessye to think you weren't a complete scoundrel."

She was beginning to think he wasn't a scoundrel at all.

Billy set the whiskey and glasses on the table before walking away. Kit opened the bottle and liberally filled the glasses. "Harry, you were right to insist we go to the west, around Kansas. No cattle made it to Sedalia. Many cattlemen held their herds at Baxter Springs, Kansas, hoping for passage. The grass is gone and the cattle are dying. I should think the winter will finish off any that remain."

"A regrettable shame," Harry murmured.

"Some good may come of it," Kit said. He touched Jessye's packet. "There is a demand for the cattle. Men of influence will find a way even if it means bringing more railroads into Texas."

"So you're going into railroads?" Harry asked.

"Haven't a clue what I want to do. I only know I no longer want to herd cattle."

He lifted his glass. "Allow me to propose a toast."

Jessye and Harry lifted their glasses.

Kit cleared his throat. "May the value of this endeavor be measured in terms far greater than money."

They clinked their glasses together. Jessye's mouth grew dry even though she sipped the whiskey. When she set down her glass, Harry took her hand and brought it to his lips.

"It already has been," he said quietly. "Jessye and I are to be wed."

"Indeed," Kit said, though neither his voice nor his

eyes reflected surprise. "When is this blessed event to take place?"

"Tomorrow," Harry said. "We've only been waiting for your arrival."

"Sounds like another toast is in order."

Jessye shoved back her chair. "If you'll excuse me, I have things to see to." She picked up the packet and pressed it against her chest. "Thank you for bringing me my money."

A soft chuckle and "nervous bride" floated after her as she ascended the stairs. She wasn't a nervous bride. She planned to be an escaping bride.

❧ Chapter 22 ❧

Harrison stood at the window, gazing at the night. It was the last time he would sleep alone. Tomorrow, he would take a bride. It was a thought that would have terrified him a year ago, but now it only brought him peace and contentment.

He heard the soft rap on his door and turned. "Come in."

He wasn't surprised to see Jonah Kane walk into his room. In truth, he'd expected the man to talk with him long before now.

"About this here weddin' you got planned for tomorrow," Jonah began.

Harrison held up a hand. "You need not issue any warnings or threats. I shall treat your daughter as though she were a queen."

Jonah rubbed his chin. "That's gonna be kinda hard seein' as how she ain't gonna be here."

Harrison felt as though a rug had been pulled out from under him. "What do you mean?"

"I mean she's upstairs packin' so me and her can slip away—"

"Packing? Slip away?" He sounded like a bloody echo, but the words made no sense.

"Yep, seems she don't cotton to the idea of marryin' you."

"Whether she cottons to it or not, we had a wager." Using his cane for support, he limped across the room.

"She's kinda hardheaded once she gets her mind set on somethin'."

"Don't I know it," Harrison grumbled.

He heard Jonah shuffling after him.

"She kept tellin' me you was a scoundrel, but I never could see it."

Harrison came to an abrupt halt and spun around. Jonah staggered back. "Then will you be so kind as to let me go see if I can persuade her otherwise?"

Jonah held up his hands. "Have at it."

Have at it? God, how long had she been planning to abandon him? She'd been pleasant, taken strolls with him. Had it all been a farce?

She was always there for him, even when she was angry. Had he mistaken obligation for love?

He reached the stairs, gripped the banister, and gazed up. He knew the pain of taking one step off the boardwalk, the agony of stepping onto it.

He took a deep breath, clenched his teeth, and started up.

Jessye placed the last of her clothing in the bag. There were things in Harry's room that she wished she could take with her, but she wanted, needed, her next encounter with him to be brief.

The door burst open and slammed against the wall.

Jessye jumped back, her heart lodged in her throat. Harry stood within the portal, looking very much like a demon risen up from hell.

"What's this I hear about you slinking away in the dead of night?" he growled.

She cursed her father, the traitor. "I wasn't gonna slink away."

He stepped into the room, staggered, caught his balance, stumbled to the nearest chair, and dropped into it. His cane clattered to the floor as he gripped the chair with one hand and rubbed his hip with the other.

She rushed across the room and knelt before him. "You're in pain."

"Yes, goddamn it, I'm in agony!"

She jerked her head up to meet his blistering gaze.

"Those damnable stairs have thirty-seven bloody steps."

She angled her chin. "You could have waited at the bottom. I would have been down eventually."

"I didn't know if you planned to go out the front or the back."

"I wouldn't have left without saying good-bye."

"So you say, now that you've been caught."

"So I say because it's the truth." She kneaded his hip. His hand closed over hers.

"You would have left me at the altar, standing there like a bloody fool."

She rolled her eyes. "I had planned to say good-bye. Granted it was going to be quick, but you would have known not to go to the church."

"We had a wager, you and I."

The solemnity of his voice shredded her heart. She bolted to her feet and began to pace. "You don't get married because one night you were too drunk to cheat and cut to the high card. You get married because you love someone and you want to spend the rest of your life with her."

He gave a long, thoughtful nod. "All right, then, I'll give you the opportunity to reverse the outcome of our original wager. We'll go best two out of three. The stakes remain the same: a wedding or one more night in my bed."

"Harry—"

"You can't call off a wager simply because you get cold feet."

"I'm not getting cold feet. I'm sober."

He pulled a deck of cards from his pocket. "Bring that table over here."

"Harry—"

"Do it. It's the only honorable way."

In exasperation, she crossed the room, grabbed the bedside table, and shoved it across the floor until it was before him. She watched him shuffle and slam the deck on the table. "Cut," he ordered.

She dropped to her knees, grabbed several cards, and shoved the bottom one in his face without looking at it. What did it matter when he would beat it anyway?

"Ah, an eight," he murmured.

He cut the deck and held the bottom card up for her perusal. A six.

Her gaze darted between the two cards and his face. She stared at him in disbelief. "I always thought you cheated."

"I only cheat when it's important that I win."

She laughed. "But you didn't win. An eight beats a six. You lost!"

"What makes you think I think I lost?"

While she struggled to make sense out of what he'd just said, he shuffled the cards.

"Forget all the cuts that have come before. Forget the best two out of three. This last cut is the only one that will matter." He slapped the deck in front of her. "Cut."

Warily watching him, she lifted a section of the deck and turned it to reveal a three of clubs. Her heart sank as disappointment hit her . . . because as much as she protested, she did want to marry him. And the odds of him cutting to a two—

He leaned forward. "Tell me you don't love me, tell me you don't want to be married to a cripple—"

"You are not a cripple!"

He smiled. "Tell me you don't want to be married to *me*, and I'll cut to the queen of hearts. Otherwise, I plan to cut to the two of hearts."

Tears burned her eyes. "Harry—"

"I know you want the words, Jessye, but I can't give them to you. However, until the day I die, I will give you the actions that show you what you want to hear." He tapped the deck. "Tell me you don't love me."

"You know I can't lie, Harry."

He smiled slowly. "I know."

"I love you, you scoundrel. But I don't want you to marry me if you don't love me."

Slipping his finger between the cards she held and her palm, he eased out the top card and flipped it over. The two of hearts.

"As long as the top card is you, Jessye my love, I will remain faithful to it," he vowed.

Her heart closed into a tight, painful knot while tears burned her eyes and scalded her throat. She shoved the table aside and crept forward on her knees until she was nestled between Harry's thighs. She combed her fingers through his black hair and held his green eyes with her own. "I can't, Harry," she whispered.

"What do you mean you can't?"

"I can't marry a man who won't risk telling me that he loves me."

Pain crept into his eyes, and the ache in her chest increased.

"You know why I can't," he rasped.

She nodded slightly. "I know. You don't trust me any farther than you can throw me."

"I do trust you, damn it!"

She shook her head. "No, you don't."

"I trusted you enough to bare my soul—"

"But not your heart." She touched her trembling fingers to his lips. "You shared your body with me, and it was glorious. Ah, Harry, it was so glorious. You bared your soul, and I've sheltered your secrets. But you won't give me your heart because you're afraid that I'll hurt you like your mother or Margarite did. I'm not either one of them, but if you can't trust me to cherish three words, I can't give you the rest of my life."

"You will never find anyone who is better for you."

"I know." She brushed her lips over his. "Tell me once. That's all I need."

He slammed his eyes closed and clenched his jaws. "I can't."

She rose to her feet. "I wish to God that I didn't need the words, Harry, because I do love you."

He opened his eyes. "Then marry me."

"The greater the risk, the greater the return. You taught me that. You've given your body to other women. I need from you something that you've never given to anyone else. I want your heart."

"You ask too much."

"Because I've had too little."

Leaning over, he snatched up his cane and slowly brought himself to his feet. He reached into his jacket and withdrew an envelope. "Here."

She took it from him. "What is it?"

"It was to be your wedding present. Now, it is simply a gift."

She opened the envelope and removed the deed to the saloon. He had signed the building back over to her father.

"I shall be the one to leave," he said quietly. "Not you."

She looked at him. "You're giving the saloon back to my father?"

"It was never my intent to keep it, but I needed something to replace what I had lost."

"The use of your legs?"

"Your love."

She felt the pain slice through her.

"I had it before we got to Kansas. I just didn't realize it until I lost it."

She shook her head. "You never lost it. Do you

think I would have stood by you all these months if I didn't love you?"

"But now you want me to earn it with words I cannot say."

"I want you to risk giving me your heart so that you'll truly understand the extent of my love."

He shook his head. "Be happy, Jessye. I shall leave in the morning."

He stepped toward the doorway. She'd gambled and lost. He'd called her bluff.

He grabbed the door, slammed it shut, and pressed his forehead against it. She rushed across the room and wrapped her arms around him, laying her cheek against his back. She felt the tremors coursing through him. "You don't have to say the words. I'll marry you because I can't be happy without you."

"I suppose if I were to say the words, you'd want me to look at you when I did."

She wrapped one arm around him and slid her other hand to his, intertwining their fingers. "Not necessarily."

He turned and leaned against the door. She saw the turbulent emotions swirling within his eyes. He had journeyed through hell, and here she was asking him to walk farther. "Harry—"

He touched a finger to her lips. "You're right. You deserve the words and so much more. A marriage should not come about because of the turn of a card."

Moaning, he worked his way down to one knee, gripping the cane with one hand. She bit back her cry at his efforts, his harsh breathing resounding around her. Why couldn't she have been content—

He lifted his gaze to her, and within the emerald

depths she saw her answer. Never had he looked at her with such intense vulnerability or overwhelming love.

He took her hand, and the trembling she'd felt earlier was gone, replaced by strength. She watched him swallow.

"I love you, Jessye. Will you honor me by becoming my wife?"

The tears burst forth, and she nodded. "Yes, oh yes." She dropped to her knees and wrapped her arms around his neck, covering his mouth with her own. His arm pressed her more closely against him as the kiss deepened into a sweetness that was joyous to receive.

She trailed her mouth along his jaw. "Oh, Harry, I love you so much."

"Good, because I'm going to need help getting up."

She leaned back, meeting his gaze. "Thank you. Thank you for the words, thank you for trusting me with your heart."

"My one regret is that I can't carry you to that bed."

She smiled seductively and rose to her feet. She helped him stand. Rising on her toes, she nipped the beloved dent in his chin. "I bet you can follow me."

She took a step back and began to unbutton her bodice. Another step. Another button. Until she reached the bed. Slowly she removed all her clothing until it pooled on the floor beside her.

Harrison caught his breath at the sight of Jessye standing magnificently before him with nothing but gossamer shadows playing over her flesh. Leaning on his cane, he limped toward her, for the first time experiencing no shame over his awkward movements.

Only now did he realize that he had been crippled long before he came to Texas. Only now, with this woman, did he feel truly healed. He lowered his mouth to hers, kissing her tenderly. She was his, not because of the turn of a card but because of the change of a heart.

How fortunate he was that she would not allow him to cheat them.

He sank on the bed. She put his cane aside. He relished the movement of her hands as she removed his clothing.

Then she was beside him, flesh against flesh, heat pouring into heat, passion yielding to passion.

Jessye felt Harry's hands gliding over her body as though he'd never before touched her. The gentleness of his exploration was devastating to her senses. She'd never felt so cherished.

He had given her his body before, his soul, and now he was truly gifting her with his heart.

He trailed his mouth along her throat and her chin until he reached her ear. He swirled his tongue along the outer shell, sending delicious shivers cascading through her body.

She sighed as he moved lower and buried his face between her breasts. She loved the feel of his body over hers. He eased up farther, cradled her face between his strong hands, covered her mouth with his own, and joined their bodies with one smooth stroke.

Her body curled as though she could hold him forever. He rocked against her, slow at first, until the power built and the sensations grew.

There was a difference in their lovemaking that she

couldn't touch but felt. No walls, no barriers . . . no more shattered hearts.

Only hearts that were healed and strong.

Writhing beneath him, she felt the pleasure rushing forward like a raging river, untamed, uncontrollable until it swelled into a magnificent wave that swept her over the edge.

Gasping for breath, she opened her eyes and watched as the current captured and carried him beyond the tide, arching over her, his jaws clenched, his low groan echoing around her.

Breathing heavily, he lowered his body until their slick flesh touched from shoulder to hip. She felt the trembling in his arms and kissed his chest.

With an exhausted moan, he eased off her and drew her against his side. "I'm thinking of asking you to marry me again. I like the way you say yes."

Laughing, she trailed her fingers over his chest. "I like the way you asked."

He cradled her cheek, tilted her face, and held her gaze. "I love you, Jessye."

Her heart overflowed. "Those are such sweet words, Harry."

He smiled tenderly, pressed her face into the nook of his shoulder, and kissed the top of her head. "Say them," he whispered.

"I love you."

Beneath her cheek, she felt his heart pound faster as he drew her more tightly against him.

"Don't let me get by without saying those words to our daughters."

"I won't," she vowed, looking forward to the day when she could keep that promise.

*   *   *

"I gets to be the flower girl."

At the back of the church, Jessye watched as her father knelt before Mary Ellen. "That seems like a mighty big job for such a tiny mite."

She thrust her petal-filled basket toward him. "I'm gonna throw out all the flowers like a fairy giving out wishes."

Tears stinging her eyes, Jessye wondered how she was going to make it through the evening without a dozen handkerchiefs. At Harry's insistence, they'd postponed the wedding a month because he wanted to include a few more guests. Damn the man for not telling her exactly who the guests would be. And bless the Robertsons for bringing her daughter and allowing her to walk down the aisle ahead of her first mother.

Sometime before the night ended, Jessye knew she needed to find the courage to tell her father the truth. He had the right to know that the child he was smiling at was his granddaughter.

She heard the organ music begin. Mary Ellen jumped before she smiled brightly. "I gots to go."

"Can I have a dance after the wedding?" her father asked.

Mary Ellen bobbed her head. "I like dancing."

Madeline poked her head around the pew and signaled Mary Ellen forward. Jessye watched her daughter reach into the basket and begin tossing petals along the aisle that led to the front of the church, where Harry stood with the preacher on one side and Kit on the other.

Her father slowly unfolded his body and bent his elbow. Jessye slipped her arm through his.

"Always wondered if you'd had a girl or a boy," her father said quietly.

Jessye swiveled her gaze to his. "You knew?"

He touched his gnarled finger to her cheek. "You were my baby. Ain't much I didn't know. It was hard watching you bear your burden alone . . . but it also made me proud to know you had the gumption to do it."

"How did you know Mary Ellen—"

" 'Cuz she looks just like you did at that age, and she's got that defiant tilt to her chin."

"She doesn't know I'm her mother. It was Harry's idea to allow her back into my life—as a friend, but not a mother."

"Looks to me like she's got a right good mother in Madeline. But I reckon a day will come when she'll learn that she's always had two."

She wrapped her arms around her father's neck and hugged him tightly. "I love you, Pa."

"I love you, too, girl, and if I ain't mistaken that scoundrel waiting at the end of the aisle loves you."

She stepped back and entwined her arm around his. "I'd best get to him. He can't stand for very long without the pain getting unbearable."

"Jessye, I got a feeling he'd stand there forever if he had to."

Jessye looked at Harry, standing straight, his hand gripping the cane. Yes, he would stand forever—and that was the very reason he would never have to.

❧ Epilogue ❧

August 1867

"I want you to leave," Jessye ordered.

Harrison wrapped his hand around hers and held her gaze. "No."

"Harry, I am about to show myself for the true coward I am, and I don't want you to witness that."

"I am not leaving," he insisted as he wiped the sweat from her brow.

"Stubborn, obstinate, oh God!"

She started breathing heavily, and her hand squeezed his. Her breaths came more rapidly, more shallow.

"Oh, God!"

"It's all right, Jessye," Dr. Hickerson said. "Just push."

"I am pushing!" She collapsed on the bed and looked at Harry. "I am pushing."

"I know, my love. We're in no hurry."

She glared at him, and he grimaced. "Of course, I realize after two days that you might feel a bit differently."

353

He dampened a cloth and pressed it to her throat. She moaned and grabbed his hand. He eased her up slightly.

"That's it, Jessye," the doctor said. "Bear down as hard as you can."

Harrison kept his gaze fastened on her face, wishing to God that he could spare her this ordeal. She released a cry and slumped back.

"You've got a daughter," Dr. Hickerson announced just before the room filled with an indignant wail.

Tears sprang into Jessye's eyes. "Is she all right?"

"Perfect," Dr. Hickerson said as he laid the baby in Jessye's outstretched arms.

"Oh, Harry, she's so beautiful," Jessye whispered with reverence.

Harrison lovingly moved his gaze over the tiny thing she held. The babe's face was puckered like a dried prune. Other than his wife, he'd never seen anything that looked as beautiful. "Thank God for small miracles," he murmured.

"She's got five fingers on each hand. And look at this. Five tiny toes on each foot," Jessye said in awe.

"And her mother's hair."

Jessye looked at him with so much love that it caused an ache in his chest. She squeezed his hand.

"I get to keep her."

He brushed his lips across hers. "You get to keep her."

More tears surfaced within the limpid green pools of her eyes. "Thank you, Harry."

"It was my pleasure and my joy."

*   *   *

"Thank God, she looks like her mother," Kit said.

"My sentiments exactly," Harrison said as he glanced at Jessye, rocking the child cradled within her arms. Kit had left shortly before their daughter was born six weeks ago. Harrison had no idea where he'd gone, and Kit didn't seem inclined to discuss his travels.

"What have you decided to name her?" Kit asked.

Jessye met Harrison's gaze. "Angela," she said softly. "Because she's our angel."

"Angela Bainbridge. Wonder what your father will say about that," Kit said.

"I suppose I should write him. He doesn't even know I'm married."

Jessye scowled at him. He held out his hands imploringly. "I've been extremely busy training the faro dealers and expanding the saloon."

A brisk knock on the door sounded before Jonah poked his head inside. "How's my granddaughter?"

Jessye smiled. "She's fine, Pa. Come on in."

"I can't get used to you living in this big house," he said as he strolled inside and shoved a package into Harrison's arms. "This came for you." Then he drew up a chair and talked to his grandchild as though she understood every word he spoke.

"What is it?" Jessye asked. She carefully placed Angela in her grandfather's arms before crossing the distance to Harrison.

"I don't know," he said as he sat in a padded chair that eased the pressure on his hip. He angled the long thin box until he could easily read the handwriting. His heart thundered at the sight of his father's elegant script adorning the paper.

"Aren't you going to open it?" Jessye asked.

Harrison nodded. "Certainly."

He cursed his clumsy fingers as he broke the string and tore off the paper. Carefully, he lifted the lid. His stomach dropped to the floor.

"Oh, isn't it gorgeous," Jessye exclaimed as she lifted the polished wooden cane from the box. A gold lion's head gleamed in the sunlight pouring through the windows.

"Looks like it cost a pretty penny," Jonah announced.

Harrison glared at Kit. "You wrote him."

Kit held out his hands. "No. You asked me not to, and I honored that request."

Harrison narrowed his eyes. "You are too clever by half. You had someone else write him."

"No, I swear to you that I did not."

"Then how did he find out?"

"I haven't a clue."

"Maybe this will offer an explanation," Jessye said, handing him an envelope.

He withdrew a letter and a scrap of newspaper. He stared at the clipping from *Blackwoods*. He'd often seen his father reading the popular magazine. This particular article was entitled "An Englishman's Journey into Kansas" and was written by Christian Montgomery.

He snapped his gaze to Kit. "You've been sending stories to *Blackwoods*?"

Kit shrugged. "Our experiences make for interesting reading. I sent them one story, and they wanted more, so I obliged them."

Harrison skimmed the article. In vivid detail, it re-

lated their encounter with the jayhawkers, the closing
words one brutal lash after another. He read them
aloud. " 'It is doubtful he will ever walk again.' You
wrote that?"

"The doctor's prognosis was grim."

"So you thought you were justified in telling the
whole world—"

"I never used your name."

"My father obviously figured it out."

"What does your father say in his letter?" Jessye
asked.

He refrained from scowling at his wife. "How the
bloody hell should I know?"

"Well, read it," she commanded.

He tossed the article at Kit. "You overstepped the
boundaries of our friendship with this." He unfolded
his father's letter, dreading the words.

August 17, 1867

My dear Harrison,

I read this article in Blackwoods *and very
nearly expired while I was eating my morning
eggs. I suppose it is pride that has stopped you
from writing me.*

*As for Christian Montgomery, a man of so
little faith does not deserve your friendship. To
insinuate that you might never walk. Rubbish.*

*I know you will despise my gift, but before you
toss it into the fire, heed my advice. Do not look
upon it as a sign of your weakness, but as a
testament to your strength. You survived, my*

son, when lesser men would have given in.

I was but a lad when my grandfather fell from his horse and broke his hip. I remember it was weeks, nay months, before he could walk again, and then only with the aid of a cane.

He was a man of presence, and the cane took nothing from that. As a matter of fact, few people noticed it. I usually didn't until he applied it against my backside.

Knowing you, you will overcome this obstacle. And I do know you much better than you realize.

You may not believe this but I sent you to Texas not to punish you, but to save you. After discovering the wretched childhood your mother forced you to endure, I could not bring myself to discipline you. I fear I caused you more harm than she did. I gave you the opportunity to waste your life—and you deserve much better. I hope you find it in Texas.

I look forward to reading more of your adventures. I would prefer to hear them from you personally, but I shall welcome Montgomery's exaggerated writings if that is all I can have.

My love,
Your father
The Earl of Lambourne

Harrison glared at Kit. "Father thinks you exaggerate."

Kit sputtered. "Exaggerate? My God, I tone the stories down if nothing else. I seriously doubt they would print the complete tale of hardships endured here."

"What else did he say?" Jessye asked.

"He hopes that I find what I deserve here." He handed the letter to Jessye and smiled. "I suppose I shall have to write him now and let him know that I received better than I deserved."

September 25, 1867

To the Earl of Lambourne
Dear Father,

My apologies for taking two years to write you. I have been busy. You were quite right. I do have a need for the cane, and I am truly honored that you sent such a fine one.

I know you despise gambling, but I must admit that I made a daring wager, and it has paid off handsomely. I gained a wife and just recently a daughter.

I have no doubt you would adore them both.

Ah, yes, we own a saloon and several gaming tables. You would heartily disapprove, but the profits have provided us with a modest home.

Should you ever have the opportunity to visit, rest assured that you shall win every hand you play. Well, not every hand. After all, there is still a scoundrel lurking within me.

Harrison studied the words he'd written. They somehow seemed inadequate. He heard his wife's soft footfalls. She wrapped her arms around him and placed her chin on top of his head.

"Tell him," she urged.

"I don't know if I can."

She moved around and knelt beside him. "What do you fear?"

"That I am not worthy of you." He dipped his pen into the inkwell and finished off the letter.

I love you, Father.

> *Your son,*
> *Harrison*

He glanced at his wife. "Happy now?"

She smiled warmly. "Yes. And you?"

He looked at the words, words that he had learned should be spoken aloud as often as possible. "Incredibly so."

She rose to her feet and took his hand. "Then come to bed and tell me that you love me."

He grabbed his cane and stood. "I'd rather show you."

"Maybe we can manage both," she suggested as she led the way toward their bedroom.

"Now that's a remarkable idea." He pulled her to him. "I love you, Jessye Bainbridge." He lowered his mouth to hers, amazed at how easily the words now came.

*G*ive in to your Impulses!

These unforgettable stories only take a second to buy and give you hours of reading pleasure!

Go to *www.AvonImpulse.com* and see what we have to offer.

Available wherever e-books are sold.

AVONIMPULSE